D1136005

Other Books by
Ronald L. Smith

Who's Who in Comedy

The Bedside Book of Celebrity Quizes

The Stars of Stand-up

Comedy on Record

The Cosby Book

Johnny Carson

Let Peas Be with You

Poe in the Media

Sexual Humor

The Stooge Fans' I.Q. Test

Sweethearts of '60s TV

Comic Support

Who'd Say That

Murder in the Skin Trade

Ronald L. Smith

A division of Shapolsky Publishers, Inc.

Murder in the Skin Trade

S.P.I. BOOKS
A division of Shapolsky Publishers, Inc.

ISBN 1-56171-220-5

For any additional information, contact:

S.P.I. BOOKS/Shapolsky Publishers, Inc.
136 West 22nd Street
New York, NY 10011
212/633-2022 / FAX 212/633-2123

Printed in Canada

10 9 8 7 6 5 4 3 2 1

Contents

PROLOGUE: 1981 1
CHAPTER ONE 13
CHAPTER TWO 30
CHAPTER THREE 49
CHAPTER FOUR 58
CHAPTER FIVE 77
CHAPTER SIX 90
CHAPTER SEVEN 102
CHAPTER EIGHT 116
CHAPTER NINE 129
CHAPTER TEN 150
CHAPTER ELEVEN 156
CHAPTER TWELVE 167
CHAPTER THIRTEEN 173
CHAPTER FOURTEEN 194
CHAPTER FIFTEEN 208
CHAPTER SIXTEEN 225
CHAPTER SEVENTEEN 234
CHAPTER EIGHTEEN 248
CHAPTER NINETEEN 263

PROLOGUE : 1981

"Let's roll, honey," Keefer said, "now you're in the movies."

He dropped his cigarette and scuffed it out on the linoleum floor and wiped what he thought was a little piece of ash from the corner of his mouth. He bared his teeth in a forced smile.

The girl, not more than 17, gamely shared the smile, still looking a little nervous.

This wasn't a Hollywood film set.

It was just a hotel room. Not expensive, not cheap. The walls were a bland shade of light medicinal green and the vaguely flowered curtains strung across the windows and clothespinned closed, glowed as they kept out the yellow of the glaring sunset flashing from New Jersey across the Hudson.

She sat on the bed, surrounded by the movie lights. When they suddenly went on, she blinked in pain at first, then she enjoyed it. All she could see was bright light.

A bank of 500 watt lamps were on tripods on one side of the Times Square hotel room, tilted at the metal umbrellas in front of them, reflecting the blazing glare into a uniform whiteness. Another lamp was attached by a clamp to a desk chair at the foot of the bed, and another was clamped to a chair positioned against the far wall, its hot glow preventing any distracting shadows from dancing on the wall during the sex.

She sat on the bed wearing a red lace bra and red crotchless panties. Keefer wasn't so used to making pornies that he didn't notice how nice the downy blonde pubic hair looked against the raunch of the red panties. The girl had milky white skin and natural blonde hair. Natural blonde hair everywhere. He hated it when the blonde had a dirty looking black bush. What was worse was when they bleached it and you could see the mound and surrounding flesh pinker than ham and pocked with irritated bumps, and the little nubs of the black roots growing out. Jeez. Go try and convince even a junkie to stick his dick into that kind of a mess.

Keefer had hopes the flighty little bitch might hang around in town long enough for him to make five or six flicks. She was worth it. Two hundred bucks was a little high for a ten minute loop but this was prime pussy. It just bugged him he hadn't been able to convince her to just do it for free. She sure seemed to give it away easy enough.

But Keefer wasn't young. Not to a 17 year-old, who thinks a few lines on a forehead means senility. Besides, she'd heard the high price up front. Some friend of a friend told her where she could make good money and get into movies. OK, she found out that this wasn't exactly the movies. But at least the two hundred was real.

Keefer had to do a lot of talking to keep this thing together. He told her that any time she didn't like something, just tell him. He insisted that any time you get in front of the cameras it's good experience. After all, he added, what the hell, what's the difference between a one night stand and this? He told her it would be a good time. He told her a lot of things, and she hung around. For him, that game was the best part of the whole thing. It wasn't easy. You couldn't feed every girl the same line. Keefer prided himself on his skill.

Keefer caught his reflection in the mirror over the bureau. He still wasn't half bad looking, if the damn lights weren't so bright. White hairs slivered in his moustache, a few clumped under one nostril, making it look almost look like a drop of snot. Any more of that, and the moustache would have to go. His eyes had crinkles in the corners, and little bumpy lumps, but some girl said it made him look friendly. His hair was still jet black, thanks to that dye stuff he picked up at Duane Reade every other week, along with Maalox and six-packs of Clorets. He brushed his hair down his forehead and around, a black circle quick-fix to hide the receding hairline. What really bothered him was little turtle of a double chin lousing up his profile. He turned away from the mirror and grabbed for his cigarette in the ashtray. Then he saw he'd snuffed the last one out.

What the fuck. He looked over to the chick on the bed. He looked back at his reflection and made a face at himself for looking back. He shook his head. "Gotta get outta this business," he said softly, as he had for nearly ten years now.

The lights in the room were getting way too hot. He took off his jacket, revealing the shoulder holster. He looked for a chair to hang the jacket on, but all the chairs in the room had lights clipped to them. He tossed the jacket on the floor.

The girl gazed vacantly up at the ceiling. She lay

back on the bed, seeming to test it. Keefer stared at her a moment.

"Are we set?" he said.

"Uh huh," the cameraman said. This was an ugly, pug-nosed teenager with long black hair curling down over his shoulders. He was 6'1" and wore a white t-shirt with a Marlboro box tucked into one sleeve at the big meat of his shoulder. Tight blue jeans white at the seat. He had a scuff of hairs trickling down his lower lip that looked like dirt. He thought it was a goatee. A real skag, and Keefer didn't like him much, but he worked cheap. The kid was one of those whizzes who knew everything about cameras, especially how to fix a cruddy 16mm job like this beat up Revere that kept breaking down. Knew about lights, too. Knew enough to save Keefer money, too, by not to going to Willoughby's to buy film, but getting it from the Orthodox Jews around the corner at Executive.

The kid didn't get stoned before shooting, so that was good. And he was hot for meeting the chicks. Fuckin' animal. He'd go to bed with some of these girls no matter what they'd been doing for that half hour he was filming them.

"Don't look right into the lights, honey," the kid said.

"OK."

"You look beautiful. Very beautiful. Hey, Mr. Keefer, it's gettin' late. You want I should just, uh, start the cameras and take care of this myself?"

"I got somebody," Keefer answered.

"Yeah? Well where is he?" the kid challenged. "We don't have all night, ya know."

Out in the hallway Keefer heard a voice. A chill

ran up his veins to his heart, as if he'd stepped in ice water. His knees felt weak. He was used to the feeling but hated himself for still feeling it. He'd die of a heart attack some day afraid of every noise outside. He recognized the voice now. And it was only Sledge.

In the hallway, Sledge was laughing. He patted the maid on the shoulder.

"You at it again?" she said with good-humored admiration.

"I'm the star," Sledge said, laughing heartily.

He gave a rhythmic four short knocks on the door and Keefer opened it. Keefer grunted at Sledge and nodded to the maid and she nodded her head, her face turning very serious. She wanted him to know she took the whole thing very serious. She liked getting those easy twenty dollar tips — the going rate for her to keep her mouth shut whenever he used the motel for a quickie fuck flick.

The maid could see into the room. She saw the young girl on the bed. She closed the door quietly. She glanced at her cart and idly straightened the piles of towels and sheets, the fresh glasses clinking in the tray on top.

She thought she really earned the twenty bucks Mr. Keefer gave her. After all, she always kind of guarded the corridor for the half hour or so it took to make one of those films. Why, if anybody was going to bust in on her friend, Sledge, or Mr. Keefer, she was ready to knock on the door first and say in a loud voice, "May I make up the room now?"

She moved the cart closer to the door. She heard a flat, muffled voice. "OK, let's get this started. You like Sledge, baby?"

"He's OK."

"Look," said another voice, "if you don't want to do it, you don't have to."

"I don't mind."

The maid backed away from the door.

But then the sound of a gunshot. Chairs moving.

"Joe, for Chrissake!"

"I'm sorry, Mr. Keefer. Jeez, it was just —"

"Don't gimme a heart attack, all right, Joe? Can we get by without that light? It don't look like it matters."

"Just makes me look blacker," she heard Sledge chuckle.

"Shut up."

The maid pressed her ear to the door. Something was wrong in there. The vibes were all wrong in there.

She waited, but she didn't hear much. Four or five minutes passed. Sometimes she heard a voice, or a grunt, but not much.

"Get ready, I'm pullin' out."

"Jeez, don't come yet! Sledge, you horny bastard."

The maid heard Hammer's deep voice. "Don't you worry, man, I can come three times, maybe four! I like this girl!"

The maid leaned against the door and smiled, shaking her head.

"Take it, baby," Keefer said, his voice the same hard breathing moan as Sledge, "when you feel him pull out, look at the camera. Look at Joe. And...yeah... that's great...Dynamite..."

The maid looked down the hallway. Not a soul. Not yet anyway. Better keep looking; you never know when there's gonna be trouble. Didn't the mayor say something about a Times Square crackdown? Again?

After a while, she heard Keefer's voice again.

"Let's go...Get him hard again. Jeez, he's already ready! Look up at him, and kind of pop your eyes, like it's almost too much for you. And then we'll try dogstyle, ok? It's going great."

The maid heard some mumbling from the girl, and from Joe, the camera kid. And then came Sledge's rumbling laugh again.

Now it was Keefer's voice the maid heard.

"I *know* there's no sound," Keefer said, "just moan anyway. They can read your lips. So look like you love it! Talk it up! Go "oh, oh," like that. Like that. That's right. Go "oh, OH." Yeah."

"Oh, ohhh," came the girl's voice. "Oh, oh owww! OWWW!"

Sledge shouted, "Shut up!"

"You're on my hair!"

"Shut UP! Look like you love every minute of it! Come on, act! Do some acting here!"

It got quiet after that.

The maid leaned against the door. She didn't feel sorry for the little bitch, not at all.

The maid walked softly down the corridor; there was some noise down in the stairway. People going down stairs into the lobby. They skipped rhythmically down, not breaking stride at all.

She slowly opened the stairway door. She heard the footsteps getting fainter. She closed the door gently.

Then bang!

It wasn't the door slamming. She looked around. It sounded like one of the doors down the hall.

But nobody was in the hallway. The maid frowned.

Must have been another one of those big light bulbs breaking. Damn, they better cut it out with all that noise!

Somebody'll hear. What's with that boy Joe today?

The maid came back and leaned against the door.

Bang!

A bullet slammed through the door, ripping splinters out of the wood. The maid cried out and fell against the cart. She struck her gut against the heavy metal edge of it, and it slowly began to tip. She shut her eyes as the corridor began to spin and go black. The cart crashed and she lay on top of it, her head snapping back on impact. Little packaged soaps spilled out of the big metal box and a roll of toilet paper bounced and began wobbling slowly down the hall.

The maid moaned, and the corridor began to blur gray, and then slowly she could see again. With the wind knocked out of her, she could only gag silently, helplessly.

She heard another shot. She stared at the disappearing toilet paper roll, rolling free down the length of the hallway, turning, actually turning, disappearing around the corner. She tried to breathe. Finally, something began to heave in her chest, the knotted muscles in her stomach giving way. She pulled herself off the cart and dropped face down to the dirty carpet, crying softly.

There was no sound except her little gasps. Nobody came out from any of the other rooms. There were no sirens. No screams. Nothing.

Hot tears ran down the maid's face, her mouth working whispered prayers.

The door to the room swung open.

The maid shut her eyes tight.

She expected a shot, one shot, the last shot she'd ever hear.

But instead there was the light sound of footsteps

going by. The sound of a woman's feet. The white girl hobbling down the corridor.

The maid didn't want to look up, but she did. She saw blood on the front of the young woman's blouse and skirt.

"I'm dying," the white girl said, almost like an apology. She stared at the maid for a moment, turned, and with a lurch ran down the stairway exit.

The maid got up slowly, still bent in half from the pain of falling on top of the cart. She leaned against the wall for support. She inched her way toward the opened door of the room.

She didn't want to look inside. She shut her eyes, weeping. Then, bracing herself, she opened her eyes and looked in.

Sledge was dead. He was naked on the bed, one side of his face a red-rimmed pit, the black skin caved in with jagged splashes of raw flesh, blood seeping away in ever quickening pools, spreading onto the pillow and sheets. The bullet had gone off point blank in front of his right eye.

The kid who was running the camera was lying on the floor. Blood was still pumping from a wound to his chest and he was gasping like a fish out of water, a heaving gasp, his eyes staring at nothing.

Keefer was grimacing, on his knees, his hands hugging his waist, his body frozen with the pain of a bullet that nearly tore his midsection in two.

"Call..." Keefer croaked.

"I know what to do," the maid said. She was cleareyed now.

A door down the hall opened a crack, then shut.

The people who rented rooms at this hotel in Times

Square knew better than to come out after they heard shots. They knew better than to even say they heard them.

When the police finally arrived, they found that Room 421 was undergoing renovations. A crew of three Puerto Rican men had finished the last mop-up of the linoleum, moving the freshly made bed back into place, speaking Spanish loudly.

One cop turned to his partner. “You speak Spanish?”

“They wouldn’t give me a straight answer even if I did.”

“Bueno,” the cop said to the guys, pointing to the way they had fixed up the room. “Muy bueno. You guys should be real proud-o.”

“Give one of these guys a few bucks and he’d cover up the murder of his own mother.”

“Sure. He probably was the one who murdered her. Yeah. The one on the end, he understood that. Didn’t you? Ablay oosted English? ‘Course not. OK pal, you won’t have to talk to any more cops. Immigration, maybe.”

“What’s your story,” the other cop said to the maid. He reached out and patted the pocket of her apron and fished out a large bottle of aspirin.

“Something paining you?” he said. “You don’t look right.”

“Just the Ritis Brothers,” the maid said, trying for a smile.

“Ritis Brothers?”

“Arthur Ritis, New Ritis, all of ‘em Ritis Brothers don’t leave me alone.”

“Sure. Isn’t this bottle a little too big for you to be

carrying around? If you had aches and pains all the time, you'd have a small re-fillable bottle with you. That looks like a fresh black and blue mark on your arm." He pressed the dark discoloration on her light brown skin. "Did somebody rough you up when James Sledge got hit?"

The maid knew better than to look down. She looked straight at the cop.

"I bumped into my cart," she said. "Ain't a week goes by I don't get scuffed and bumped."

"You saw who did it," the cop insisted.

The cop was searching for a reaction. He didn't get it.

"You know James Sledge, don't you? And you know where we found him? We found him in the alley down on 10th Avenue in back of the parking lot. Yeah. Mr. James Sledge, man with a record for a few robberies, a little numbers running. And lately making some dirty 8mm movies. I hear that a lot of them were made in this hotel. You saw him in here, right? You brought bed linen up to this room?"

The maid shook her head at the detective.

"Somebody shot him in the head."

The maid nodded uncertainly.

"Looks like a hit. Like somebody really wanted your friend dead. He was your friend wasn't he?"

The maid kept her head still and her eyes straight ahead.

"OK, if that's how you want to play it."

She knew how to play it. She knew Sledge wasn't registered. She knew the manager took good care of things and never said a word. And that was what he always said for her to do. And Mr. Keefer too. She was proud about how she played it. The dumb cop.

The cop was stupid. He hadn't a clue.

Nobody would ever know what went on.

CHAPTER ONE

"I think I have a really good opening for this," Rob thought to himself. "Start off hot and dirty." He sat on the Broadway local, a pen in one hand, the eight page/ 2,500 word story rattling in the other. He made typo corrections each time the train lurched to a stop.

The story about fucking was like fucking. He thought it was pretty clever when he did it, but now, in the morning, he was wondering how good it really was.

But the story was about fucking, so even if it was terrible, it couldn't be that bad. The readers of Rabbit Magazine didn't care about perfection.

It was easy money, that was the main thing, Rob told himself. A few hours, and $200. Even a shrink couldn't do much better than a hundred bucks an hour. The trouble was, he couldn't manage more than a few stories a week. The rest of the time he just brooded.

He wasn't expecting to be writing porn at age 37. Just a few more years to the big 4-0, and nothing in the bank and nothing to show for it.

Fired. The promising reporter, booted. It was a long time ago, but it was a fresh wound.

Rob burned at the memory.

He tried to concentrate on the story and check it over one last time. But his mind re-played that last scene over. That last insult to the injury...

"And give me your press pass."

Like, what, he was going to use it to sneak into a goddam baseball game or something?

The shame of handing it over like an admission of failure.

Christ, the dead-end jobs since. The wastes of time.

She said it was murder, all right. She could name everybody in the room. "What good will it do now?" she said.

And he felt sorry for her.

She kept her job. He lost his.

Rob looked up.

The train pulled into 225th Street. The 9 train had barely gone a few stops toward Manhattan. It started at Riverdale, the clean tip of the Bronx where the middle class had fled with their kids. Where Rob had grown up attending Barnard School for Boys. But the area was, inevitably, getting worse. And just a few stops down it was pretty damn slummy.

At 225th some high schoolers got on, girls screaming like they were being shot at, guys sullen and bellowing, gesticulating to each other as they swaggered down to the back car. They owned that back car, where they could all smoke cigarettes and turn up Hot 97 on the boom box. The girls giggled and squealed and shouted at each other in mock rage over a borrowed lipstick or an accidental jostling caused by the lurching train. Not even 2pm and they were through for the day, ready to play in mid-town.

Nobody bothered to look up. Older people, sleepy and somber, wore expressions of fatigue and foreboding.

Rob didn't belong to either group, and he tried to

feel thankful about that. He wasn't a school kid anymore, free to goof off. And he wasn't some old, unemployed character going to visit some friend, or take in a movie.

But, as some of his pain in the ass friends liked to tell him, he was "middle aged" now. His college diploma was gathering dust on a closet shelf and his big chance on a New York newspaper was way, way behind him.

What now? Keep writing porn? Start at the bottom writing for one of those dumb free newspapers? Move to New Jersey?

After college, it had taken years to work up to The City Daily and that crummy little desk next to the gurgling water cooler and the ninny idiots who gathered around it and babbled, distracting him while he sat at the computer, trying to get the throbbing ache behind his eyes to clear just long enough to polish that opening paragraph and make it read right.

It had taken years of typing, of going on research errands for other reporters, of re-writing copy from the newswire. And finally he was getting by-lines.

When they fired him, it was like getting fired from every newspaper in the city. Nobody wanted him. For years he tried to break through the cliques at the big magazines, sometimes getting a few thousand for an article in Ladies Home Journal, or a few hundred in Cable Guide, but somehow the editor moved somewhere else, contacts dried up — magazines were a dead end for a freelancer.

His resumes were being used for coffee cup blotters all over town, or mailed back to him with "thanks — not hiring." "Your clips were very interesting," but, no. Not even a freelance piece? No. Everything's staff written.

He passed thirty. Thirty five. There was that year editing manuscripts for that scholastic book publisher on Madison Avenue. Day after day corresponding with windy professors and trying to make sense of manuscripts about the art of library science and a bibliography of ethnic references in Shakespeare's plays. There was another year or two out of writing entirely, working for that computer company in Queens, proofreading software and taking Advil every day and overdosing on Murine. Twelve hours a day it was, what with the hellish commute.

So here he was on the subway, knocking out a story for a skin magazine and glad to get it.

Half out of work. Half an adult. Leading a half-assed existence.

"Don't worry about it," Julie told him before he left the house. He stared down at the story. The fuck scene was good. He flipped a page, then another. "When she unhooked her bra, her heavy boobs swelled forward into his face, and he hungrily caught a thick, sweet nipple in his mouth —"

A stocky woman boarded the train, her eyes tiny beads, mouth stretched down in a frown. She caught sight of the seat open next to the quiet young man reading, and she grimly hurried through the closing doors to wedge down into the seat. She stuffed herself into the small space between Rob and the wall of the car, taking half of Rob's thigh and elbow into the expanse of her rump and meaty ribs.

He shifted as far to the side as possible. He looked down at his paper: "She felt the thick tip of his cock nudge at the tingling, thickening wet folds of her pussy..." The woman started to read over his shoulder.

Rob rolled up the manuscript.

"Is that another dirty one?" Julie had asked, noticing the neatly stacked sheets of paper on the dinner table.

"Another two hundred buck one, if that's what you mean."

"I'm not in it, am I?"

"No. I wouldn't write about you."

"No?" Julie smiled teasingly. "Then who gave you all this expertise?"

"It's just a job," he answered, bored and a little annoyed.

"Why don't you try writing something else? There's all sorts of things around you."

"What? Birds and trees? Who wants to read about birds and trees? Everybody wants to read something dirty."

Even this fat slob next to him on the subway. Rob looked at her. Maybe she wouldn't buy a dirty magazine. But she'd buy one of those gothics — one of those romance novels — just porn with a silk lining and a good alibi.

The air conditioning was off in the car. The fat woman's body was expanding like warm, rising dough. He couldn't get at the story now if he wanted to. The fat woman's sweating flesh made cementing contact with his arm. Every breath she took he could feel. She was dozing now, leaning on him with her melting fat. He could smell her poached egg breath as it came out in grunts from her moist mouth. He stared at her slack face, and the mole with the hair in it. He felt her trembling fat flesh pressed wet and sweaty against his own. The every day pornography of life.

Rob's eyes began to close as he slowly leap-frogged between daydream and consciousness, nodding his head each time the doors opened. Yes, 125th Street. That's right. 59th. He roused himself as the train pulled into 42nd Street. He struggled forward like a worm caught between a huge thumb and forefinger. He pulled loose from the seat and rushed through the exit doors before they hissed shut.

There was a newsstand on the train platform. When he was working for them, Rob always stopped to catch the headline on The City Daily, and compare it with the the others. Now he looked down at the display of sex mags. Where was his, Rabbit, compared to the competition? Usually way up and over to the side. A gaunt Pakistani with a permanent curl of disgust on his lips silently stood guard over his wares.

On most newsstands, the sex magazines were covered with plastic bands censoring the cover photo. They were tucked into pockets so only the names stood out. But in this Times Square subway stand, the bizarre lunatic fringe of sex magazines hung proudly. Haughty girls stared out, some smiling, some sneering, some bending over, some standing stupidly. One cover had just a pair of tits, another just a huge butt.

The titles made no sense, vague code words most of them: Gem and Nugget and Velvet and Fling and Flick. The others transformed the average hard-up slob or restless hubby into something special: a Dude, a Duke, a Hustler, a Stag, a Playboy. Then there were some dopey ones with names that made little sense at all, like Rabbit.

Normally, Rob would've walked up a few blocks to

the giant building that housed The City Daily.

Now, he stayed on Forty Deuce. He walked from the subway station down 42nd Street to 9th Avenue.

Sometimes when he walked, Rob liked to pretend he was a football player steering slowly through the slow maze of the opposition. The slow shuffle-footed old bag ladies were blockers. The beggers and drug jivers were tacklers. The bicycle messengers were part of the suicide blitz. The trick was to slip through the crowd untouched, unpoked, unstepped on. Each block he got through without someone stopping and putting a hand on him and saying "Yo, slick, a quarter" and each block without some bunch of thieving kids knocking into him as they ran away from a store owner — that was a touchdown.

There were no touchdowns this day, just a technical foul when the wind blew up a page of newspaper that adhered to his shin and wouldn't be kicked off.

Rob pushed on till he came to the thin, beat-up building between 9th and 10th. It had two shallow sockets carved into it that housed stores — a cramped little space where some sort of illegal alien sold cigarettes from behind a bullet-proof window, and another crammed with tourist gifts from ash trays shaped like toilet seats to "I Love New York" knives. There was the standard "Going Out For Business" sign on the door, the one tourists mistook for meaning going out of business.

A guard sat in the building lobby reading The City Daily. Rob nodded to him, and he just glared. He stuck his tongue out, scraped a finger over it like he was trying to strike a match, and then turned a page of the newspaper with the moistened digit.

Rob got off the elevator on the sixth floor and walked over to the rippled, opaque glass door for Bernice Publications that had the chipped lettering on it: Be nice Pub ica icns, Roo 600." There was a push-button lock on the door. It was very easy to remember the combination: 6.0.0.

The magazine office was drab and shabby, with dirty beige carpeting on the floor, balding and scuffed near the door. The white walls were smudged with fingerprints and lines from where idle pens or keys scraped along.

On the right was a closed door, heavily lacquered. It said, "I. Krantz, Publisher." Down the corridor, a far distance from the publisher's door, was a large room honeycombed with cubicles. The hum of different radios buzzed in the air. An old issue of Rabbit was on the floor. It was a real old one, since it showed pubic hair on the cover. It had to be from the early 80's during one of the cycles where newsstand mags had gotten raunchier. The cover lines blared: "Sandy and Serena: Sibling Revelry," "Ins and Outs of Anal Sex!" "Shaved Bald and Balled."

Rob picked up the magazine and thumbed through it. Then he walked down a few cubicles to the little one that was piled with all the back issues. The magazines from the last three years lay promiscuously strewn over themselves on warped wooden shelving. Nobody seemed too concerned about keeping up the archive. Rob tossed the issue onto a shelf.

Rabbit, the name a knock-off swipe at Playboy's bunny logo, never tried to be anything more than a girlie magazine. There were no celebrity interviews, no articles on cars or music, just tons of dirty pictures. A bunch of letters and a few sex stories were used for filler to lessen the expense of all the photos on glossy paper. The twenty or thirty pages of text was printed on cheap pulp that wrapped around the first and last pages of the magazine.

Rabbit, along with a dozen other cheap men's magazines, had survived on the lust of guys who couldn't get enough from just Playboy or Penthouse, and wanted a few more each month. It survived on guys who wanted something raunchier than those slick titles, and on guys who figured that these were the magazines that had "the real thing." Rabbit was in its twenty third year, and probably had just as many editors.

Last year's editor was a guy named Goodman. He was knifed by a black junkie for no other reason than the guy didn't like his looks. Come to think of it, the junkie had a point. Too bad it was such a sharp one. Rob had met this year's editor, Larry Slezak years ago. Slezak was a freelance photographer back then, and he did the photos for a story Rob did for New York magazine on the death of the Central Park children's zoo. They'd changed their minds and cut the story, giving him a kill fee.

Slezak had found that porn was what paid, and he enjoyed taking pictures of naked girls. He was happy to take the editor's job at Rabbit.

"See," Larry teased when Rob called up about writing some fiction for Rabbit, "you're starving, waiting to get some kind of Pulitzer prize. Now you're writing for a sex mag, where every page is a pull it surprise!"

Rob paused at the entrance to the cubicle.

Larry was talking to another writer. It was Toby, an extremely serious guy in his mid 20's. He was thin, despite the shapeless white shirt and pleated pants he wore. He was pale, his hair woolly and jet black, cropped unreasonably close to his head in back, pudding bowl style. It might have been considered some kind of hip nerd style, but there was nothing hip about Toby. It was just a bad haircut, with the hairless white areas behind the ears sharply defined, the back razored up too far, exposing too much thin white neck.

Toby sat stiffly, his long white fingers spidering over his knees, his head forward listening intently to whatever Larry said.

"Hi Toby," Rob said, pulling up a chair in the cramped editor's office. He nodded to Larry Slezak, who gave him a cursory nod that could've easily meant goodbye as much as hello.

Toby stared at Rob for a moment.

"How's it going, Toby?"

"Oh, all right." He turned his head from Rob to Larry as if it was on a tight ratchet.

"Listen, Toby," Larry said, "you're a good writer, but you have to loosen up. You sound too educated. I mean, look here:" tendrils of semen dripped from her cunt." That should be "gobs of cum." If she's just been fucked — *really* fucked — that's what she's supposed to have in there, right?"

Toby nodded uncomfortably.

"Now look over here: you have the guy eating out the chick's pussy and you go, "He wanted to stay pressed between her legs forever, he felt the softness of her thighs against the sides of his head, the tongue licking homage to her pussy." Look, Longfellow, the reader wants his wad's worth. OK? Spell it out — he sucked that clit and lapped that juice!"

Larry glanced at Rob and winked. "Now take this guy over here. He used to have a real job and write for one of New York's fine, fine newspapers. But now I've got him down to gutter level. And I'm putting him in every issue and he's making *piles* o' dough."

Rob nodded to Toby. "I upped my income. Up yours."

Toby didn't get it, or didn't want it. He got up out of his seat. "What kind of story should I do next?"

"I don't know. Whatever you want. We haven't done anything with amputees for a while."

"Amputees," Toby repeated, obviously not thrilled.

"It doesn't have to be amputees. How about foot worship? You're good at that stuff. I loved that story you did, "I Am a Bathroom Slave." Did you read that one, Rob? It was in the June issue. This guy licks this chick's pussy clean every morning in the bathroom and stays there all day. The clowns at the printer's believed it was real. They're goin' "Ay, da guy's a fuckin' douche bag! Man, that's dis-gustin'."

Larry smiled. "Listen, Toby, do foot worship, or female domination. First person. She's dictating it into a tape recorder while she makes him eat her out and fuck her with a dildo or something. OK? I'm doing your work for you! Do I get a cut on each story?"

Toby seemed deep in thought.

"Unless you'd rather do it, Rob."

Toby looked at Rob with alarm. Rob leaned back in his chair and shook his head good naturedly. "It's all yours, Toby."

"I'd better be going," Toby said. "When do you want it?"

"I needed it yesterday," Larry said. That was his standard line. Toby awkwardly brushed past Rob and out into the hallway. "Next," Larry announced. "What do you have for me today, my good man?"

"Fresh porn," Rob said, handing over the story. Larry scanned the first paragraph and then tossed the manuscript onto the top of his crowded 'in" basket.

"Fine," Larry said. He smiled his patented smirk. He showed his teeth when he smiled, two matching grids of white that didn't vary in size or shape along the front and down the sides. It was a wolfish smile, and it would've been unpleasant, almost threatening on someone else. But there was boyish mischief in Larry's gray eyes. He was just thirty, his face was smooth, with even a touch of baby fat on the cheeks that were only lightly speckled in spots with stubble, indicating that he could never grow a thick beard if he tried.

He combed his hair straight back, a pony tail dangling a few inches down his neck. He always wore a plain blue shirt and had a tie deliberately unknotted around his neck.

"Toby kills me," Larry said. "He takes things way too seriously. But he'll learn. I have to yell at him 'cause he holds back too much. He's too timid. So I end up giving him the raunchiest assignments I can think of. It's funny to see how far I can go with him."

"What's the story with him, anyway?"

"I don't know," Larry said impatiently. "He's just weird. He used to write copy for some classical music mag till it went under. He can write some decent stuff. It just took him a while to learn. It's not so fuckin' easy to write good smut. Even your first stories were a little too inhibited. Why, you even had story lines!"

"It used to take me hours," Rob said. "Now it's easy. I just write these first person stories out like I'm taking dictation from somebody. They go right through me to the typewriter."

"Sounds logical, whatever you said. So give me a good blowjob story. Some kind of "I Love to Eat the Meat and Drink the Cream" deal.

"Does that sound kosher?"

"Make it a woman telling the story. If it's a man, it just sounds like bragging: "She gave me a blow job," yeah, yeah, sure. You know when Kinsey did his report — maybe 30% of chicks gave head. Now it's like 90%. Don't say that porn hasn't affected the world! You know my girlfriend, Tee? She tells me she can get an orgasm just sucking me off. Is that heaven? She likes to play with herself and suck dick. Do I have a good girlfriend or what?"

"Then you should write the story."

"Me? I haven't written anything in years. I've got some hot pix for ya." Larry rummaged around in his desk drawer. "I have a hot chrome here somewhere. Where did I put that slide?"

Larry found a color slide tucked in a small envelope. He squinted his eyes as he held up his magnifying lupe to it. He twisted the neck of his lamp, the light bright and blinding. He held the slide up to the lamp and leaned over the desk a little.

"Yeah, just as good as I remembered. Take a look at the cover girl for the next issue of Rabbit."

He handed the slide to Rob, careful to keep it against the magnifying lens. Rob held it over the lamp.

It was a shot of a giggling girl with long, silvery blond hair. She had a throw pillow in front of her crotch, her breasts thrust together by her arms as she held the pillow.

"You're kidding," Rob said. "That's Tee."

"She could be a cover girl, right?"

"Sure. She looks like she enjoys posing."

"She digs it."

Larry took the slide back and dropped it on the desk.

"Wait a minute, I got more."

He rummaged around and found an entire clear 8 x 11 plastic sheet containing 20 different poses.

"She'd let me run these shots, she really would. I had her sign a model release just in case. But I know mumsy and dadsy would go nuts. Her parents on *Lon-Giland* would get a warrant out on me. But shit, they're great shots. This is the stuff that keeps you young. She makes me want to come four times a night."

Larry smoothed his hair back along the sides. It stuck tightly for a moment, a few stringy strands hung over his ears.

"And when am I going to get a look at your girlfriend? What's her name? Julie? How come I never see any color slides of ol' Julie? Does she have big tits?"

"Does Tee want to be a model or something?"

"I don't know. Who knows what she wants." Larry reached into his pocket and pulled out a pack of Newports. "She dropped out of school 'cause she didn't know what she wanted to do. I give her an allowance, just like a kid. She's what, 19? She can get anything she wants out of me. So what does she care about anything else." Larry exhaled. "So what's with this cock holster of yours? Gonna get married?"

"I hope so."

"You hope so? Jeez, that's like hoping to be strangled. *Rent*, don't *buy*. Cunt doesn't improve with age. Take a look at these pix. She'll never look like this again. A year or two from now she's gone."

"Gone?"

"I'll have dumped her. Or more likely she'll have left me."

Rob looked at the pictures of Tee. She was posing against a wall of books. The pictures were so sharp he could even make out the titles. "Cosmos" by Sagan. Alot of Asimov. More science books.

"You're into astronomy?"

"Me? Nah."

"Tee?"

"No. You know, Rob, for an ex-investigative reporter you ask dumb questions."

"I was just noticing the books on your shelf."

Larry glanced at his watch.

"What makes you think they're on my shelf? No wonder you were fired. I better get to work. I have to write captions for some photos. Here I am, putting words into these girl's mouths. That's not what I'd really want to put in their mouths."

He looked at a picture of a brunette lounging on the sheets. He showed it to Rob. "The caption's gonna be: 'Bed me and spread me!' Not bad? I write these fucking captions — guys are really jerking off to ME."

Larry laughed. "Think of all the guys jerking off to *your* words, Rob! They think you're some hot slut! Here, sign this."

Larry handed him a voucher. Rob signed for the $200 story, putting down the title, his name, address and social security number. He scratched out the part that read "all rights" and made it "first North American."

"You keep doing that," Larry said. "The publisher gets pissed off. What do you think, somebody's gonna make a movie out of one of these fuck stories?"

"If I sell all rights, you can keep re-printing my stuff with no pay. What about those Rabbit annuals, and 'Best of Rabbit?' When you reuse a story, I should get paid."

"You should. But you won't. What are you going to do, sue? Stop writing for us?"

Larry picked up the phone and punched in some numbers. "Tee, it's me. Yeah. I'll be home in a few hours. Hey, I showed your slides to Rob just now. Rob says you're really sexy. You know. Rob. Sure you met him. One of my writers. The cute one? Ohh, I don't know about that. He's a little too old for you. Hey, he's old enough to be your father! Right? He's 37! He remembers when Paul McCartney was with The Beatles! Listen, I told him that if he paid me a hundred bucks you'd give him a blow job."

Larry held the phone away from his ear, pleased at the joke. Tee's voice came through tinny and loud in protest.

"Kidding! Listen, Rob said you could be on the cover of Rabbit. He really did. Yeah." Larry held the phone out to Rob. "Tell her."

"Very nice shots," Rob said toward the receiver.

"Hear that? He showed me some spread shots of his girl and we both agreed you were better."

Rob waved goodbye.

"Hold it," Larry said. He shouted to Rob, "Hey, I liked your idea about doing a piece on Times Square. That's right up your asshole, investigative reporting. Make it about 3,000 words. You can mention that these dried up lesbian feminists are trying to close down every damn store. This stupid "beautify 42nd Street" crap. But mostly tell our horny reader out in Iowa about all the hot peep shows and hardcore mags and stuff he's missing."

On his way out Rob was surprised to see Toby sitting in one of the empty cubicles. He had a copy of Rabbit in his lap, but it didn't look like he was reading it. He had a vacant look in his eye as if he'd been thinking about something or listening to something.

CHAPTER TWO

When Rob left the magazine office, the afternoon sun was hot and glaring.It stoked up the restlessness of the Times Square crowd.

The air was sickly sweet and smokey. A vendor on the corner was selling a soupy mess of hot pralines, stirring a stick into the diarrhea of brown syrup and nuts. Next to him another vendor was shouting "Sheekabah, sheekabah!" as black smoke burped from a small grill clotted with baked grease that periodically produced a festering flame. Fatty hunks of grayish meat perspired on wooden shishkebab sticks."Shine! Shine!" a voice rang out. "Shine 'em up. Look good for the ladies, Slick!"

A hoarse voice parroted "sparra kawta" over and over. The bum came over to Rob. "Sparra kawta."

Rob tried to sidestep him, but the bum had cut him off. The man was just a few years older than Rob. Rob could tell that by the graying hair at the temples, and more pronounced grooves down each side of his nose toward his mouth. He thought that if he kept on writing porn for rent money, this was what his fate would be.

"Sparra kawta!"

Rob barely had the change on him for a newspaper these days. He sometimes caught himself grabbing one off an empty subway seat when the train pulled into those last few stops in Riverdale.

Three nickels and a penny.

Rob dropped them into the bum's cup.

"Have a good day," the bum said, his eyes knitted in sincerity. Rob sometimes thought about trying to have some spare change with him. But something in him, especially these last few months, insisted "don't be played for a sap." As he walked past the bum, he found himself wondering if the guy really need his sixteen cents or not. Then he found himself wondering why he was so worried about sixteen cents.

Rob walked up to 8th Avenue, and mid-block, into Girl-a-Rama, a porn store on the south side of Forty Deuce. The entrance was framed in hundreds of flickering lights, the walls painted with polished red enamel, shining like fresh wet blood. There were little mirror squares all over the walls and ceiling inside. The place had once been a penny arcade, now refurbished to retain the bright and gaudy facade, but twisted by the demands of porn.

Here the booths that could have dispensed 4 photos for a dollar showed hardcore porn. The little stool seat was the same, but instead of smiling into the camera behind the little pane of glass directly across, there was a TV screen flickering anything from straight fuck-suck action to grainy European footage of dwarfs and piss drinkers. Thirty seconds of peeping for a quarter.

Instead of rows and rows of ski-ball machines there were racks and racks of magazines. The most popular were the standard hardcore shots of pretty girls in action. But there were also magazines of transsexuals with giant breasts and cocks, interracial combinations, orgies, and S&M scenes divided evenly between magazines of men lording over slut slaves in bondage, and those showing mistresses dominating spanked wimps.

Where there were once kewpie dolls and stuffed animals for arcade prizes, there were glass cabinets displaying vibrators and dildos, some made out of rubber and very realistic, others more like plastic bats; impossible large, studded with strange bumps and knobs, twisted into curves and angles. There were folded up plastic dolls with open mouths and fried-egg staring eyes.

The opposite wall had box covers for porn videos — $5, $10, $20 for the ordinary, up to $50 for the imported tapes of women with dogs or horses, couples crapping on each other or biker sluts grinning while sticking pins in their breasts. A lot of porn stores didn't bother with the crazy stuff. Too much risk and not enough sales. Most guys were very predictable: they wanted a few hot Playboy-quality blondes and brunettes fucking and sucking. That was what they were missing and that was their jerk-off fantasy.

"Like what I've done with the place?" asked Bernstein. Bernstein was about 55, a friendly man with a warm brown eyes and an ironic sort of half smile. His moustache was gray, his hair was gray, and he walked with a slight stoop, as if he'd spent years in a shoe store helping patrons into Hush Puppies.

Some porn store managers were nasty. A few were dangerous. But Bernstein, like quite a few others, was just a very ordinary man who happened to drift into the business. The hours weren't bad, the pay was good, and he had a few good burly bouncers to take care of any problems. Bernstein was proud of his store. "My stock is all computerized. I'm never out of stock. It takes something really crazy, like that Democratic convention, for me to be out of something for too long."

For years, Girl-a-Rama would get little mentions in Rabbit. In return, Bernstein would give the publisher or the editor a nice gift basket of smut.

"A whole article on Times Square?" Bernstein said. "That's good. But it may be too late. I don't know how long I can keep my lease. You know, when the city really wants to do something, you can't fight and you can't win. It's a shame. The people who really need porn should be able to have it.

"They claim that the porn stores promote loitering and prostitution and crime, but do you see young punks in here? No, they hang out in front of the theaters showing horror movies and kung fu pictures, and Herman's Sporting Goods so they can ogle the expensive sneakers, and the fast food joints. They know that if they come into the porn stores they'll get bounced. We want quiet, affluent customers, not thieves, loudmouths and troublemakers."

Bernstein looked at Rob admiringly, "And you're going to write me up again? In Rabbit Magazine? That's very nice. Very nice. We have your magazine here, you know. Right over there."

Bernstein pointed to a rack of magazines. Rabbit and other men's magazines, with their covers ripped off, were selling for half the regular price. Just small, every day corruption. Instead of sending back the unsold copies of Rabbit every month, the newsstand dealer would just rip the front cover off and send that, proof that the magazine wasn't sold. Then instead of destroying the magazines, they'd somehow end up in the 42nd Street porn stores.

Rob asked Larry Slezak about that. "So what can we do?" he said. "Get our legs broken? You know what I'm talking about. In every business, there's some *business* you just don't mess with."

Bernstein and Rob stood in the middle of the store, the target of fleeting glimpses from the men solemnly riffling through the magazines and staring at the beautiful girls so eagerly paying lip service to everyone's cock but theirs.

There was the guilty, unwritten law of the porn shop and its customers. Nobody talked, nobody leered at the pictures, nobody snickered or laughed out loud. Whether it was the businessman grimly staring at his copy of "Hard Hung Hunks" or a down and out old man spending half his social security check on a bunch of copies of "Panty Teasers," they all kept their silence. They stood, each a measured distance apart from each other, not wanting anyone else to see what it was that was turning them on.

Like the druggist who carefully averts his eyes from the pimply kid buying Clearasil or the fat lady with the large tube of Preparation H, the counter men in the porn stores always maintained a stone face and the customers always pretended they were not going to be rushing home and jerking off to what they were buying.

For Rob, the sight could be amusing or depressing depending on his mood.

"I moved the paperbacks over to here," Bernstein was saying. "They don't sell much anymore. Nobody reads. Nobody goes to school! And I took out the 8mm films completely. Nobody owns a machine anymore. It's all video. Listen, have you seen any of the new videos? You really should. Pam Future's got a new one. Some of the customers ask for her. And they like the new brunette, Mindy Hooters. Got a bunch of them with Spanish dubbing, too. And here's a good one." It was a lesbian feature, Scarlett Tara and Leigh Vivianne in "Cunt with the Wind."

"That's really somebody's idea of clever," Rob said. But Bernstein didn't understand the cornball art of pseudonyms. Bernstein opened the glass case and took out the video. "You're going to talk about the videos for sale? In that case...make sure to mention I have a fine selection of fetish stuff." Bernstein picked out a transsexual orgy tape, a foot fetish video and, after a pause to rub his chin in deep thought, an enema video. He piled the videos as if they were shoe boxes.

Bernstein waved to the counter clerk, a poker-faced Indian who looked like he needed a good night's sleep that would last for a month. "Raj, put these in a bag. No charge. This is for Rabbit magazine."

The Indian nodded grudgingly.

Bernstein said, "Look at these peep machines. All new. Listen, don't mention the animal stuff. Not even in Rabbit. We might be getting rid of it, anyway. It's not worth the trouble, it really isn't." "Well, the animals aren't consenting adults. What I'm doing, Mr. Bernstein, is a kind of overview of what's going on in the Square. Especially for tourists coming through. We're telling them where to shop, and what to avoid."

"Port Authority! I'm more afraid of being around the bus station than I would be in Times Square."

Bernstein fished into his pocket for some change. He opened an empty booth and stuck a quarter in the slot. He eased out and ushered Rob into the cramped stall that smelled strongly of ammonia. On a TV monitor he saw the slightly grainy color footage of a girl attempting to lick the red tip of a dog's penis .The dog balked at this, circled the nude girl and ducked out of camera range, totally unaware that this was supposed to be good for him.

The girl stubbornly crawled after the dog, her panties around her ankles. After looking at the camera for instructions, she managed to grab hold of the animal and press her fingers underneath it, against the furred sheath. The red tip of the penis finally emerged again and she dove for it with her face. The picture went black. Another quarter for another thirty seconds.

"European," Rob said. Bernstein nodded, as if he had imported fine wine.

A well dressed old man with a cane carefully counted out eight quarters in the palm of his hand, and unzipped his fly as he entered the vacated booth showing the dog sex film. A black janitor with a mop and bucket slowly moved into another recently vacated booth, grumbling to himself.

"I managed to find good copies, too. The others stores? All third generation prints. Oh — the upstairs — you've got to see this. This is what the customers are really going for these days."

He and Rob walked up a narrow flight of yellow and green tiled steps to the second floor. In the old days of the penny arcade, there were live attractions on the second floor, like the bearded lady and the sword swallower, each selling souvenir photos and doing a show for a nickle or dime.

Now upstairs was the live sex show. The thundering dance music was loud and hypnotic both for the dancers and the masturbators. From the outside, the area looked like a bank of phone booths at a night carnival. The walls and ceiling were painted jet black, non-reflective. The better for customers to sneak in and out anonymously. The booths were also painted black with a dim light bulb jutting out of each door. If the light was on, somebody was inside.

Inside each booth was a single glass window facing front. A metal sheet was over the glass and it raised when a quarter was inserted in the slot next to it. After thirty seconds the sheet descended, shutting out the view. The hemisphere of 18 booths stood in a semicircle in front of a small stage where a nude dancer writhed, swayed, or simply walked from booth to booth.

Businessmen, blacks, college kids, blue collar boys, they were all reduced to the same hungry level, a fraternity of penis-holding peepers, each with their own reason for wanting a 25 cent peek at a naked woman who they knew probably hated them. Some college kids were trying to fit three in one booth, whispering loudly to each other. Bernstein raised a hand and called out, "Fellas," and that was enough .They dispersed into separate booths.

The place smelled strongly of the ammonia. Rob noticed a bucket of detergent and water off to the corner. The booths had to be washed out often. Bernstein slipped Rob a quarter and he entered the cramped, dark booth. It was eerie and claustrophobic to be in the empty black booth, but there was something comfortable about it too; a safe hiding place.

Rob put the quarter in and the metal sheet over the window slowly lowered. At the moment a large breasted black woman was on the stage, smiling broadly and nastily. She dance-strutted slowly from booth to booth.

The semi-circular arrangement made it possible to see her at all times, some getting to see crotch and tits, others ass. The woman could see into the booths where, distorted by blue and green stage lights, the men's faces glowed sickly. Sometimes, if the cops were being lax, there was no glass between the dancer and the customer, and the men could push a hand through and fondle a breast or kiss a nipple, and hand the girl a dollar tip for it.

The black girl moved back to the center of the platform, taking a breather. She planted her feet on the floor, only her legs moving to the music, her breasts swaying, the suffocating heat of the lights seeming to melt her nipples into her areola. She tweaked them from time to time to make them stand up for a good view.

When she saw a face that looked particularly awed, she stopped and gave it a little extra, like Bernstein told her. She fed the guy's eyes while he pumped in the quarters. She made sure he got a good look at her when he was coming. To make a guy lose control —from behind glass — that was good dancing. She had pride in that.

She could also tell when a guy was about to lose interest. She'd do an extra shake, even charge toward him, act like she wanted to bust through the glass and fuck him. Only him. Of course, if it was lunch hour, or right after work at 5pm when all the booths were crowded, then fuck 'im. Somebody else would be more than willing to take his place.

She flashed a lust-hate smile, watching the irregular rhythm of the metal sheets lowering and rising in each booth. She eased up purposefully to one of the booths, kicking her leg up high, practically shoving her snatch into the window. Look at it! Look! She grinned at the shocked reaction, the feverish eyes. She strutted back toward the middle of the stage. The metal sheet stayed down in that booth. The guy was done, all right. He wouldn't soon forget her. Time for the bucket and mop in booth #9. She caught a glimse of Rob and clearly was annoyed at his calm expression. She was heading for him when the peep show window shut.

Bernstein offered a handful of quarters, but Rob politely declined. The manager led Rob down the row of booths and through a door marked "Stay OUT." it was the dressing room. Two girls lounged on a couch, naked, smoking. They ignored the two men. A fat white girl with cellulite thighs and bad skin was wiping sweat from her neck with a towel. The white women rarely had the good bodies. Light skinned blacks and Hispanics made up the bulk of the better looking models. A good looking white girl had many more lucrative options in the sex world, like lap dancing for yuppies in some fancy East Side topless bar or lunch hour dive around Wall Street.

"Can't you turn down the heat, Mr. Bernstein?" the white girl whined, putting the towel down and sitting with her legs spread wide.

"Why? You want to get goose bumps from the cold? Who pays to watch a plucked chicken!"

Bernstein looked at Rob and winked. Then he said, "I take care of my girls, I really do." He nodded to a Puerto Rican girl just entering the room. She took off her bathrobe and tossed it on the sofa. She checked herself out in the full length mirror. She spread her legs as she stood. She pawed at her pubic hair and squatted.

"Can you see the string?" she called out.

"Not unless you really squat," one girl answered.

"I cut it far as I could. Don't want for to have to go in after it."

Bernstein whispered to Rob, "She wants to be a secretary. This job pays for her night classes. She has two children to support. I really want the girls to save their money. If I catch a girl hooking, she's out. Drugs? Out! I get lots of girls who want to be actresses some day. You know, this is a good way to lose your inhibition in front of a crowd. Want to talk to one of them?"

"No, that's OK," Rob said.

"Don't be shy."

"I'm not," Rob answered. It was like being in a locker room or a doctor's office. There really wasn't anything sexy about it and he and Julie had some good sex last night. It made this sight about as exciting as an all-you-can-eat buffet in a school cafeteria.

"We'll go over to the conversation booths," Bernstein said.

"Phone sex?"

"Yeah, but it's better than phone sex. Phone sex, you have to use your imagination. Here you *see* her while you talk on the phone. And it's only a dollar a minute. You can talk to Chrissie. She's been with me since the conversation booths were put in a few months ago. If you're going to write up what's going on in Times Square, this is it!"

Just past the peep show area was a smaller room. It held a set of five cabanas, each one double the size of a phone booth. For a dollar token, a man could enter one side of the booth, and his choice of girl would be on the other. A sheet of clear glass was between them, floor to ceiling. Two-way phones were on the wall so that they could talk. It was a scene one might expect at a very liberal prison. For a minute the man could see the woman, talk to her, ask her to strip and pose — he could do whatever came naturally or unnaturally.

At a dollar a minute, this was the only time premature ejaculators could feel pride about themselves. Only a few men were milling about in the room. The girls stood in front of their booths. Each wore an unrevealing robe, each a different color. Regularly one of the Indian employees would call out sternly, "Dollar change. No just looking!"

Some men stayed as long as they could, hoping for one of the girls to let her robe fall open to reveal her bra and panties. If a girl thought a man was interested she might give him a little teasing smile to jump start him. One of the girls disappeared into a booth. A man slowly walking to his side of it, casually, as if *she* was paying him.

Bernstein rubbed his salt-and-pepper moustache with his finger and said, "That was Chrissie." He motioned for Rob to follow him. They went behind the change counter into a little room hardly bigger than a closet. Inside was a push button telephone. Bernstein picked up the phone, punched 4, paused, and handed the phone to Rob.

"What do you think of this, huh baby?" Rob heard a husky male voice say.

"Oh that's a nice one, honey," Chrissie told him. "I like it."

"You'd like to suck on it."

"Oh that's a nice one, for sure, honey."

"Bend down for me baby, like you wanna suck it. Can you...take your top off for me?"

"Sure, honey. Like this?"

"Yeah. Now kind of, get down low, like you're gonna do it."

"Oh, I'd like to suck it..."

There was silence on the line. Rob knew what was going on now, the naked girl miming a blow job, her mouth inches away from the cock behind the glass, the man looking down, his own lust making the fantasy real.

"Yeah, you're sucking it, you're sucking it, suck...suck...swallow it, you're swallowing it...tell me...say you like it."

"I like it..."

"Hold your mouth open..."

A few moments later, the man's voice appeared on the line again, this time it was well modulated, matter-of-fact.

"Maybe you'd like to meet me after work."

"No honey , I can't. That's not allowed."

"We could have dinner. That's all. Nothing wrong with that."

"Thanks, but I really can't."

"I could show you a real good time."

"I'll bet. Look, you take care, baby, drop by again and see me some time."

Rob put the phone down.

"I can monitor all the booths," Bernstein said. "I catch a girl selling herself after her shift, and she's out. They don't have to do that here. They get good pay. Hundreds and hundreds a week. Pure cash. So why should they spoil it all and be hookers?"

Chrissie was lounging outside her booth when Rob and Bernstein came back. She was a light skinned black girl wearing a long black wig. She had a calm, friendly look to her face and rich, dark brown eyes with little light brown flecks in them. She seemed to have the warm good nature of a receptionist or a nurse.

"Hello, Mr. Bernstein," she said. "Hello," she added, nodding pleasantly to Rob.

"Why don't you talk to Chrissie for a minute?" said Bernstein. "I don't think so," Rob said. There was a metallic strain to his voice. "I don't think my girlfriend would understand."

"What kind of an investigative reporter are you!" Bernstein laughed. "You don't have to DO anything. Just talk in the booth. It'll give you an idea what a booth is like. Can't have you talking out here, for God's sake. Here, just talk to Chrissie. In there."

He waved his hand and one of the Indians came over. "Five tokens for this gentleman." He handed the coins to Rob. Rob caught the resentful eyes of the meandering customers nearby. Who was this guy who got to talk to the beautiful girl for free, the bastard!

There were a few dry crusty patches of white on the glass that the clean-up man missed. Rob backed up a little. He caught himself wiping the receiver of the phone against his sleeve before holding it up.

"I guess a job like this could be depressing if you don't have the right attitude," Rob said.

"Oh, yeah,' Chrissie said thoughtfully, "but most of the men that come in are very nice gentlemen. They just talk, you know, that kind of thing." She spoke quietly, almost apologetically. "They're just lonely."

"Women get lonely too, but they don't get so pathetic."

Chrissie shrugged lightly. "Least we make some money out of it."

"Do you have regulars who drop by?"

"A few. Yeah. Some men I see a few times a week. They just want to talk. Doesn't matter what they say. I don't care what they say. That's what I tell the other girls when they first get here. It's just loneliness talking. Loneliness ain't natural. That's the only unnatural thing. You're not supposed to be that way — not for too long. I see them through and they get less lonely, and maybe that helps them."

"Helps them?"

"To, you *know*," Chrissie said with an appraising smile. "Like you say. To feel not so *pathetic*. Then they can find someone of their very own."

"That guy who just left — I guess you see men like that a lot. They'll stay here till..."

Chrissie smiled broadly at Rob's self-consciousness.

"I don't mind what they do. It makes them feel good. It's just play is how I look at it. I'm not harmed to play games."

"Well, I don't want to take up any more time..."

The veneer of the investigative reporter was eroding. "It was nice talking to you." Rob hung up the phone.

"See you," Chrissie said.

Bernstein was saying on the way downstairs, "Chrissie's going on vacation next month. That's another of my rules. Every girl who works for me more than three months gets a regular vacation. Three months on, a week off. I take care of my girls. I keep them fresh."

He paused at the landing. "Speak of fresh. Here's spring cleaning for you."

There were several large cardboard boxes piled up near the stairwell. They were filled with shopworn old magazines and paperbacks. One held a lot of reels of film with a coating of dust on them. "I cleared out this stuff from the top floor storage when I put the Talk-a-Date booths in. Want any of it?"

Rob shook his head. Then he realized he was hurting Bernstein's feelings. So he said, "I don't know. What are the films?"

"How should I know," said Bernstein. "Take some. I'm just gonna throw it out anyway. You have a projector? You know somebody with a projector? Then take it."

Rob picked up a handful of the reels from the bottom, avoiding the dusty top layer. He came up with some 200 foot reels, which came in boxes about the size of a compact disc jewel case, and a few 50 footers, which were barely three-minute long porn films in a box barely the size of an audio cassette.

"These must really be old," Rob said.

"Take some books, too."

"What's this thick reel? This isn't super 8 is it?"

"No," Bernstein said, squinting at it. It was a plain white box, thick, about the size of a double-CD set. "it's 16mm. Sometimes they shoot the film in 16mm and then make the copies in the smaller size. Shooting 16mm was a pain in the ass. You had to change the reels ever three or five minutes. The quality was better that way, but not everybody bothered. I'll get you a shopping bag—"

"I don't have a 16mm —"

"Give it to somebody who does."

"I don't even think I still have an 8mm projector. I had all my old family home movies transferred to video."

"Then why are you taking all of my films?" Bernstein

said with mock-brusqueness. "Don't forget the paperbacks."

Rob noticed a few really old 60's porn paperbacks, the kind that used words like "vixen" and "his hard manhood" and nobody did much except mash their lips together in passionate embraces and then "unite." That was the kind of porn he remembered when he was a kid. He took a few with funny looking covers.

The clerk behind the counter carefully put all the stuff into a paper bag, sealed it with tape, then sealed it again. He handed it to Rob with grave seriousness, as he did with all customers.

Rob glanced at his watch. Julie would be home soon from work. He walked down the corner to 42nd and Eighth. He heard the crackle of a police radio. Then he saw two cops standing over what looked like a dirty pile of clothing.

The bum's stubbled face was indistinct from his shabby gray overcoat. The corpse was just a twisted pile; shoeless black feet pointing one way, knobbled legs bent the other. The arms were folded between his thighs as if he had been trying to keep warm, even though it was easily 80 degrees out. The dirty face bore no resemblance to anything human. The toothless hole of a mouth was caved inward and hidden by the stubble, the shut eyes crushed amid the wrinkles and bags under his eyes.

Another bum, lying against a chain link fence a few yards away, coughed out some laughter.

"Hold that guy in case this isn't a tick or tox" one of the cops said.

Rob knew the cop meant that the old bum probably died of a heart attack or the toxic effects of alcohol poisoning.

"I killed him and I'm glad," a crazed, growling voice said behind Rob. He turned. It wasn't a crazy person. It was a crazy writer.

"Cy Kottick," Rob said.

Cy looked deadly serious.

"I had to kill that bum. It was a sex thing. I've become...a hobosexual!"

Another police car pulled up.

"Did you see Slezak already?" Cy asked.

"Yeah," Rob said. "This is his lucky day. Toby Shell was in when I got there. And now you. The whole crew."

Cy held up his hands.

"You see anything? I'm not writing another word for that fuck till I get paid. That's what I'm going up there for. I want the dough, see? They're always late with the pay. Always. It's almost as bad as that guy on 22nd Street."

"Which publisher is that?"

"They're all the same. They think writing is just typing. They have no respect for writers. They hate literacy. They'd as soon run a fuckin' laundry but they couldn't stand the idea of something clean."

Cy was intent on making himself angrier than he was. He lived up to his pen name — if it was a pen name. Rob had no idea and neither did Slezak, or the accountant. Cy insisted on signing his vouchers by that name, and that was the name on the checks. He lived in a transient hotel way over on St. Marks Place and always brought his checks to a check cashing place on 14th Street.

Cy didn't need much, and he was proud of that. He knew every thrift shop in town and what each one specialized in. He knew that the one up around 89th on the East Side always had great $5 shirts with big name brand labels — stuff given up by Yuppies that had outgrown them or simply changed wardrobes every season. And there was a place on Houston that got in a lot of shoes and hats. And there were plenty of cheap places down on Delancey to buy irregular jeans.

Cy was about 45, with straw-colored hair and a straw colored beard that thinly traced the outlines of his cheeks and jaw. He had sharp features, a pointed, longish nose and high cheekbones. His eyes were a piercing shade of light blue. He hinted about being a Vietnam veteran, and his rangy, slouching posture made it easy to imagine him sneaking through some jungle somewhere. The hollows of gray around his eyes also suggested that he had seen enough to make him the borderline psychotic his name implied. Larry said that Cy had divided his time in Nam between fucking and killing and wasn't sure which had changed him more.

Rob reached into his shopping bag and popped some of the tape off the package. He handed Cy one of the old porn paperbacks. Cy grinned. "Small Town Tramp" by Stu Pitt. Has to be a classic. Why isn't there a library for this stuff? If you want to know what went on with a generation, read its pornography."

"What does the porn you write for Rabbit tell us about the world today?"

"It's fucked."

CHAPTER THREE

"'She got de butt, she got de butt.' That's what they say!"

Julie took another sip of the cold white wine and put the glass down. "Where do they get it from? These two kids in my class — Lincoln and Marty — they're not even twelve yet and they're teasing this girl all through recess, shouting "she got de butt" at her till she cried."

"Don't blame this stuff," Rob said, pawing through Mr. Bernstein's gift of porn movies, "that's from MTV, honey."

Julie was a career school teacher. Rob was hearing more horror stories from her and her school kids than he could read in The City Daily.

"Did you bring home the school projector?"

"This is the only one the recreation instructor let me take. I hope it's ok. It looks pretty old." Julie pointed to the big gray box near the door. "It was heavy, I could barely carry it."

"It's not an 8mm. It's a 16mm. I hope I still remember how to run one of these things. Damn it, I knew it. I only got one 16mm film from Bernstein. This'll be a pretty short show."

"Good."

"Good? Didn't you like that video we saw Saturday

night? The two guys on one girl? You said that turned you on. I *know* it turned you on. They could've called that one 'fuck along with us.'"

He had fucked Julie from behind, reaching over and keeping a finger in her mouth to suck on, like she was getting two men at once. They kept the video sound on while they did it, the music and the moans almost making it seem they were starring in it.

They had been living with each other for a year now, and had known each other for another two. If he had some kind of steady job, they probably would have married by now. They were living in her one room apartment. He'd given up his cheap studio, which was in a once-prospering building down around Van Cortland park.

The South Bronx had slowly been swallowing up the North Bronx and Riverdale. Every year the boundaries changed, the burned out buildings extending cancerously upward. From 161st Street to Burnside, then up through Fordham, the little shops and neighborhood stores were exhanged for check cashing parlors and bargain stores where everything was made to sell for ninety nine cents.

Rob remembered when his grandparents finally moved out of their apartment on Burnside. It wasn't the crime, or being forced to stay home. It wasn't the ruin of quiet nights or the loss of friends or the hostility of the new neighbors who couldn't understand why dance music at 2 a.m. was something to complain about. What had finally made them move was when the synagogue closed. Even God had been forced away.

Riverdale was all right for now, Rob reasoned, and Julie's salary as a teacher would get better over the years.

If only he could get his career back on track. He looked at the projector. A projectionist in a movie theater was doing better than he was. A school janitor. A few more years, and he'd have to make a decision on whether to take some job with a pension just to have security.

"Be careful," Julie called out.

"What?"

"The cord. It's frayed. See? They wrapped some electrical tape around it over here, and over there, but it's very loose."

Rob examined the cord. It was scuffed and worn. The projector was definitely ancient, as balky as an old toaster.

"You'd risk death to watch a dirty film?" Julie said.

"Cut it out," Rob answered.

Rob threaded the projector. And snapped the big take-up reel on the bottom. The little roll of 16mm film looked pretty dinky.

"Almost ready."

Julie drained her glass. "Well I'm not watching this one. I have a whole bunch of test papers to try and read. Can't this wait till *after* dinner, Rob?"

"This'll be quick. I'm just curious —"

"Compulsive is more like it."

"Turn out the lights, ok? I'll show it against the wall. Move Arthur out of the way."

Julie swept the avocado plant off the dining room table and walked into the bedroom. She closed the door. Rob stared after her for a moment, then switched on the projector. The ratchety machine started to run, splashing the wall with light. Rob adjusted the focus.

Now here was a willing woman. Lying back on the bed in just her hot red undies. For an old pornie, the picture was sharp and clear. He could see the lace biting into her flesh, each downy pubic hair grazing along her inner thigh. She ran one black-polished fingernail around and around her stiffening pale pink nipple and trailed her hand downward.

She eased the hard-shelled nail inside her pussy and nudged it further in, to the knuckle. She gently slid it out, her white skin glistening with the wetness.

The projector grinded tensely in the quiet apartment, the sound of it making the picture seem somehow sleazier, more forbidden. It was dirtier watching a porn film on the projector, the image flung up against the wall like that, big as life.

The camera panned clumsily up to the blonde who was already sucking on some black guy's dick. She had her eyes closed. Rob looked at the light dusting of freckles across her cheekbones, the whiteness of her eyelashes. Her face was distended with the thick meat, the contrast sharp between the black going in, the white of her skin, and the red slash of lipstick moving in between.

A black hand rested on her head, guiding her face forward, the body pushing forward, the girl just seeming to be there, her eyes closed, no more expression now than a Noh mask.

Rob glanced at the reel and saw that the film was already nearly half over. She kept sucking and sucking.

And then she opened her eyes.

The lights caught them just right. Fiery green they were, a beautiful mysterious green, olive green only so bright the light reflected and danced in them.

Her skin was so smooth and white, white like a model's even with the light freckles. The hair honey blonde and soft. But it was the eyes. This couldn't be — there was something about her. It just couldn't be — it just couldn't be...

Carrie Sinclair?

Carrie Sinclair!

The grinding sound of the projector matched what was grinding in Rob's head, the gears ripping illogically into his brain.

It can't be. It can't!

"We just saw her," Rob said half aloud, "what was that movie in the Riverdale Twin — I think it's her... it's a *young -Carrie Sinclair—* she looks so *young...*"

The reporter's sneer curled as he watched the black hand on the black cock, rubbing up and down, slowly, slowly, working that cock over and over, stiff and hard, right in front of the face, the face with the eyes closed again, closed over like the Noh mask.

She barely flinched when the come hit her, a few thick wads that skidded against her cheek, hard to see at first, her skin so Nordic white. The porn stud knew what to do, pushing his meat closer, taking aim. The next spurt plopped heavily on her lower lip.

Now the camera tilted slightly, and the girl moved backward, and the black man awkwardly tried to get into bed with her. This would be the fuck scene. He was running his hand over her shoulders and breasts, and she was looking to the camera for instructions, and he was smirking and saying something. The camera tilted down, out of focus, the screen filled with white flesh.

Then the screen went black.

Rob looked up at the projector. The reel was still unspooling. He blinked and looked at the screen again. Blackness.

"I've gone blind — my punishment for watching this stuff."

Rob slapped at the stop switch and flicked on the lights, his eyes squinting momentarily. As patiently as he could, he pulled the reel off the spool and slapped down the ratchets holding the film in place as it wound in and out of the machine. He held the film up to the light.

Nothing.

OK, reporter, he thought to himself. He tried to remember his photography course from college. "It's not underexposed. Then it would be white or light gray. And it's overexposed if it's black. Or is it the other way around? But this part doesn't look like it was used at all. What the hell did the cameraman do?"

Rob found the part of the film where the image changed from a picture to nothing. He ran his finger over it. He didn't feel any splices. He held it up to the light. He didn't see any splices.

He tried to remember everything Bernstein had said in the porn store. And it was beginning to add up.

Plain white box. A 16mm print. 16 mm used for the original copies before they were duped into 8mm and Super 8.

So this was an *original*. *Nobody* made a dupe of it. Nobody. Nobody finished it. It must've got lost somewhere along the line years ago. Ten years ago at least. But that's her. That's HER! And nobody knows it!

Rob nodded his head as he expertly re-threaded the film onto the projector.

"Are you finished?" Julie said, opening the bedroom door.

"You've gotta see this!"

"Oh, Rob," Julie said, "let's watch it later. Maybe I'll be in the mood. I just don't *feel* like watching it now."

"But it features one of your favorite actresses."

Julie glared at him.

"At least, I think it is." Rob said. "That's why I want you to see it. I'm not sure — I need second opinion."

"Second opinion?"

"Come on, sit down. I want to show it to you! Just a little bit. You only have to see just a little bit. Come on!"

Julie stood with her arms folded. She let Rob gently push her from behind, toward the living room and the projector.

"She's a lot younger, but it's her," Rob said confidently. "You just tell me who. Let's see if you can figure out who this is."

"All right," Julie said, "let's get it over with."

Rob turned off the lights at the same moment he gunned the projector.

Julie paused for a moment.

"Oh, that's disgusting," Julie said, more out of bored disappointment than anything else.

"Just look at the girl. Who is it? Come on!"

"I'm supposed to know this girl?"

"Actress."

Rob jammed a lever on top of the machine and froze the picture.

"OK, can you tell now? Or should I run it from the beginning?"

"Rob..."

"Isn't this the star," Rob coaxed, "of 'Night in Rio'...which we saw at The Riverdale Twin...'"

"Carrie Sinclair?" .

"You know what she's going to do for me?"

Julie looked at Rob. Rob flipped the projector off and answered his own question.

"She's going to get me back on The City Daily, that's what she's going to do. Or she's going to make me rich. Or both!"

Julie sat down on the couch. She nervously twisted a finger into her long light brown hair. She kicked off her slippers and tucked her feet under her. She was wearing a light printed skirt at a knit top with a modest neckline. Teaching some unruly kids at school, she didn't need them trying to look up her dress or down her blouse.

Rob came to sit down beside her. He nuzzled her neck.

"You think that wretched little film turned me on?" she said coldly.

"Huh?"

"Rob, you can't *do* something like that. What's gotten into you? When you first started bringing home these porn videos and things, it was ok. I'll admit, sometimes it was even sexy. But now you don't even send out your resumes, you don't even try to write articles for real magazines —"

"It's all cliques, I've told you that," Rob said angrily. "I'm tired of writing on spec. I'm tired of writing a whole story and sending it out and having nobody even read it. I don't need form rejection letters anymore."

"So you're going to make money off this creepy little film you snuck out of a porn store?"

"I didn't sneak it out of anywhere! That girl knew

what she was doing. That was Carrie Sinclair, all right. The same old story. The oldest one in the book. So this was old Carrie's start in show biz. Before she got wise and started blowing producers instead."

"Is that what you think when I do that to you? You think that I'm just a cocksucker? Am I a slut?"

"If you did it in a film, maybe yes."

"What are you, for writing dirty stories?"

"Don't start playing games with me, Julie. You want to live in this crummy place till all of Riverdale turns into a war zone like the Bronx? Don't you want to live in a place where guys don't call you "Mommy" and "Mama" on the street when you try and walk home with the groceries?

"Just because you've had some hard luck with your career, that's no reason to do something so...so low!"

"Take a look at Carrie. She knew how to get ahead in the business. Here's a scoop, and it's going to get me ahead. It's going to get me back at The City Daily!"

"This isn't a scoop. This is sneaky and dirty, and I can't believe you can be so mean."

"You don't even know her."

"Her? Don't you mean 'it'? Only an 'it' has no feelings."

Julie shook her head. "You really think you'll get somewhere with this?"

Rob nodded. "I'll make a killing."

CHAPTER FOUR

Rob crawled up the steep steps to the elevated subway at 238th Street. On this, the next to last stop on the line, far up into the North Bronx and just touching the Riverdale suburb, the train was always empty. Rob went to the front car and sat down.

"Make a pass, grab some ass, licky licky boom boom down on the grass!" Three black teenage girls were laughing, a boombox playing rap was at their feet. They were standing at the front of the subway car, looking out the window.

"I'm drivin' this train," one of them said, shoving one of her friends with her shoulder.

The tune played its repetitious refrain over and over. Finally the engineer slowly opened the door to his cramped cabin and said, "OK, Ladies, that's enough o' that."

The music stopped.

"Yes," one of the girls said solemnly, "we *ladies*." Then they all burst out laughing.

Rob wondered if they were the kind of girls in Julie's classroom. They were wearing white blouses and the same dark blue skirts. He looked carefully at the blouses. Were those junior high school tits or high school tits, or were these girls just big-for-their-age elementary schoolers? At thirty-something, Rob found all school kids beginning to look the same, just as to school kids, anybody over 20 was one age: near death.

When the train finally hit the tunnel and made its way underground into Manhattan, Rob studied his reflection in the darkly mirroring window. He thought, for a minute, that he might almost pass for college age. At least, in this light. His dark brown hair, still reasonably free of gray and hardly thinned at all, was neatly combed. He'd kept it short, ever since he got the job at The City Daily.

He'd had a beard and moustache in college, but had shaved it when he started really looking for a job — the first years when he realized poetry not only couldn't pay the rent, but he couldn't even sell any to the little journals each caught up in its own brand of arch obscurity. The fuzzy college days were gone, and Rob now prided himself on his strong features. He had dark eyebrows that lent more intensity to his cool blue eyes. He liked the white, keloid scar that ran for about an inch just off his right eyebrow on the side. It made him seem like a boxer. But to anybody who asked, he admitted it was just a dumb bicycle accident, riding smack into an overhanging metal fire box on Kingsbridge Road, where he used to live as a kid.

The sound of the boombox erupted. The girls turned the music back on as they left the train at 145th.

Rob thought of Julie. Did she really want to spend her life teaching art to impudent school kids? The big dream was that she'd be illustrating children books. And he'd have his own newspaper column.

"You could quit your job if this hits big," Rob said last night.

But Julie said nothing.

What was with Julie, anyway? Didn't she realize this was the perfect shot here, the perfect shot to get back on The Daily City?

The City Daily building was up on 45th Street, just off Eighth Avenue. It was close enough to Forty Deuce to prevent most everyone from feeling any liberal thoughts about the porn world. Too many secretaries had to endure being mistaken for hookers, or for sluts, or for runaways. Too many timid office boys had to turn eyes-front when big angry black pimps swaggered by, or crazies suddenly demanded attention. There were too many lunch hours gone sour with the homeless and the juvenile delinquents and screaming streetcorner religious fanatics who somehow had enough money for microphones and P.A. speakers, the better to shout at the world. And it was all the fault of smut. If Times Square didn't have so much porn none of this would be here.

A big, nearly block-long hotel had just been built on the next block, all with fresh new Japanese money. But somehow that only increased the number of conmen and hookers and sleazeballs in the area. Nobody could figure that out. The hotel was expensive, too.

"Hi, Elise," Rob said to the mousy, serious-looking girl sitting at the reception desk. She just stared. With her tangled dyed auburn hair, round face and hard-bitten pout she looked like a hungry woodchuck. She could have been fifty, sixty. It was hard to tell. She wasn't married and in all the years of working the lobby of The City Daily, never had a man even hit on her for a date. Her job at reception was to give everyone a chilly reception, and her face was in an almost permanent scowl.

"It's me. Rob Streusel. Remember?"

She nodded suspiciously.

"Is either Mr. Simon or Mr. Colman in?"

Without a word, the girl stuck a plug into the switchboard and paused for a moment.

"Mr. Simon is away from his desk," she said a second later.

"What about Mr. Colman?" Rob asked.

"Mr. Colman is away from his desk," she said.

"You could've at least tried his number before telling me that," Rob said. He looked around. Staff reporters and secretaries and clerks and typists were bustling back and forth. The security guard was smiling efficiently at each one of them.

"Listen, Elise, put me through to Michael Krebs, ok? Is he in?"

Rob stared at the far wall of the lobby. He turned it into a screen, and on it he replayed the Carrie Sinclair porn movie. The movie star sucking on that cock. Rob smiled to himself, thinking about how he'd manage to find a way of describing that for a "family" newspaper audience.

Rob was thinking about the euphemisms when Elise said, "Michael Krebs is in his office."

"Good. Well, tell him I'm coming up for a second."

"You can't go up, Rob," Elise said. "It's the policy of the paper when it comes to ex-employees."

"You do remember me."

"That's the policy."

"You've got to be kidding," Rob said. It was a very dumb thing to say to someone as serious and by-the-book as Elise. She looked offended, her overly mascara'd eyes narrowing, her little face turning more squirrelly than usual.

"Come on, Elise."

"I didn't make the rules, Rob. You *don't* work here anymore."

"Can I talk to him? Where's a phone?"

Elise pointed to a house phone at the far end of the reception desk. It had a little orange light on it and it was lit. Rob picked it up.

Michael had always been one of his friends at the office. He worked in the sports department, and sometimes they'd have lunch and talk about how lousy the Yankees were when they were growing up — the days of Horace Clarke and Danny Cater and nobody able to get a batter out except Stottlemyre.

Once when Michael had mononucleosis, and had used up his sick days, Rob had covered for him and gone to three night games in a row at the Stadium, taking care to write his copy in Michael's style.

Rob shook his head. Maybe he'd still be at The City Daily if he had easy writing like that; just covering sports.

Rob had seen him at a Yankee game a few years ago. Michael had seemed pretty friendly. He didn't offer an assignment or anything, but he did seem to mean it when he said, "I hope you're doing ok."

"Hey Mike — I can't come up. They won't let me upstairs, is that crazy? Can't you get somebody to clear me?"

"Gee Rob, no."

"Can you come down here?"

"No, no I can't Rob. I mean, I'm on deadline right now."

"I got a great story. Listen, how about this: a big movie star who made a porn flick that nobody knows about!"

"Gee, that sounds like something for the gossip page, doesn't it? You want me to connect you? What are you, giving it in as a tip? You know Dawn Landgrebe, she doesn't give any credits in her column."

"No, I have a movie that has..."

Rob looked at Elise looking at him. It was a dirtier look than any full-crotch close-up in any porn film.

"Look, this film has a *big* star, Michael. Listen, you're the only one I still know at the paper, besides...Simon and Colman." He still hated to mention by name the managing editor and the publisher.

"Why don't you write a query letter to Mr. Colman or one of the other editors?"

"Thanks, Mike." Rob put the phone down.

"You'll have to leave now," Elise said.

The lobby of The City Daily was cool, a sanctum of granite and marble. Rob pushed the heavy revolving door and found that it was broiling out on the street. Rob hadn't noticed how hot it was until now.

The newsstand across the way from the building had nothing but copies of The City Daily all over the front of the booth. That, Rob noticed, had to be because this particular newsdealer was stone blind. Somebody on the staff was probably hired to go down and sneak all the competing papers off and replace them with theirs.

Way in the back, with protective wrappers around them, were the offensive magazines that, if some people had their way, would not be deemed fit to print.

Rob made out the dumb bunny ears that formed the two "b's" in Rabbit Magazine.

"All right, pricks," Rob said under his breath, looking around the lobby of The City Daily. "You don't want to pay any attention to me, I'll find another publication that will."

He headed down toward Forty Deuce.

"Glad you dropped by," said Larry Slezak, "I'm putting out the call. I got my deadlines fucked up. Need some shit as soon as you can. Write a story, any story. I'm not picky."

"Yeah? When do you need it?"

"Yesterday. I gotta call Cy. He'll knock out some good filth for me. Hey, do you want to hear something really gross? This is the latest from Cy. Get a load:

'They come after her and before she knows it, the chick is pork-assed and cock-mouthed, grunting and drooling and frantically digging into her clit with her free hand, almost waving her strumming fingers as if she'd like a third man on her. The dog style dig is getting more and more manic. She raises her ass up, and it's a tight fit, she squirms quite a bit until he hits deep into that dark pit, not stopping till he's shot his load into her butt. He pulls out and her asshole is still wide, so wide you could drop a golf ball in there. And she'd probably love it. She's got her hands pulling her cheeks apart, ready for more. Another man steps in, adjusts himself, rubs his already hard swollen cock, and slams in. He's missed the asshole, going for cunt. But he's a smart boy, he jams two fingers into her ass. She shivers and shudders her body wet with sweat, and she comes, comes, comes..."

"What's that all about?"

"I told Cy to do an article: German whore houses where anything-goes-orgies are a way of life."

"Not that he went to one."

Larry laughed. "His imagination is a hell of a lot

better. So what's with you? If this is a social call I'm so, so flattered."

Rob looked into Larry's leering face. He thought about what Julie had said. Now, the anger he had felt at The City Daily had cooled. He had to push himself to ask the question.

"Larry, did you guys ever do a celebrity nude? What does Krantz pay for something like that?"

"You've got nudies? On who?"

"Well, it looks like it might be Carrie Sinclair."

"Bring it in!" Larry said, his eyes bright, an open-mouthed look of delight on his face. "Shit, that bitch is hot. I don't think she's ever even done an R-rated movie! Didn't she make a bunch of beach movies? I swear I've seen 'em on USA cable. She's always in a bikini, and that's as far as she goes. I don't think she's even shown tits on screen! This could be great. Can you go back home and get it?"

Larry was leaning so far forward in his seat, he was practically in Rob's face.

"I don't even know if it's really her," Rob said, backing off.

"You know it is! Bring it in, for Chrissake. Don't be a putz!"

"I was wondering — if it really *is* Carrie Sinclair, then it's worth a cover. What's the circulation of Rabbit? About a hundred thousand, or something? Let's say this issue is a sell-out. Would that be worth a dollar a copy?"

Larry gave Rob a "come on, you're nuts" frown, his mouth sliding into a sour grin.

"Wait a minute, you're saying a hundred thousand dollars?"

"You guys would be making a big profit. What if you raised the cover price an extra dollar?"

"Any other bright ideas?"

"Well how about if you doubled the print run? You print up 200,000 copies. Anything you don't sell, you keep on hand. Over the years they'll be collector's items. You could charge ten dollars each for them mail order."

"For Chrissakes, maybe I can get you five hundred bucks. Maybe a thousand if these pictures are really great. You've got eight by tens?"

"It's a film. It's film footage."

"We'd have to convert it. That's expensive to do, you know."

"Yeah. I'll bring the stuff by some time."

Larry reached out and grabbed Rob's wrist. The hold was surprisingly strong.

"Come in tomorrow with 'em."

Larry's eyes were white, the pupils only small dark spots in the center.

"I don't even know for sure if it's Carrie Sinclair," Rob said.

On the subway home, Rob checked out the newsstand and the headline for The City Daily. Something about the President and taxes. Was this their idea of a grabbing headline? The newspaper was fifty cents now. Rob bought a candy bar instead. He ate it in a few gulps as he waited for the train.

Back in Riverdale he walked into the pizza joint right next to the station and bought two huge slices of pizza with everything on it. As he sat, spinning the oregano container around and around with his free hand, he tried not to think about the bastards.

No breaks anywhere, from The City Daily to Rabbit magazine. That company boy Michael Krebs was one thing. But what was Larry trying to pull, playing it close to the vest like that? Five hundred bucks for a celebrity nude?

Rob got out of the pizza parlor and the sunlight splashed over him, the hot breath of humidity coating his face, the oregano from the pizza stinking its aftertaste in his throat.

He put the shower on cold and put his face in it. But when he came out dripping into the bedroom, it was so humid in the apartment he didn't even feel cold. He flicked on the oscillating fan that dumbly shook its metal head back and forth.

The phone rang.

"Yeah?"

"Rob? That you?"

"Yeah."

"It's Larry. Larry Slezak. Listen, I was thinking. You know, I could really use an assistant down here. An associate. Something like, maybe a managing editor. A managing editor is what I need. I've been thinking about it for a while now, and I want to talk it over with you. We could go as high as $20,000. And we wouldn't need you to hang around the office every day or anything, so you'd still be free to do freelance. Could be a good gig while you get your bearings."

Water dripped down Rob's face all over the phone.

"I don't know. I just got out of the shower."

"You're not making sense, Rob. Listen, what were you talking about before? About a film? Bring it down with you tomorrow. I want you to meet the publisher. Can you do it?"

Rob wiped at his eyes. Larry's voice was harsh in the receiver, loud. "Come on, Rob. I want to see if I can help. You really looked pissed off or something today. Why don't you give yourself a break?"

"Yeah. All right, I'll try and make it."

"What time?"

"I don't know. You're in all day, aren't you?"

Maybe Julie was right. It was muggy in the apartment and it only made him restless. He wasn't used to it. He needed a job or something. Rob looked at the cruddy portable typewriter set on his desk with the stack of paper waiting. It was so much better at the newspaper, when he could knock out stories on the computer. He looked at the beaten-up desk that he'd promised himself would go after a few more pay checks.

$20,000 was nothing. Julie was making more. But at least it was a job again. New furniture. Maybe a move into Westchester, so Julie could get into a better school.

He sat on the bed. He tried to think. From six floors down he heard the sounds of kids yelling and playing, some car driving by with Salsa music thumping at full volume. He thought Riverdale was hot stuff when he first moved in. A big improvement from the Bronx. But the guys he knew in college were already living in Manhattan now, on high floors with sound-proof windows, making real money. Or else they were out in some suburb on Connecticut talking about how they saw David Letterman drive by. It was embarrassing to live in Riverdale. And nobody ever wanted to visit him. It was the end of the earth to them.

"Don't you want to work with *her*?" Larry said, holding up a cover of Rabbit, pointing at it with his finger, tapping on the tits. Larry's mouth was a leering open smile. He was sitting sideways in his chair, in profile, leering back at Rob like an old vaudevillian trying to tempt with an old soft shoe. "Do it for *her*. She needs you. She wants you. Without you, she has nothing to say. Nobody to write her captions. Don't you want to put words in her mouth?"

Larry shuffled through the mess of papers on his desk; "I just got something in today, this is great." He found an envelope, opened it, and fished out a bookmark-sized piece of paper. He handed it to Rob.

It was a four-for-a-dollar set of photos taken in a public photo booth. A girl not more than 18, with thickly painted dark pink lips, tawny brown bangs obscuring her face, and a snub nose had her tank-top up around her neck. She was holding her small breasts, squeezing them as she pushed them toward the camera like she was selling lemons.

"Do you believe this?" Larry smirked, "got her name and address here. She wants to be in our amateur photo section."

The joke was that Rabbit didn't have such a section. All the photos on those two pages were old stock photos from past girlie sets. Real photos never made it in. The publisher had a policy against using them, figuring the people might be really crazy and sue, or that the photos might have been stolen off some hapless person's nightstand and submitted for a prank. It amused Larry how many Polaroids came in, and that so many were from the Bible Belt, where bored housewives were the most virulent swingers.

"She's not half bad," Larry said, snapping the photo out of Rob's hand with one quick swipe. "It's better than all the damn mail we get from guys in prison!

Look at this letter: 'Every night I touch myself...reading Rabbit.' And looking at the pictures! That makes her a dyke! I could bring her home to Tee and have a three-way. Shit, where's she from again? Yeah, right over the river. Hoboken! Hey, you could call her up and get some action. Wouldn't that be a change? Aren't you tired of the same old thing after all these years? You play ball with me..."

The smile left Larry's face. His eyes stared intently into Rob's.

"Listen, what's the deal with this film, Rob? You brought it, right? Give it up. Let me take a look. This16mm? Sound?"

Larry got his magnifying lupe, which was lying like a round chess piece atop a few color slides on his desk, all of them marked with one word: "Tee."

"After I look at your film slut, you can have another look at Tee," Larry said. He put the lupe to his eye after unspooling a portion of the film which coiled into his lap. He held the film up to the glaring bulb in the cheap lamp on his desk.

"I'm supposed to know who this is?"

"I told you who it is," Rob said.

"Uh huh. Yeah. Looks a little like Carrie Sinclair, but see, there's no way you can prove that it's her."

"It's her. She's just ten years younger."

"Yeah, but anybody using it would have to say "Carrie Sinclair lookalike" or something like that. How old is Carrie Sinclair? You know, we could get busted if we print this and it turns out she was under age. What you're giving me is a big headache."

Larry smoothed back his hair with the palm of his hand.

"And this is the only copy?

"Yeah."

"Nobody knows about it except you?"

"Me and Carrie Sinclair, I guess."

Larry put the film down. He pointed his finger at Rob and then back at himself. "You and me." Then he jerked his thumb backward toward the office that said I. Krantz.

The publisher's office was large.The carpet was very thick and plush, but an ugly shade of brown. Rob looked at the walls, one of which was filled with homely photos of Irwin Krantz and his wife and his kid. They were on a boat. They were on vacation. They were in front of a big house. The son was about 35, wearing shapeless green corduroys in the summer and a plaid shirt that was baggy at the waist. He had blank brown button eyes and a little brown moustache that looked more like smeared fudge under his nose. His teeth were Chiclet thick and stood atop his lower lip, giving him a hungry, weasel-like expression. His hair was straight and spilled awkwardly over his large ears. Irwin's wife wore the same severe expression in every picture, and always seemed to be staring at her son.

The other wall held what looked like diplomas and citations, most of them seeming to state that Mr. Krantz was a fellow in good standing with various publishing groups and organizations. The furniture was all dark mahogany, the lighting subdued. The surroundings were opulent compared to the sparse metallic furniture and bare white plasterboard walls of the outside office. A retail magazine rack, the kind in a coffee shop, made out of wire and able to turn, stood off near the plump sofa. It held copies of the mid-range sex magazines that were the competition; titles like Caper, Bolt and Sultan.

The expanse of the thick sofa extended to Krantz himself, squat and heavy.

As Larry and Rob walked in, Irwin Krantz was on the phone. He was looking at the wall as he talked. In profile, the heavy-set publisher was nothing more than a series of fat bubbles ascending to the bald dome on top. He was leaning over and his shoulders were sloped, and there were bulbous ripples of fat at the base of his skull where his neck was supposed to be.

The fleshy ripple of neck was thick, almost goiterous, scabbed with puffs of gray-white hair that looked like thinned dabs of cotton. It was obvious from those woolly tufts that he hadn't been to a barber in a long time. The little hairy knots became more cohesive as they reached the thinning, curly ring of gray hair that cut a two inch swatch in a horseshoe around his head.

The profile deteriorated down the other side of his body, a slide from his round small forehead to his pug nose, a ripple at the lips, and then a dead drop inward on the chin. The bubble gained force from the tie knotted severely at his neck. The slope ran outward from his chest to his stomach where it overlapped the tightly buckled belt by several inches.

"Yahhh," he said languidly, "Right. You take care of it. That's what I keep you on retainer for. G'bye. Yahh."

Krantz turned his face slowly toward Larry and Rob as they stood in front of his desk. His small eyes were impassive, dead and dark brown. His mouth began to work.

"So, what do you two want?"

“Irwin, I’d like you to meet Rob Streusel.”

Irwin Krantz remained expressionless. For a moment his firm, prominent lips seemed to shudder slightly, as though about to speak, but he remained silent. His eyes shifted to the sofa. Larry walked over to sit down in it, and Rob followed.

Irwin Krantz remained inert for what seemed like a full thirty seconds. He lifted a pudgy hand, a gold ring biting into the pinky flesh. He reached for a clear blue Bic pen and held it. Krantz muttered to Larry, “Does he know cunt?”

“He’s been writing for us a long time,” Larry answered. “You liked that piece he did about peep shows? That line, what was it, you put a quarter in a slot to look through a slit and see a slut!”

Irwin Krantz’s lips seemed to form a smile but it could as easily have been a sneer.

“He really know cunt?” the publisher said.

“This guy knows cunt inside and out,” Larry said. “I told you

about this guy. He used to be an investigative reporter once, but he’d rather work for us.”

Larry looked at Rob. “We’re an expanding corporation, Rob,” he said in an unnatural-sounding voice, “we’re planning on setting up several new magazines in the near future. We might do one on movies, like a knock-off of Premiere, with reviews and interviews.”

Irwin Krantz nodded his great head slowly and then he put his elbows on the desk and sank his head down into his hands. His cheeks were soft and they slid upwards into his eyes as he propped his head between his palms. The fat of his cheeks drew up, making his eyes slant. The pressure from the hands on the sides of his face pushed his mouth wide into an unwanted, thin v-shaped grin.

"You could become the editor of your own magazine," Larry told Rob. Larry was looking at Krantz all the while.

Irwin Krantz leaned back in his chair. He let his thick hand drop onto the small cardboard stick-up calendar on his desk. He turned it idly over and over. Rob saw the words printed in mock-gold lettering on the calender pad: "Courtesy of Delmo Auto Repairs, Day or Night."

Larry said to Krantz, "Rob would be a fine addition to the editorial department." He added to Rob, "we'll be moving to new offices someday soon, too."

There was an awkward silence.

"That's it," Irwin said with boredom. The publisher's face was bloodless, expressionless. The doughy face had come to life for a moment or two. Now it was inert, almost not even blinking. Larry and Rob got up and walked out slowly, quietly out, as though not to wake him.

"What was all that stuff about new magazines?" Rob asked when they were back at Larry's cubicle.

"Irwin likes to think he's a big mogul, that's all."

"Has he read any of my stories?"

Larry smirked. "Irwin's a publisher. Publishers are illiterate. You should see what happens when he decides we have to re-do a cover line. He spells it all wrong and if I don't check it, it'll go out screwed up."

The phone rang.

"Rabbit. Oh, hi, Toby. No, tomorrow's fine. Not too early in the morning, this time, all right? I don't want you waiting around in the hallway for an hour till I get here and open up!"

Larry looked at Rob and said, "Leave the film here. The art department can blow up a few frames and make some stats and we can see exactly what we've got here."

Larry re-rolled the film and put it back in the white box.

"I'll hold onto it," Rob said.

Larry put the phone down.

"Look, if it's really Carrie Sinclair in that film, I want to find out, and the sooner the better. We could get it into the next issue: Rabbit Exclusive: Carrie Sinclair's Hardcore Porno Past!"

"I don't know, Larry. You said yourself that this could be trouble."

"Yeah. Look where you are! Isn't it about time you took a risk? Look, here's the deal. You get a full-time job — that's $20,000 to start. For nothing, for just finding that film. That's one hell of a finder's fee. You'd be fuckin' stupid to turn it down."

"When am I supposed to start this job?"

"I'll work out the details with Krantz. Don't worry. Wait a minute, will you? Toby's still on the line. Hello, Toby, can I call you back? I'm in the middle —"

Rob noticed a copy of The City Daily, lying folded on the floor next to Larry's desk. "I gotta go, Larry."

"Stay here, read the paper while I talk to Toby," Larry said, scooping up the paper. It was two days old.

"Toby? Yeah. No, I told you, don't see me first thing in the morning, the first thing in the morning I'm not here. Yeah...yeah..."

Rob flipped the pages of The City Daily. The anger vibrated inside him as he flipped past the gossip page, the one he was told *might* take his story, for an unbylined fifty buck "tipster's fee."

One of the big items on the gossip page was a photo of a pretty star and a camera crew blocking traffic in the little park across the way from the U.N.

Filming scenes for her new spy thriller, with its big climax at the United Nations Building, was Carrie Sinclair.

CHAPTER FIVE

Carrie Sinclair's publicist motioned to Rob as he stood just outside the hotel room door. The air was suffocating in the posh hallway, a smell of musty carpet and the musk from heavy air freshener. The publicist, white haired and maternal, whispered, "Be careful."

Rob adjusted his tie, annoyed with himself for dressing up. "Be careful?"

"Yes, didn't you see? One of the papers today had some kind of blind item about her. Something about her making a film a long time ago. An editor from some terrible smut magazine says he has seen it and insists it's Carrie."

"Rabbit magazine?"

"Yes. That's the one. It isn't Carrie of course. She never made a film like that. We'd deny it but it isn't worth the effort."

The anger showed on Rob's face. The publicist said, "You hate those gossips, too? I don't know how they get away with it."

"It's amazing what some people try to get away with. I didn't see the piece. What did it say, exactly?"

The elderly woman shook her head in exasperation. "I don't remember it completely. It doesn't matter because it isn't true."

Rob nodded. Fuckin' Larry Slezak. What the hell was he trying to do?

He knocked on the door.

Carrie Sinclair's suite at the Waldorf Astoria was large and spacious, well lit. The windows were open and there was a fresh scent in the air. There was a tray on the elegant coffee table in front of the couch and it held a large bowl of salad and a tall bottle of mineral water.

The room service waiter had just set it down. He couldn't have been more than 18 and he was clearly nervous in the presence of a beautiful woman, much less a rising film star.

"Vegetarian salad with fresh basil," he said, hunting in his pockets for the bill. "If you could sign this."

Carrie glanced at the tray.

"You didn't mention the bottle of Evian water," she said, "I don't want you to get into trouble. You better write it in."

"Oh, oh, it's all right," the kid blurted.

"Nonsense, I can afford it, believe me." She smiled, "The studio is paying for everything. That makes it so much easier doesn't it?"

The kid exhaled a nervous laugh in response.

"Shall I write it in on the bottom here?"

"Oh, no, no, it's a gift then. A gift for you, Miss Sinclair."

"Well, thank you very much..."

The kid suddenly reached into his coat. Carrie Sinclair flinched for a moment.

"Could you..." the kid fidgeted, "sign this for me? Please, Miss Sinclair? To Joe."

It was a photo of Carrie in a bathing suit from one

of her early beach-horror movies. "I don't look quite that good anymore," Carrie said. She noticed the elderly publicist and Rob standing in the doorway and added with deliberate if humorous emphasis, "and I don't make pictures like that anymore!"

She signed the autograph. The waiter nodded his head several times in unspoken thank yous and walked out beaming.

Carrie motioned Rob to come in.

"I hope you don't mind if I eat during the interview. Can I get you something?"

Carrie Sinclair was incredibly beautiful in person. Rob couldn't tell what was so different about her, but perhaps Julie could have explained it. Carrie had enhanced her naturally light blonde hair with darker, honeyed streaks that blended sensuously in curves, gliding down to her shoulders.

Her eyebrows were also honeyed, adding deepness and character to her face, drawing attention to her eyes, lightly touched with mascara, bright olive green, flickering with light and mystery. The beautiful hair and Carrie's pouting lower lip, pinkened just slightly more than the upper lip, led Rob's eyes in a dizzying mobius strip around and around her face.

Carrie had a pug nose, but the art of her hairdressing and make-up made it seem to disappear entirely into pertness. Rob noticed the slight freckles across the bridge of her nose, not quite hidden by her ordinary make-up. Not hidden in that porn film he had uncovered.

That feeling came back. Julie called it shyness. At The City Daily it was "the lack of the killer instinct." Or just plain gutlessness.

That was years ago, Rob said to himself. He could still see the woman's face. The man she had known was murdered. But there wasn't anything she could do. Getting her name in the papers wouldn't help. She could lose her job. Lose her life! Please, she'd said, please just leave me alone!

"Come in, come in," Carrie said.

The publicist backed away and closed the door. Carrie invited Rob to sit on the couch next to her.

"You can put your tape recorder on the table here," she said. "Did you check the batteries?"

Rob turned his tape recorder on.

"It works. Thanks."

"Good," said Carrie, "I hope you don't mind, but I always ask. I had a writer who didn't realize till the very end that his batteries were shot. I had to do the whole thing over."

"That was nice of you."

"Better that than have them make up the quotes. There's enough of that as it is."

Carrie looked at the full salad bowl like a young girl looking from a balcony down to a department store toy department. She tentatively picked out a spinach leaf and popped it in her mouth.

"My last film is still playing in some of the New York theaters," Carrie said, "so you can ask me about it if you want. And thanks for that photo."

"The photo?"

"In your paper a few days ago. It may seem silly to you, but no matter how big you are, you get a little nervous if you don't see your name in the paper every now and then." Carrie brought the salad bowl into her lap. She was wearing a soft, light cotton skirt with a floral print and the salad seemed like an extension of it.

"I look like the Earth Mother," Carrie said, her palms upward, regarding the salad in her lap. "It's like it's coming right out of my skirt."

Rob had noticed.

"Fire away," Carrie said.

"You mentioned the film with the picture? The kid from room service?"

Carrie licked a bit of basil off a carrot stick and looked quizzically at Rob.

"I mean," Rob said, "the photo that you just autographed for that kid. You said you don't make films like that anymore?"

"Oh. *That* picture. That was, oh, years ago. I forget whether that's the one where I'm carried off by the manatee monster into the Amazan or the one where I'm the Olympic swimmer but there's a plague of piranha invading the lake. One was "The Horror of something or other," and the other was "The Terror of something else."

Carrie re-arranged the napkin so it was under her lap.

"They put some kind of dressing on this. One drop of oil and this skirt is ruined! Silly, isn't it? We knew when we were filming that manatees are only in Florida, and they're just these big harmless lumpy things. And there's no way piranhas can live in a lake! And why in the world would they travel all the way from thc Amazon river ,and somehow *crawl* on land, and then *jump* into a lake just to take a bite out of me!"

"If I were a piranha, that's what I'd do."

Carrie laughed lightly.

"Thank you," she said.

"I was wondering, Miss Sinclair, if any of these old films embarrass you at all."

"Embarrass me? Why should they embarrass me?"

"Well you said you didn't want to think about that beach film, for instance."

"I don't want to think about it only because I have so many other things to think about *now*. I'm working on a very fine movie right now, so that's what I'm concentrating on. It's a wonderful thriller, sort of in the Hitchcock tradition. But don't write that; just say it's a thriller. Everybody says their film is in the Hitchcock tradition, don't they? That means it's copied. This one isn't like that at all. But there's a wonderful chase scene across 42nd Street and over to the United Nations."

"I meant, you wouldn't want to see that old beach film, right?"

"I don't know. I looked so young in it. It's like it was another person. I really don't mind. Do you really want to talk about this? You're not one of those bad-movie buffs, are you?"

"No, no..."

"Good. Because I really can't tell you much about John Carradine and Neville Brand or any of that. Mr. Carradine was only on the set one day and they did process shots of all his scenes underwater. He seemed nice but I hardly met him."

"No, but I was wondering. You made, or there are reports — there are reports that you made some amateur films very early in your career."

Carrie used her fingers to place an olive atop a piece of mozzarella cheese. She put it in her mouth.

"No, what do you mean amateur films? Like in college or something? I didn't go to college. My father couldn't afford it. He couldn't even afford high school, really. Buying a new text book was enough to start a fight. What do you mean?"

"When you first came to New York."

"What are you talking about?" Carrie asked impatiently, but still trying to appear polite.

And, still trying to appear polite himself, Rob looked down and said softly, "42nd Street. You made a film — with an actor..."

He could hear a little intake of breath, the barest gasp.

"I don't know what you mean."

"A black actor —"

"What?"

"A film you made —"

"That newspaper piece this morning!"

Carrie's eyes narrowed. "Who are you?"

"Just a reporter, I just — I just happened to dig it up. The film. I found the film."

"The *film*," Carrie Sinclair gasped. "Then the film really still exists? My God, the film exists? Does it show everything?"

"Yes. Yes it does, Miss Sinclair," Rob said, struggling to keep his reporter's control. He hadn't expected the hurt. He hadn't expected the surprise. He looked into Carrie Sinclair's eyes, which were brighter, paler, very wet.

"Well what have you done with it? Did you take it to the police?"

"The police?"

It was definitely illegal to sell or to make porn films back then, and sometimes the actors got busted.

Especially if they were under age. Carrie must've been under age when she made it!

The actress stood up, the glass bowl thumping onto the table, rolling around and around and around on its base, clattering and clattering until it finally, finally came to a stop.

"What do you want? Who are you?"

"I'm Rob Streusel, I'm a reporter. I was with The City Daily —"

"Was? *Was*? You're not with a newspaper?"

"Uh, well—"

"You *cheated* to get this interview with me! You creep! What are you trying to do?"

"Nothing yet— "

"Yet!" Carrie's hands formed little fists. She shook them and then dropped them in anguish.

"Miss Sinclair — Carrie — we can keep the cops out of it —"

"What? You're with the Mafia! Oh God, oh my God." Carrie pointed wildly at him. "Oh my God! You're with the Mafia, that's it!"

"Jesus, no! Miss Sinclair —"

"I didn't know — I had no — I had no idea what was going to happen. Oh God, oh God!"

"No, please, Miss Sinclair — I found the film and I took it over to Rabbit Magazine —"

"You *bastard*, you scum! You put that thing in the paper? How could you?"

"I thought I could get ten thousand, or fifty thousand — for a moment I thought — "

"Is that all you care about? My GOD is that all you care about?"

"But I didn't sell! I wanted to meet you first —"

"For a counter offer?" Carrie said. Her face was cold with the hurt. "You are the lowest. The lowest. Look at what *happened* in that film — the *destruction*, my GOD!"

Rob tried to put his arms around the distraught star, tried to understand what she was talking about. Destruction? Her virginity? Being degraded by making a pornie? Against her will? She's saying she was under age and made it against her will? Was she a junkie? Did she need the money? She looked like she was enjoying...

"Help me! Help me!" Carrie cried.

Rob, his eyes wide, didn't know if she wanted to be kissed, if she wanted him to hold her tighter — did she want him to just hand her the film?

But she wasn't saying "Help me" to him.

From one of the other rooms in the suite, two bodyguards came running. They looked like Secret Service men; dark glasses, big shoulders and black hair, close-cropped. They wore blue suits with black ties.

One of them wrenched Rob away from Carrie and the other spun him around and grabbed him by the throat.

"Where's that FILM!" Carrie shouted, the tears making ugly black rims around her eyes, her face drained of all color, her lips almost white with fury.

By reflex, Rob gasped, "I don't know!"

The hold on his neck got tighter.

"He has the FILM! HIT HIM!" Carrie shrieked. "Hit him HARD!"

Rob stared helplessly, at the big fist waving menacingly in his face. The bodyguard was cruelly impassive. Rob closed his eyes, shut his mouth tight, drew his lips in, his whole body tensed, his heart throbbing up and down in his chest like a thick rubber mallet.

The fist buried itself in the pit of his stomach, knocking the air out of him in one embarrassing, ridiculously cartoonish guffaw. Rob keeled over in half and stayed that way, stiff and dazed with the pain.

A claw-like hand grabbed him around the neck and began to pull him up, the fingers jamming into his throat. As he involuntarily stood, Rob's stomach muscles felt like ripping rope, the strands pulling away with prickling waves of pain.

The bodyguard released the vise-like hand from Rob's neck. He gagged, trying to get a breath. He wavered to his knees before being brought back up by the hand at the back of his neck.

"Where is the FILM!" Carrie screamed.

Rob's face was frozen, the fingers that dug into his neck seeming to paralyze him, the words he wanted to say were stuck to the back of his throat.

The bodyguard landed one chopping punch to his kidney and Rob crumpled.

The men stood over him.

Rob stared up at Carrie Sinclair, looking for mercy in the cold blonde's face, a face turned hateful. Her stare of loathing shocked him almost as much as the punch.

Somebody was knocking at the door.

"Room service, Miss Sinclair. Can I take your tray?"

Carrie wheeled around.

"Just a minute," she said, sweetly. Rob gagged, still trying to catch his breath. Carrie was smiling now, no sign of tension in her face. God, she was a great actress.

Carrie looked at the clock.

"Damn you, PIG!" she spat.

She looked over to one of the bodyguards, "I've got another interview scheduled for 2:30."

"I'll bring him into the bedroom and fuck him over," the goon said helpfully.

"RABBIT!" Rob cried out.

Everyone stared down at him. The bodyguards reached down and hauled him up by his shirtfront.

"Rabbit," Rob said, "I brought the film up to the Rabbit office."

"What's he saying?"

"Rabbit Magazine," Carrie said with contempt.

"Oh. I heard of that," one of the men said.

"Take his wallet," Carrie said. "I want to know exactly who this man is and exactly where he lives. Get his driver's license."

"I don't drive," Rob wheezed. He looked at the bodyguards.

"I take the subway," he said apologetically.

One of them ripped his wallet in half as if the leather was paper.

"Library card," Rob half-whispered, one of the big gorillas holding up a blank-looking piece of white plastic. "No address anymore. They just — they just use bar codes."

"Shut up!"

One of them grabbed him by the arm and flung him down, knocking his head against the carpeting. The right side of Rob's face began to burn, a patch of skin rubbed raw. He could feel a bump rising slowly over his right eye."

Rob stumbled to his feet.

"He's cut," Carrie said, wincing.

The bodyguard put a paw up against Rob's face and looked at him carefully.

"The blood ain't running *into* the eye," he said. "He's OK."

The other read from a card in the wallet. "Rob Streusel. 2835 Webb Avenue, Riverdale..."

"He's not Mafia?" Carrie said.

"Hell, he's not even YMCA."

"You get that film to me," Carrie said to Rob. "Now GET OUT!"

The bodyguard flung Rob against the door and Rob banged off it with a groan. He didn't know if the sick cracking sound was one of his ribs or the door knocking against the frame.

"Wait a minute," Carrie said, rushing forward. There seemed to be a look of concern in her face. Rob stood dizzily on his feet in front of her, a trickle of blood running down his cheek.

Carrie raised her hand and slapped Rob across the face.

"Now get OUT," Carrie said as she walked away.

Rob could hardly feel the doorknob, could hardly turn it.

He nodded weakly to the astonished kid from room service, and slowly made his way toward the elevator bank.

Beyond it, he made out a sign. He sleepwalked down past the elevators. There was an alcove where the sign said "Ice." Rob pushed one of the buttons and cubes began to tumble out. He gathered a few in his cupped hands.

He blinked up at the door a few yards away.

"Stairway Entrance."

Rob jostled the door open, dropping a few ice cubes.

Eventually, in the dim quiet of the stairwell with its calm blue enamel-painted walls and stairs, he came to his senses.

CHAPTER SIX

Rob put a finger in his ear and tried to block out the roaring sound of the subway cars. The pay phone on the platform smelled of peanut butter and sweaty feet and he tried to keep the crusty receiver away from his mouth. After a few rings, Slezak picked up.

"Rabbit."

"Larry? What the fuck did you do it for?"

"Hi Rob," Larry said pleasantly. "You saw the paper?"

"I never said I'd give you the film."

"Just testing the waters, Rob. I'm doing you a favor. We'll find out how much that film is worth. Maybe we can sell it to some collector. Maybe if there's a lot of publicity, I'll be able to convince Krantz to hire you to be my managing editor. He might give you a bonus for bringing in the film. You should be thanking me!"

There was a draft coming through the air, cool and accompanied by a distant rush of noise. A moment later the soiled lights of an incoming train became visible in the murk at the end of the platform. Rob waited as the noise grew louder. The subway car shot quickly out of the darkness and the roar was bright in his ears.

"Talk to you later," Rob yelled. He hung up the phone.

He turned around as a scuttling figure slipped behind him. It was a bum checking the coin return.

Rob timed his steps so that he would get on at the back of one of the subway cars, where there would be a two-seater. He didn't want to be sitting in a long seat with people on every side of him. Not when he felt like passing out.

There was nothing unusual about a beat up guy on the subway. Blood was still seeping through the strawberry scrape marks on the side of Rob's face, but the ice had helped soothe the burning sensation and the feeling of swelling around his eye. This was the first time in his life that Rob actually found some relief in riding the subway. If nobody was looking at him, it wasn't that bad.

When he got home he turned on the bathroom light and cautiously approached the mirror. The pressure on his eye felt like somebody's big fat thumb was pressing up against it, but in the mirror, it hardly looked swollen at all. And for all that blood that kept moistening his palm when he touched his face, there were only a few scratchy marks. Rob thought about all the boxing matches he saw on TV. It was exactly like that — blood all over the place, then back in the corner they wipe it away and it's nothing.

Rob opened the medicine cabinet and found Julie's box of Q-tips. He was about to put one up to the deepest cut, like they did in the boxer's corner, but realized he had no idea what it was supposed to accomplish. He dipped one in vaseline anyway and smeared it lightly over the very pale pink line where the cut was.

He put some vaseline on the wide raw scrape that smeared down one side of his forehead and immediately it began to itch and sting.

The key clinked in the front lock.

Julie was there in a second.

"Oh, Rob, what *happened*?"

"Fell. Fell down the stairs on the elevated. It's ok, it was just the last few steps but I clunked my head."

"God, it looks like somebody punched you. Does it hurt?"

Rob grunted. She kissed the back of his neck as he stared at himself in the mirror. She put her arms around him, rubbing his chest.

He felt guilty for getting so momentarily becoming infatuated with Carrie Sinclair. But that was her job. An actress. She was crazy. A crazy bitch, turning on him like that. He saw that little film over and over in his mind. She didn't look like she was coerced or anything.

All that nutso talk about ruin and destruction. What ruin? What destruction? She didn't even really do that much in the damn film. Gives a lousy blow job and the film ends.

And the Mafia? One minute she's afraid, next minute it's ok to have the goons push him around like a putz.

The sting of the scrapes and cut seemed to burn now.

"I want to see something," Rob said. He broke away from Julie's suffocating, well-meaning hold around his waist. She sighed seeing the Q-tip lying on the sink and shook her head, placing it in the bathroom waste basket herself.

Rob picked up two pencils. He took the 16mm reel of film and an empty reel and put each through one of the pencils. He sat down carefully and wedged the pencils between his thighs. Primitive but effective; he rolled the film onto the empty reel as they both spun on the pencils. When he got to the middle of the reel, where young Carrie was in bed with the black guy, he stopped. He held the film up to the light. The image was small, but he could see what he needed to see.

Two people on the bed, naked, and that was it. Then blackness. There definitely was no splice in this. It was all one reel of film, all right — obviously it had been processed, put in a box, and forgotten. So what was so destructive about a blowjob?

He rolled the film back on the little five inch spool. The bitch. She'd kill him for the film, just to save her reputation. Larry was right. The fucking hypocrisy of it. He and Larry used their real names on Rabbit. Stephen King used his real name when he wrote for Cavalier. And for Chrissake, what's wrong with a stroke mag? So some lonely people can have something to jerk off to and keep them sane?

But this bitch — so high and mighty. It would serve her right to run her story on the front page of Rabbit.

Rob remembered telling the bodyguards — Rabbit had the film at the office. Well, what the fuck. Maybe that's where the film actually did belong. Give it to them, like he was thinking of doing, and let her bodyguards try and do anything about it.

Rob laid down on the bed and tried to sleep it all off. Sometimes in the jangle of his thoughts, trying to soothe his thoughts and just stop thinking, he thought of the sweet smell of the hotel room, and the fresh, friendly way Carrie Sinclair had greeted him. Nice to him, she was. Till he brought up that film.

The phone rang loudly. Automatically Rob leaned over to turn off the alarm clock. The second ring brought him halfway to his senses. He blinked as he tried to focus on the digital clock's red, squared numbers. 11:03.

He was shocked by the bright light yellow coming in from the window. It was morning, not 11 at night.

"Hello?"

A strange, hoarse voice called out, "Is this Rob?"

"Yes."

"Irwin Krantz. We talked about you coming aboard."

Rob put his hand to his itching forehead and the side of his face. The moment he did, the pain of the scrapes vibrated.

"Irwin Krantz," Irwin Krantz said again, "Rabbit magazine. We have an issue to get out, and we could use your help."

"Sure. We — we talked about my joining as uh, managing editor. But I didn't think we made any final decisions."

"Yeah. We'll talk about that when you get here."

"Is Larry in yet?"

"No," said Irwin Krantz. "I don't know the full story of course, but Larry is dead."

6.0.0.

Rob tapped tentatively at the buttons in the locked door of the Rabbit magazine office.

The office looked the same. Quiet. Empty. The door marked I. Krantz was closed.

Down the corridor, the lights were off except toward the back where the art department's cubicle was. Rob followed the tinny sound of a radio, and saw the art director and the paste-up girl working on the magazine, laying out the stats and some of the copy. They didn't hear him. He turned and walked back past Larry's darkened desk and cubicle.

He knocked on Krantz's door. There was no sound

from within. He knocked again. He tried the doorknob.

The door was unlocked.

Knocking again as he pushed it slowly open, Rob entered.

Irwin Krantz sat behind his desk. There was mild expectation in his glazed expression, and he motioned Rob to sit down on the sofa.

Rob crossed slowly on the thick carpet, eyeing the magazine publisher. He could hear the husky asthmatic sound of the fat man breathing. Krantz stared down at his fingernails, noting each pale white half moon at the base, and the shine coming off the nails. He moved his tubby fingers from side to side, seeming to admire the roundness of each nail, perfectly filed by a manicurist.

Now Krantz's dark little thick button eyes fixed on him. Rob was almost sorry he'd made eye contact.

"You were here with Larry, asking about a job."

Rob nodded.

"I remember. You've written for us for quite a while. You're Rob."

"Yes. Rob Streusel."

Irwin Krantz slowly nodded, his lips thinning out into what passed for a paternal smile. Little crows feet flicked at the corners of the button eyes. He seemed to force a hoarse chuckle.

"Streusel. Like the cake."

"Yes."

"Like the cake."

"Yes," Rob said again.

"Cake."

"Right."

"All right," Irwin Krantz sighed, the indulgent smile

slowly wiping from his lips. "Larry was in the middle of an issue when he died. I need somebody who knows the magazine to finish it up."

"Sure."

Krantz nodded his head slightly, with satisfaction.

"Mr. Krantz, what happened to Larry?"

"Killed," Krantz said pleasantly. "These things happen all the time."

"How did it happen?"

"I don't know," Krantz said. "His girlfriend called the office about it this morning. We all feel badly, of course. Rob, I'll pay you just what I was paying Larry Slezak. You'll get a payroll check in two weeks."

Krantz's labored breathing was the only sound in the room. Rob's feet seemed lost in the plush carpeting and he couldn't feel them.

"I hope you can stay out of trouble," Krantz said.

Rob moved off the sofa. Krantz waved his chubby hand limply, then pointed a finger. "I'm serious. Look at you. What were you in a fight about?"

"Nothing. It was an accident."

"I hope you won," Krantz said, looking down at his papers. He picked up a clear Bic pen and began to scratch at one of the sheets.

Rob waited for him to look up again, but he didn't.

He paused for a moment, then walked out, softly closing the heavy wooden door behind him.

He glanced into Larry's cubicle then looked away. He walked quickly down the corridor toward the music and the people.

Rob leaned over the drawing board and stared at the full page photo of a bent over backside.

"That's what we like. New faces."

He wasn't expecting a laugh and he didn't get one from the sullen paste-up girl, Cheryl. She was about 20, working part time, taking art classes at night. She always dressed in the latest style, looking like something out of a teenage fashion magazine. The tight tiger striped leotards and the oversized blouse tied in a knot in front didn't suit her. She looked too old, which made her look even more sullen than she would have. She had jet black hair, dyed evidently, tinged with very dark blue. Her heavy mascara was also blue-black. Her eyes, large and brown, were the only things in her head that seemed alive. Her white-pink lipstick was smeared along a thin-lipped, rigid mouth.

"Hi Rob," she said, looking up briefly. "Wasn't that terrible about Larry?"

"What exactly happened?"

"I don't know."

Cheryl took up a grease pencil and jotted some numbers on the nude's ass. "90%" on the fleshy part, "30%" on the background. More numbers indicating exposures for the printer.

"We just found out about it this morning," she said. She looked up with a dubious, bored glare. "You're not the new editor, are you?"

"Yeah."

"Lucky you."

"Temporarily, anyway. It just happened. I'm not even sure this is all happening."

"Is Cy still here?"

"Cy? I didn't see him. He was here?"

"I thought he was getting the job. But I guess he didn't. I'm glad. I couldn't stand having Cy Kottick for the editor. He's just too crazy."

Rob saw a pile of boards on a stand near her desk. About ten pages had been completed, including the cover.

"I thought Larry was saving the cover for a special girl," Rob said. "Did he say anything about having a special cover or anything?"

"Nope."

Cheryl was trying to align two columns of type to the fresh page in front of her. She smoothed one column down with a clear acrylic roller and then took black, string-thin Chartpak tape and carefully placed placed it down between the columns. That made the black line that separated the columns. Rob watched how easily she got it straight.

"Do you need me right away?" Rob asked.

"Soon enough," the art director interrupted.

"Hello, Mr. Fitzgerald."

"Hello, Rob."

Raymond Fitzgerald insisted on formality when addressed. He always wore a look of severity, and Rob was always unnerved by the man's stare, as if there was something offensive in Rob's not wearing a suit or perhaps wearing the wrong shoes or last year's tie.

Mr. Fitzgerald spent his money on clothing, and his shoes were always shined and buffed to a glow. Unfortunately the crispness of his shirts and the stiffness of his bow tie only called attention to the fading body it was covering. He was 60 years old, his arms thin and mottled with white curly hairs. His moon face was a pot pie of little acne scar bumps. His hair was a faded brown and tightly cropped in a lather of small curls around his head. The thinning hair was a source of nuisance to him, and he would scowl at the way his scalp was clearly visible through the ringlets. He sometimes could be caught positioning an errant curl on the top of his receding hairline, his left hand not quite concealing a little round mirror.

Mr. Fitzgerald was listed on the masthead as "Creative Director," which Larry always said was the first tip-off that the guy was gay.

For his part, Mr. Fitzgerald was happily convinced that all the other men in the office were latent homosexuals. Otherwise they could not possibly stand to look at naked women all day.

"The deadline is very, very tight," Mr. Fitzgerald said.

"What do you need from me," Rob asked.

"Larry didn't go through all the slides for the four pictorials, so I don't know what he wanted to use or not use," Mr. Fitzgerald said with exagerrated annoyance. "And since Krantz never lets *me* pick them out..."

"I'll go through them," Rob said.

Rob remembered Larry chuckling and telling the story of the Creative Director trying to decide on his own whether to send back some freelance nude shots that had arrived in the mail addressed to his attention. He had asked Cheryl, pointing to one shot, "Is that a pretty vagina?"

Larry dead.

"Do you know anything about Larry?"

"No," Mr. Fitzgerald said with deliberateness marking his disinterest, "not a thing."

Outside of the art department's cubicle, the honeycombed area of office cubicles was gray and unlit. At one time, there was a desk for a secretary handling subscriptions and Krantz's correspondence, and another desk for the accountant, but budget cuts had reduced them both to part-time status. In fact, Rob had never even seen them come in.

Rob snapped a few switches on the wall and overhead fluorescents shuddered for a moment and then spilled out white light, so bright it was startling.

Rob went to Larry's desk. He tried to make sense out of the mess on it — the papers, the letters, the slides, the half-empty wrappers of gum and Life Savers and cigarettes.

It all happened so quickly. But now, the moment he sat behind the desk, it hit him. Larry was gone. There was no more Larry Slezak in the world, and there would never be one again.

He fought with himself to accept that this wasn't such a bad idea. The fuckin' wiseguy. Asking for a 3,000 word story for the same price as a 2,500. "Hey," he'd say, "I'm giving you a chance to really let loose and put everything into the piece you want!"

The phone rang loudly. Larry always liked to have the volume turned up loud, whether it was a radio or a phone.

"Hello?"

"Yeah. Is this Rabbit magazine?"

"Right."

"Can I speak to the editor? What's his name?"

"I'm the editor. Rob Streusel."

"Listen. I'm interested in getting that film that was mentioned in the paper. Can I see it? Is it in the office?"

"There's no film in the office. That story was — nothing."

"What did you say your name was?"

"Rob Streusel," Rob said. When the phone suddenly clicked, he was sorry he'd repeated his name.

As far as most anyone knew, Larry Slezak was the editor, and maybe it would have been wiser to keep it that way.

He knew that Larry liked to use cocaine. Maybe that was it. It was probably like that basketball player, what was his name? Len Bias? Larry just snorted too much. That was it. Maybe. Or hell, you could get yourself killed just crossing the street in mid-town.

He stabbed at the touch tone phone.

"Hello, Tee? It's Rob Streusel, one of the writers at Rabbit. I met you once or twice up at the office..."

"I know. Oh God, Rob," Tee said, sniffling, "it's so awful, it's like hell. Why would anyone want to kill Larry?"

Rob felt the chill steal over his body as he found himself say, calmly, "I'd like to come over. If there's anything I can do."

"The police are here."

There was a loud thump, as if the phone had dropped. There was a muffled sound that Rob couldn't make out. He strained to hear what was going on. Finally, he heard the phone bump a few times and then a loud male voice barked out, "Who is this?"

"Rob Streusel. I'm the new editor of Rabbit Magazine. Is Tee all right? Who are *you?*"

"This is the police. If you're coming over, get to it. You saw Larry Slezak yesterday, right?"

"Right."

"Then get over. Right now."

CHAPTER SEVEN

Larry's girlfriend was curled up on the couch, weeping softly. She was wearing dark maroon capri pants, vintage polyester that she'd found in an antique clothing store. She had on a white t-shirt with the printed faces of a heavy metal band on it. There were two cops still in the apartment and the detective.

"Oh Rob," Tee sobbed, still in a fetal position, looking up at him, "I came in...and he was dead!"

"Is this the way the apartment looked when you arrived?" Rob asked the girl.

"I'll ask the questions," said the detective. He was professionally grim-looking, working a stick of gum with a fast, insistent rhythm. Thin and wiry, he liked to clench and unclench his fists, as if he couldn't wait to punch somebody. His dark eyes stayed on Rob in an unnerving stare. He chewed his gum restlessly, and the contrast between the fixed glare and the nervous chewing made the detective seem just on the edge of losing it.

"Can I see some identification?" Rob said.

The detective fished out his wallet and it flopped open, exposing the credentials of one Sgt. Keim.

"Let me get this straight, pal," the detective said, "You're another pornographer?"

"I'm an investigative reporter," Rob said, "I also write fiction."

"You're a reporter? For what?"

"I was on the staff of The City Daily."

"*Was*? Uh huh, ok. And now you write pornies." Sgt. Keim's eyes gleamed, a smirk of challenge was at the corner of his mouth.

"I wrote articles for Larry, and some stories. What happened to him?"

"You saw the deceased yesterday? What did you talk about?"

Rob thought about it. The job at Rabbit. The film.

"Well?"

"We talked about the magazine. That was about it."

Rob asked himself questions, lightning fast: did Larry really want him to join Rabbit, or was it a ploy so he could get the film, and get it cheap? Did Krantz really want the expense of another editor? Maybe they both wanted to get the film away from him. Hire him, get the film, and fire him.

"Well?" the detective said.

"We talked about the business, that's all. My next story assignment. Stuff like that."

"About you becoming the new editor?"

"How'd you know that?"

"Routine police work, Mr. Ex-reporter. We had to know who would be showing up for work in Larry Slezak's place. You just saved us a trip over to your smut office."

"Now I can't give you free copies of Rabbit."

"I don't need 'em," he said. "I'm happily married. That's something a guy like you probably knows nothing about. You and your readers. How long have you been the editor?"

"Just...since this morning."

"So," the detective mused, "you wouldn't be making much money if Larry Slezak was still alive."

Rob took a deep breath.

"Look, this all happened so quickly. But listen, do you know how much money Larry made as an editor?"

"Yeah. Matter of fact, I checked into that."

"Then you know it isn't a motive for murder."

"In this town a penny on the sidewalk is a motive for murder. "OK, the killing happened some time around 10pm. Where were you?"

"Home. With my girlfriend."

"Anybody else can verify it? You got a doorman?"

"No."

"Any of your neighbors see you enter the building?"

"No."

"Just your girlfriend, huh."

"Yeah. So what?"

The detective didn't look up from his pad as he scribbled his notes.

"So," he said calmly, "I'd like to know where you got all those cuts and bruises on your face."

Rob had forgotten about that.

"Well?" the detective said, "You having trouble remembering who beat you up?" He scratched something heavily onto the pad. "Wouldn't happen to have been Larry Slezak, could it?"

Tee let out a whimper.

Rob turned to her — he wanted to say something — but he didn't. He had to cling on to his silence as if he was clinging to a clear plastic ladder. Nobody could see anything and he knew he looked stupid just hanging there, but that was all he had.

"I fell," Rob said lamely.

"Maybe you'll remember what really happened if I take you downtown and book you, Murder One."

"Go ahead," Rob suddenly said, "blame me because the subway has broken steps and idiots pushing you and you fall over down a whole flight and when you get to the bottom they all just walk around you and don't even help you up!"

Sgt. Keim's eyebrows raised slightly.

"Nobody helped you up?"

"No."

"Maybe because it never happened. You're in deep shit, Mr. Porno Writer," the detective said. "We'll be talking again. Right now you can crawl back to your office."

"I have to stay here and talk to Tee for a minute," Rob said.

The detective looked at her. Rob looked at her.

She looked at Rob.

"It's OK," Tee said softly.

"We'll be going," the detective said. "But maybe we'll be right outside this door."

The detective motioned to the cops and they left but not before they paused to fix their eyes meaningfully on Rob.

"You know I didn't have a fight with Larry," Rob said.

"Why didn't you tell them what really happened?"

Rob sighed heavily. "Because, the people I had the fight with would not have backed me up. Carrie Sinclair's bodyguards weren't too happy with me — because I asked her about the porn film."

Tee stared at him, as if she was still making up her mind.

"Larry told you, right?"

"He told me something about a sex film with Carrie Sinclair in it."

"Right, right. That was my film. I found it and I told Larry."

"He was going to sell it for $100,000 to The National Inquirer."

"What?"

"Or Penthouse. He was laughing. He did a few lines, and he was telling me about how we were going to be rich. I didn't know what he was talking about. When he does drugs, sometimes he talks crazy."

"When was this?"

"It was when he got home, around 6."

"What else did he say?

"I don't know. I said he'd put a down-payment on a nice co-op, you know? He was talking about a car, and driving to Atlantic City and stuff. Then he was making all kinds of calls."

"What kind of calls?"

"He called Toby, and Cy, he called all these numbers in California, 'cause he said the offices were still open out there. He was trying to think of who he could sell that film to. He figured he could get a bidding war going."

"He just kept making calls?"

"Yes. I got so bored. We were going to go out, and he kept saying in a minute, in a minute. I got hungry, so I told him if he wasn't going to go with me, I'd eat by myself. He said fine, he didn't need my company. I went to the Chinese place on the corner, and I ate. And I thought I'd be nice, and I got him a take out order of Chow Fon. But when I got home..."

Tee began to weep.

"Do the cops know about the film?"

Tee shook her head. She picked at a box of Kleenex and pulled out three or four tissues. She sat back down on the couch, arranging herself so her long legs hung over the side as she leaned back on the pillows.

"Did Larry call The Waldorf Astoria? Did you hear him make a call to Carrie Sinclair?"

"I don't know. He was calling all night. Talk, talk, talk. And then I went out."

"Tee, I'm sure that what happened had something to do with this film. When an actress is becoming a big star, and millions of dollars are involved — she's not going to let anything get in her way."

Tee squirmed in the sofa, pushing her knees up against her chest, hugging her legs to her. Rob could see the visible panty line under her tight pants. He dragged his chair alongside her, and looked in her eyes.

"Look, I don't want to ask, but I have to know. Was the apartment messed up when you came in...like there was a struggle?"

"No."

"Did the cops say there might've been a struggle, or a fight or anything?"

"No. Nothing like that. Larry was sitting behind his desk."

Rob looked over there.

"With the lamp turned up like that?"

"Yes."

"Please forgive me, but I used to be a reporter. And...I still am. Tee, how was Larry murdered?"

"Shot," Tee said quietly. "He was shot. In the head.

They said it was close range. The gun was right up against his head."

Tee began to moan, the tears flooding down, she lunged for Rob and clumsily held on to him. The warm body shivered in his arms, the legs locking on top of him, the hot tears dripping onto his neck.

"It's so terrible," Tee cried, her words muffled as she pressed her face against Rob's chest.

Rob put his arms around her and patted her gently. He stared blankly at the walls.

"It's OK, Tee, it's OK," he said.

He tried to keep his mind clear. He searched the apartment with his eyes. It wasn't the kind of apartment he would ever have envisioned for Larry. For a writer, he didn't seem to be a reader. There were no book cases, and hardly any books. There was a wall unit mostly filled with bric-a-brac, and the junk Larry liked to collect for a hobby. Mostly sports memorabilia, oddly enough. A few framed autographed pictures of sports stars he'd written to as a kid.

Only a few shelves had books in them. One shelf was solidly filled with magazines. Probably copies of Rabbit.

Tee moaned and rolled over on the sofa, burying her face in one of the throw pillows.

Rob looked closely at the book cases. He walked along the wall, turned, looked briefly into the bedroom, then started back. There was no carpet on the floor, it was just polished wood. He squatted and squinted at the floor; it looked pretty clean, no sign of scuffling feet and no dropped objects. There was nothing under the sofa or the furniture.

Rob stepped over to the desk area. The cops had

gone over everything already and now the address book was closed and the envelopes and papers neatened. He looked over at Tee to make sure she wasn't looking. He quickly snatched up the envelopes and went through them.

He looked carefully around for anything else. A magnifying lupe was on Larry's desk. He might have been looking at slides. That would explain the lamp turned up the way it was. Or he was looking at film. Rob glanced over to the wall unit.

"Tee, does Larry own a projector?"

"Yes. He shows slides all the time."

"Not that kind. A movie projector."

"Movies. Gee...yes. Yes, he does. I remember. Once he showed me some old home movies he made."

"Where's the projector?"

Tee sat up and thought for a moment. She went straight to the hall closet. She looked up.

"It's probably in back of those hats up there."

Rob slid the desk chair over to the closet and lightly stepped onto it. He caught sight of the old 8mm projector. There were a few blue cans of film along side. He touched the top can. There was no dust. He saw a little tongue of film sticking out from one of the cans, as if the can had been closed quickly.

If Carrie Sinclair's bodyguards were here, they could've twisted Larry's arm and gotten him to take the projector and film cans down. They could've held up the film, looking for the one with Carrie Sinclair on it. They wouldn't have known that it was 16mm, not 8mm.

Rob leaned down to examine the blood stains in the wood. The idea that it had come leaking out of Larry's head began to nauseate him. He stood up and brushed himself off.

A blonde hair was adhering to his pants at the knee.

Rob moved back to the sofa. He put his hand on Tee's shoulder and patted her again. She was still crying quietly to herself. He ran his hand over her hair.

He looped one strand of Tee's hair over his finger and pressed his thumb down on it. Then he tugged the end quickly, breaking off the hair easily, without having to pull it out by the root.

He draped the hair across his thigh and it stood out from the black fabric of his pants. He placed the hair he found under Larry's chair next to it.

Tee rolled over and sniffled, moaning out loud, "I've gotta get out of this place. I'm going back home to Massapequa Park."

"To your parents?"

"Yes. For a little while, anyway."

Rob brushed away the identical blonde hairs from his knee.

"Going home's a good idea, Tee. Take some time for yourself."

"A week with my parents is all I can stand."

"Then what will you do?"

"Do you live on the West Side, Rob? What's it like?"

"I live in Riverdale," Rob said. "What do you want to know about the West Side for?"

"Oh, yeah, yeah, that's right. You're in Riverdale. I—"

The front door rang several times.

Tee opened it, and there were the cops and the detective.

"Everything all right in there?" the detective said.

"Everything's fine," Rob answered, getting up. "If you need anything Tee — just call." He stared at the cops. He said, "Tee, call any time. I care about what happens to you. And not just for a few minutes before I go on my coffee break and go roust some homeless or something."

"You're asking for another beating," said Sgt. Keim. His eyes did not leave Rob's. He took a piece of silver foil out of his pocket and smeared it over his mouth. He crinkled the wad of gum into the silver foil and then grabbed Rob by the wrist. He handed Rob the foil, which was surprisingly hot in his hand.

"I'll stick to you like gum to paper, you just remember that," the detective said. "You just try and pull that apart, friend."

"Garbage doesn't bother me," Rob said, chucking it into the empty trash can near the desk.

"Good shot," Sgt. Keim said. "I bet you never miss. Especially at point blank range."

At the Rabbit office, Rob checked all the mail that was addressed to Larry Slezak. Another wave of nausea seemed to rise up in his throat. Handling Larry's mail gave him a queasy feeling and he had to sit there and fight it.

Most of the mail was freelance submissions; bad stories written by beginners who figured there was no art at all to writing porn. Rob glanced through the stories, his annoyance and preoccupation with their stupidity slowly erasing the feelings of uneasiness at sitting in the murdered man's chair.

"She felt his maleness enter her, the burning sensation of lust throbbing in her veins..."

Rob tossed the story into the return envelope and

scrawled "Sorry," across the query letter. That crap went out in the 1950's.

"I was splitting her wide open, my giant cock pumping quarts of cum into her pussy hole..."

Rob looked for the return envelope and didn't find one. He tossed the bullshit boaster's fantasies into the garbage.

Footsteps were coming from down the corridor.

"Oh, you're finally back," Raymond Fitzgerald said. The art director tapped a bony finger onto the messy desk. "Did you pick out the pictures for the "Tara" set? We have to return the ones we're not using. Larry held onto them for, I believe it has to be three months already, and the agency is very upset."

"Yeah, here. Two full frontals, a back shot — I picked out both vertical and horizontal versions so you can lay it out any way you like. Do the standard with it. Let's start with her stripping, then she's on her back, then she wants it with her legs spread dogstyle, and the reader turns the page for a good crotch close-up."

The art director nodded. "And the final page on the bottom let's have a shot of her face, with her eyes closed, like the reader's just satisfied her."

"A face shot? Larry never ran face shots. Every photo has to have nudity. How about a shot where she has her eyes closed but it's on the bed and you can see her tits?"

"The more things change," the art director said grimly, "the more they stay the same."

Rob thought about Larry and the lupe on his desk.

"All the photos of the girls are from agencies?"

"Oh, yes, it's a matter of policy. We'll never use pictures from individual photographers, or amateurs. They're unpredictable and besides, most of them only shoot their girlfriends and are they ever homely. Not that they ever think so. The agencies give us what we need. They're all out in California where the model-actress-wanna be's are. We get the pictures cheap. And so, of course, are the girls."

"You know, Raymond," Rob said, "I've noticed that a few photos in each issue always seem to turn out too dark, or out of focus. I hope we can do something about that."

Raymond pressed his lips together.

"That's not my fault," he said loudly. "It's the printer. The printer doesn't follow my specs. And the photographers don't give us the best chromes."

"But you're the art director. Don't you know when something's trouble ahead of time?"

Raymond looked up at the ceiling. "If you give me any more pressure, I might just quit. Or worse. You don't know who you are dealing with!"

"Don't get upset, Raymond."

Raymond had some slides in his hand.

"These are from the movie review pages. We need captions for these, and these two are dupes. Please call the film company and tell them to send us the originals. The focus is impossible on these."

Rob held up the slides. They looked fine, but he didn't want to tell his art director that. Raymond had on an "if looks could kill" expression. One slide showed a porn starlet seemingly awash in white stuff. He looked closer and saw that she was lying on a kitchen table, whipped cream all over her chest. Cherries were stuck into the whipped cream at each nipple.

"Very tasty," he said. "I like this. This can go double-truck with this. I like the way the whipped cream is melting a little, so it really looks like she's doused with come."

"Lawrence said something like that when he showed that chrome to me," the art director sniffed. "I didn't realize you were so closely a disciple."

Rob checked the rubber-stamped copyright mark on the slide and called up the film company. He looked carefully at the Rolodex on Larry's desk.

"Hello? I'd like to speak to Ann Hester. Oh, hi. This is Rob Streusel over at Rabbit. I'm filling in for Larry Slezak for a while. We're reviewing "Kitchen Witch" but we need a better slide. These are like second or third generation."

"I can send you the originals if you take good care of them," the publicist said.

"Just the ones with the whipped cream. Those are all I need."

"Fine, when do you need them?"

"I needed them yesterday."

"Well then I don't see how I can help."

"That's just an expr — listen, if you can send them Priority Mail, that'll be fine."

"Now you can do me a big, big favor, Rod. Can you give me some quotes?"

"I don't have the review handy."

"That's ok. Just make up a quote. Something we can use on the box cover for the video. We're shipping the video at the end of the month so whatever you say, that would be just fine. We'd love to have a rave review from Rabbit Magazine. Please, Rod, just think of something. Right now."

"Sure. How about, uh, here: The Whipped Cream Scene Will Leave You Creaming."

"What? Something shorter, darling. Something short but very hot, that'll make them want to buy."

"Look, just write whatever you want and say it came from Rabbit."

"No, no, I need *your* quote. *You* say something."

Translation: Ann was too dumb to make one up. Rob looked \at the slide.

"How about 'You Won't Believe Your Eyes — Ever Again.'"

"Let me write that down...ever...again. What else, Rod?"

"I don't know. Maria Romero is the hottest find since Sterno."

"Since what?"

"She's got the hottest can since Sterno...She's hot enough to melt the cassette housing...I don't know...Tina will melt your contact lenses...Tina will blow your mind and everything else..."

"I don't know," the publicist was saying.

"Hottest film of the year?" Rob mumbled.

"That's good! That's very crisp. You really think so? I'll write that down."

Rob shook his head in minor amazement.

CHAPTER EIGHT

It really was a job like any other, Rob thought, getting off the subway after a stifling, long ride. The subway had been packed and all those bodies radiated enough sweaty heat to render the faint air conditioning useless. So some people were going to shuffle tax forms or bank statements or invoices. He was going to shuffle through sex stories and photos.

He stopped at the door. The handyman was leaning over the doorknob, working on it with a screwdriver.

"What's going on?" Rob asked.

"Guess it broke," the handyman smiled. Rob had seen the man before. He had the happy grin of an imbecile and lived in a happy world where if things were broken, they could be fixed.

The handyman let Rob in, and then began to tap at the door knob and check the screws.

"Who called for the handyman?" Rob asked.

Raymond Fitzgerald was adjusting the art department radio to WNCN and paused to contemplate the strains of Pachelbel's Canon. When the station was tuned in to his satisfaction, he said, "I called. The doorknob was loose."

"Is that all?"

"No, not all," Raymond said. "I think someone was in the office. Things were moved around. I'm not quite sure, but it looks that way. Did you notice anything in Larry's cubicle?"

"My cubicle? I couldn't tell, the place is still a mess. I haven't had the time to sort through everything that he left behind."

"The radio was moved. I could tell because the reception is off. And I had a very fine scissor and if I can't find it, then it must have been stolen."

Rob nodded and returned to his desk. He sifted through some of the papers on it, but there was no way to tell if anyone else had been through them. He opened a drawer. Whoever it was hadn't taken any of the loose change Larry had left behind.

He busied himself making calls. Cy Kottick was supposed to have a story in, and he had called Toby about taking a few photos of Times Square, ones that could be used to illustrate that article about the porn stores. He especially wanted a good shot of the Girl-a-Rama joint.

He hadn't finished writing up the place. He began to knock out the story from his notes, and was relieved when he glanced at his watch and saw that a few hours had slipped by. He kept at it, and didn't stop until the phone rang.

"Rob?"

"Hi Julie."

Rob glanced at his watch.

"Oh, shit. I know what you're going to say; I'm working late already. I'm leaving right now. I had no idea it was after 6."

"Rob — there's been a break-in."

"Shit. When? Are you OK?"

"I just got home. It must've happened during the day. I called the super —"

"The hell with that fucking idiot, call the police!"

"I did, I did!"

"Jesus. Godammit what did they steal?"

"Nothing. That's just it. Nothing."

"Are you *sure*?"

"They must have been surprised or something."

"Surprised? What do you think, we've got Bozo the Clown living with us or something? They weren't surprised. Shit. Are you sure nothing was taken? Will you look around?"

"I did, dammit! The place is a mess, but nothing's missing."

"Wait a minute. Check the bathroom."

"Rob!"

"I mean it! Listen to me. Go to the bathroom, open the medicine cabinet, and look for a white box next to the aspirin. A white box about 5 x 5 marked Band-Aids."

Rob slapped at the desk, over and over, waiting.

"Rob?"

"Is it there? Is it still there?"

"Yes, it's still there," Julie said. "What's that roll of dirty movie film doing in the medicine cabinet?"

"Well, it's sick stuff isn't it? It's that three minutes of porn they're after, that first roll of 16mm that they made. I'll be home as soon as I can. Don't open the door for anybody. When the cops come, make sure they show ID. Don't just open the door for two guys who say they're detectives or something."

Rob took a cab home, spending the ride trying to make sense of what had happened. It wasn't easy, especially with the cab driver playing loud Jamaican music in stereo through the front and back speakers.

There was no one in the lobby. That immediately

made Rob edgy. It was a big lobby area, with two couches opposite each other on either side. Neither were flush with the walls, and Rob leaned down to see if he could spot anybody hiding behind one or the other.

Before he got onto the elevator he took a long look at the viewing mirror that was screwed into the corner of the car. There was nobody in there either. Rob took the elevator up and when he got out, looked both ways carefully. His building, once considered "luxury" had become almost slum-like; bulbs burned out and not replaced for weeks, the carpet dirty gray with dark splotches mottling into the pattern. It was the decay of the Bronx now firmly infecting the once upper middle-class refuge of Riverdale.

The elevator doors shuddered and closed slowly, with the grinding noise of a hostile dog growl.

On the floor just to the side of his front door was a scrap of paper with writing on it. It was folded over.

"She doesn't even notice it on her way in?" Rob said out loud. Julie could never be a reporter, that's for sure.

He bent over to pick up the paper, but it didn't give. Rob got down on one knee and examined it.

He never saw what hit him.

One man threw a flying tackle that knocked the air out of him. The other was right there, pinning a hand around his throat.

"Don't say a word," one of them said hoarsely into his ear.

Rob's eyes popped wildly, he tried to breathe but nothing was coming in. His eyes hurt as he twisted them to get a good look at the man who was speaking, standing above him. But the other man had him down on the ground, his strong fingers crushing around his neck.

The man above him was maybe 60, with a white moustache. His eyebrows were still dark, creating a stern, evil look to his brown eyes. His skin was blotchy red, sunburned into ugliness, meaty and bloody. He wore a shabby, non-descript brown suit and had his hat pulled down low.

The other one was younger, maybe Rob's age, 37 at the most, his black hair still thick and full, combed back off his face and straight back, Italian-style. His complexion was olive, his nose hooked and bent slightly to one side. He had no lips, just a cruel line twisting downward in a frown. He had the kind of impassive greenish-gray eyes that never seem to focus on anything, looking through their target.

"We're going in and we're getting that film," the older one said.

"You want my money, take it," Rob gasped, "take it."

"Cut the act, asshole." The hand gripped tighter.

"Wallet...in...pocket..."

"Cut the shit. You're no actor," the younger one sneered.

"We want the film," the older man said again.

The other one, still gripping Rob easily around the throat, shook his head in exasperation and looked up. "Hey, *Brains*, waddya talkin' to the motherfucka for?"

He kept hold of Rob's throat with one hand. The other one cranked up slowly and slammed into Rob's groin.

Over the strangled, gurgling hiss that came from Rob's throat, the young thug said calmly, "Now, I reach into his pocket, and I take out the key. Simple, right?"

Rob watched helplessly, still gasping for breath,his

stomach hollowed out with pain.

The young thug smiled as he watched Rob writhe. "I could kill you," he said. He brandished the keys.

"Let's get in," the other one whispered.

The thug was still smiling at Rob, a mean smile. He liked to see a look of pain.

Rob finally caught his breath. He strained to take it in. He exhaled it slowly.

"Shut up!" the thug said, lurching low to slam a fist into Rob's gut. "I took care of him," he said to the older man. But his partner, glancing nervously down the corridor, was not amused.

"Come on, open the door."

The younger one glanced at the deadbolt lock and then went through the keys.

"Medeco. This is the one."

He sank the key into the lock and quietly turned it.

"Beautiful," he whispered to his partner. "I got the touch." He checked the bottom lock.

"Wait a minute!" his partner hissed.

He was eyeing the blinking elevator light and it was nearly at Rob's floor. He hauled Rob to his feet, making him stand, even if he was still bent over at the waist. The three men watched the blinking elevator light. It passed the floor and went on.

"OK, it's ok. Will you get the fucking door open?"

The bottom lock gave way.

"Now let's get the film," the man with the white moustache whispered.

"Yeah, sure. And anything else that might be good," the other one said.

Then he gave Rob a quick elbow in the stomach that sent him thudding back to the ground.

"Just making sure," he said to his glaring partner.

He pushed the door but it stopped dead with a little rattling noise.

The men looked at each other.

He pushed on the door again. It opened an inch or two but stopped.

"Hey, *Bitch*," the younger one called out brazenly, "take the fuckin' chain off the door!"

There was no sound in the hallway, save the hum of the elevator in use.

He gave the door another push.

"You hear me, BITCH? You take that chain off or your man gets his balls beaten off!"

He hauled Rob up by his throat, as if he was a dead turkey.

"Bitch, take a look. Take a good fuckin' look! We got your boyfriend right here!"

The goon grabbed Rob and before he could dizzily fall back to the ground, shoved him against the door.

"Now open up!"

The young thug grabbed one of Rob's hands and pushed it into the door opening. He grabbed the door knob and pulled the door shut on his fingers.

"Rob! Oh, Rob!" Julie cried.

"Don't open it —" Rob shouted, the pain crackling into his knuckles.

"Don't be a hero, asshole," the older man grunted. "Give us the film and nobody gets hurt."

"All right, all right," Rob gasped.

"Hold it! The elevator!"

The men looked wildly at each other.

"Unchain it! Unchain it now!" one of them yelled at Julie.

The elevator settled on the floor and the door rocked open.

Two uniformed policemen got out.

"The stairway — hurry!"

Rob made a wild grab for the man closest to him, the older one with the white moustache. The man easily squirmed away from his weakened grasp. Rob swooned against the door and slowly slid downard.

As the cops rushed after the two men, Rob struggled to his feet. He staggered for a moment, and mustering all his strength, pushed his lead feet and his limp legs forward. He got to the stairway which was echoing with grunts and curses.

"This is for real," Rob thought to himself. For some reason, he was strangely amazed that the cops weren't shouting "Halt!" as they ran down the stairs. "The cops know that the men aren't going to stop," Rob reasoned dizzily, "so they don't call out, like they do in the movies. And they aren't firing any shots. Because...because, I guess, they're out of range. Or out of bullets or something..."

Rob fell back, the hallway seeming to rise up like an ocean wave and sink him.

The noises got further and further away from him.

"Oh Rob, Rob," Julie was whispering, "are you ok?"

"Get...back...inside," Rob said, wincing, rubbing at his eyes, unable to focus. "Jesus...everybody's beating me up."

The elevator doors opened. It was the cops.

"We put out an APB on them, they won't get far," one of them said.

"One of 'em was like 60," Rob said, catching his breath. "The other guy was big, 6 foot one or something, black hair. Much younger." He saw that neither man had his pad out. "I guess you can take my statement later. I don't believe it. I mean, I'm about to be killed and there you are!"

The cops looked at him.

"You called us. Apartment 4-P., Streusel, right?"

"Yeah. But I just got home."

"Woman called about a break-in, about a half hour ago."

"Oh shit— yeah. Yeah. I forgot."

"You Mr. Streusel? You just get home?"

"Yeah. I was working. I'm a reporter. A writer."

The cops looked at him doubtfully.

He realized what that look meant. And he felt pretty stupid himself. A reporter who couldn't even figure out why the cops had come.

"So what paper you write for?"

"I used to write for The City Daily. I, uh, got let go."

No wonder, one of the cops seemed to say with his eyes.

"When we got a report of a break-in," one of them said, "The lady didn't say the thieves were still on the premises."

"They came back," Rob said.

"Ever seen them before?"

"No," Rob said. "It's strange. No."

Rob was thinking to himself, Carrie Sinclair must have a fuckin' army on her side. These two jokers were different from the two other bodyguards that roughed him up in her hotel room.

After the cops left, offering little hope for an arrest in what was one of the minor and plentiful crimes in the area, Julie got out the ice cubes. Then she got out the blender and crushed the ice cubes up.

"You don't have to—"

"I know what I'm doing," Julie insisted.

"The ice cubes are fine."

"No they aren't. Now just wait a minute."

Julie piled the crushed ice into a bowl, took out the other ice cube tray and crushed those in the blender too.

"Will you stop making the noise with the blender?"

"Hold out your hand...now slowly...see? It's soft. Nice and cool and soft. This'll help your hand."

She pushed Rob's hand into the bowl full of snowy crushed ice.

"How does it feel?"

"Like it got slammed in a door and then frozen."

"Now let's go over to the sofa and sit down. Come on."

Rob led the way, his hand in the bowl.

Julie was wearing a pale blue blouse open at the neck. Sweat glistened at her cleavage, and the ordeal and excitement made her chest and cheeks blush a deep pink. She wiped a few strands of light brown hair from her face. She sat down, tucking one leg under her, exposing the lace fringe of her white slip. Her lip quivered.

"Rob, I'm scared. I'm very, very scared."

"Don't worry."

"Don't worry! Just shut up, is that it? I'm just here to fuck, is that right? Is that why we're living together? Is that all I am to you after four years?"

"No, of course not."

"*Talk* to me, Rob. *Tell* me."

"I can't."

"What do you mean, you can't?"

"I don't know, that's why. I just don't know."

"Rob, somebody's trying to get that film you have. They'll kill to get it! You could've died if the cops hadn't come! What if I had been home alone when they broke in the first time? I'd be dead now! Rob?"

He stared down at his hand in the ice.

"Rob? We're supposed to be partners. Why are you shutting me out this way? You're treating me like I'm nothing. Don't you know how much I love you? It's you I'm worried about most!"

"This *is* love," Rob said, looking at the crushed ice in the bowl. "You didn't have to crush up the ice..."

"Thanks loads."

"You had the chain on the door That was smart."

Rob twisted his hand in the ice a bit.

"That film in the bathroom cabinet! They hunted for it when we were gone, and they would've killed for it now. It's crazy. It's just a porn film, isn't it?"

"Just a porn film with Carrie Sinclair in it."

"I know, I saw it."

"She sent her bodyguards to get it. I should get the cops to have them all arrested."

"Then why didn't you?"

"I-I don't have proof. I don't know what the hell to do."

"I do.*Give* it to her. Give her the film. If I made a film like that, I'd want it back, too."

"Would you beat somebody up to get it?"

"Maybe I would."

"I went to see her and that's what happened. I told her I had the film and that I was from Rabbit —"

"Well, God, Rob, if I thought of having my picture

in Rabbit, I'd beat you up myself."

"Thanks."

"It's true. I wouldn't want everyone seeing pictures like that of me. Don't you think Carrie Sinclair's human? Any woman would feel that way. Rob, what do you think I did before I met you? Think I never made love to another man? You think there isn't somebody out there who doesn't have a few dumb Polaroids of me naked?"

"What?"

"No, there aren't, but there could be. One of my old boyfriends took some Polaroids of me —"

"It was that guy, what's his name, somebody Chevalier, right, he had a French last name —"

"It doesn't matter. For Christ's sake, that's not the point. I took them back after we broke up. But what if I hadn't? Or what if I missed one or two? Don't you understand? What did this woman do that was so bad, Rob? Why does she have to be reminded of it now? She was a dumb kid and she made a film she probably regrets now. And some people don't understand. You included."

"When I first saw the film, I thought I could use it to get my foot in the door at The City Daily."

"They fired you. They're not going to rehire you."

"They thought I didn't have the killer instinct. They thought that I didn't have guts. All because I didn't want to interrogate that woman."

"What woman?"

"You know, you know. She witnessed a murder or something, and she just didn't want to talk about it. I handed in the story and it was nothing. Just another city shooting of some guy in a hotel room. She didn't want any trouble, she said. A real reporter would've never let her get away with that. And that was it. The last straw. Fired."

"Listen, Rob, I'm proud of you for what you did. I mean it."

"Thanks."

"But I'm not proud of you for trying to show how tough and unfeeling you could be and exploit Carrie Sinclair!"

"My hand is killing me," Rob said.

"You'll live."

"All right, all right. I'll talk to her," he said at last.

"Don't talk to her, just send her back the film and promise that you didn't make a copy or anything. Just forget about it."

"Forget about it. Yeah."

Rob stared at the floor. But how could he forget that the psycho actress put out a contract to get the film at all costs. She ordered them to beat him up to get the film. And she even gave them the green light to commit murder!

On the floor of an apartment in another part of town there was blood. Blood still in the cracks of the wood. As far as Julie knew, Larry Slezak was still working at Rabbit, and Rob was just his managing editor.

Rob rubbed his sore hand and with a grimace, made a fist. Only Carrie Sinclair knew what had really happened to Larry.

CHAPTER NINE

"We just got into three-way sex and it happened when my best girl friend Melinda came over to the house. My husband Charles was reading a copy of your magazine, Rabbit, and he didn't put it away in time. Melinda saw it, but to my surprise she started to look at it with him. We got to talking about sex and all the weird things in the magazine and Melinda, Charles and I, we sort of decided to swing!

"Before long, Melinda was lying stark naked on the bed and my husband was eating her out. I was tremendously excited watching it. I just had to get down there and give him head while he did it. As my face bobbed up and down, I kept looking at the way Charles's tongue worked up against Melinda's pretty bush. I found myself so aroused I wanted to do it too.

"Charles shot his load down my throat and I swallowed it all hungrily. He lazily rolled over, and I went to work on Melinda, completing the job, snuffing my face into her pussy. She worked herself around so we were in the 69 position and she began to tongue me too. Now it was almost as if I was licking myself, like a cat. And it was like firecrackers going off! Next thing I knew, I was getting the fucking of my life, Charles was on fire, screwing me hard, Melinda gently twisting my nipples. I groaned like there was no tommorow. His cock was harder than ever as he put himself into me, and I came, came, came..."

Rob put down the letter. It wasn't from a reader, of course. Rabbit readers were barely literate.

"Pretty good, Toby."

"Thanks."

"Larry was paying what, fifteen bucks a letter?"

"Yes. It was too bad about Larry."

Rob looked up from the letters. "Yeah, it was," Rob answered, looking into Toby's blank face. Toby uncrossed his legs and nudged his glasses back up the bridge of his nose. Toby always seemed to dress like some kind of elementary school student. He had shiny black shoes on, his pants were black with a crisp crease in them, and he was wearing a long-sleeved white shirt buttoned up to the neck with no tie.

"It's gotten very warm out," Toby said in his bland, unassuming voice. Rob wondered if it ever got warm enough for Toby to wear a short sleeve shirt.

Rob glanced at his watch. Carrie Sinclair and her camera crew were going to be doing exteriors over at the United Nations building again, and they usually broke for lunch at noon.

"There wasn't any air conditioning on the train coming down here," Rob said. "I was sweating like a pig."

Toby looked like he was going to speak again, but he didn't, his lips half-puckered. He re-crossed his legs.

"Larry always told you to get a little dirtier, but I think some of your stuff adds a touch of class. "...his tongue quivering bright pink against the brighter pink of her moist, sweet labia. They formed a delicate ridge for his tongue to furrow..." That's almost poetic, you know?"

"I used to write a lot of poetry," he said. Toby fidgeted with his fingers. "After a while I just stopped. The poetry magazines kept rejecting me."

"They weren't rejecting you, just your poems. Probably no good reason, either. It's who you know, that's probably what it is. You shouldn't give it up."

"No, when you're working with words that are pregnant with feeling and meaning, delicate lines, and they knot together into something important —" Toby paused. He took a deep breath. "Well, nobody wants those kind of words anymore. I can make money with technical writing. I did some instruction booklets for a line of toasters. I took some photos, too."

"Really?"

"The pictures they had of the thermostat — the bread brain — they didn't look clear enough when I was writing up how it worked. So I went to their office and photographed a model using a close-up lens. They paid me an extra ten dollars."

"That's a start. Maybe you can do portraits of people some day."

"I've hardly ever had a chance."

Rob remembered Larry Slezak talking about how Toby hadn't had a steady girlfriend in years.

"Sometimes people who know me and know I can take pictures, they'll ask me to do some. It's sort of word of mouth. People like photos, and they look at them and like them right away. Poems don't make sense to people. I type and re-type them over and over because they always come back dog-eared and crumpled."

"Yeah, well, you should keep trying."

"I try, I do try," Toby said, now getting agitated, "when you're on the outside, you try anything to get in there, anything. You just want to be accepted. You wait and wait. You want somebody, anybody to be interested. You think they're interested and they're not."

"Look, deadlines here seem to be coming up quickly. I'm counting on you. Did you take those photos of the Times Square stores?"

"Yes. Yes, I did. I developed them and I should be able to make some prints next week."

"You developed them yourself? You must have been a chemistry major! Great. Whenever we need a photo to illustrate a piece, I'll throw it your way. I need to depend on my regulars. Larry didn't seem to plan ahead too well. I need some more stories, soon as you can. OK?"

"Sure. OK, Rob." Toby kept silent.

"Fine."

Rob could see that Toby was in one of his pensive moods. He stood up and Toby, seeing it, stood up too. Toby looked around nervously.

Cy Kottick framed the door to Rob's cubicle. Toby managed to squirm through, mumbling something as he went.

"Yeah," Cy said to him.

Cy looked at Rob.

"Did you hear that?"

"No. Toby speaks so softly sometimes."

"He said 'Scussmee.' That's what he said. What exactly does that mean? Every time some putz gets in my way, it's always 'scussmee.' Doesn't anybody know how to say, "I beg your pardon for being in your fucking way?"

Cy stayed lounging against the cubicle wall like a gunslinger, one hand dangling dangerously at his side, the other locked into his belt by his thumb. His blue jeans were white at the knee. He was wearing a long black frock coat, something out of the Wyatt Earp era. It was so old the black was more a dirty gray. His black shirt was a contrast to his white skin and hay-colored inch-thick beard.

"What's up?" said Rob.

"My dick," Cy grunted. He slouched into the chair opposite Rob.

"Dressed in black, huh. Mourning the sperm that died on the sheets last night?"

"Strangled in my fist," Cy said. His mouth was drawn down in a frown, but his blue eyes were alive, the light lines under them seeming to crinkle under the pressure of the straining orbs above. "I was being thrifty last night. Aced a hooker out of thirty bucks by jerking off. You know what I hate?"

"I have a pretty good idea."

"You get a blow job, and you pay good money, and they won't swallow. They go turn their backs and spit it out. They spit my kids into some Kleenex. Imagine the great geniuses stifled in the mouths of whores and spat down the drain."

"The world couldn't take another Cy Kottick. It's hot out, Cy, why the black coat?"

"I'm proud of my dandruff. Isn't this a great coat? Guess how much? $7.50 down at Canal Jean."

"It looks warm. It's a fall coat, isn't it?"

"Yeah, well I'm sick of waiting for the fucking seasons to change. I'm sick of everything. This summer really shits. I walk down the street and half the people I want to fuck and the other half I want to kill."

Cy tossed a manuscript on Rob's desk: "Rag Time: Sex with Menstruating Women."

"Gee, thanks a lot, Cy."

"I mention how you can make edible tampons out of breadsticks."

"When did I ask for this?"

"You didn't."

"Did Larry?"

"Nope."

"I don't think we can print this, Cy."

Cy pointed a long, bony finger at Rob. "I thought things would be different with you being editor. They sure would with *me* being editor." He glanced at his fingernail, which was black-edged with dirt. He grinded it against his upper left canine tooth. He looked again and grimaced, wiping his finger against his jeans. "I've been writing for this rag a lot longer than you have. They're afraid to make me the editor. I wrote to that prick Krantz. I need a full time job, but something that isn't really such a big deal. Like this."

"If this job isn't such a big deal, why bother?"

Cy ignored Rob and picked up a copy of Rabbit. He saw that it wasn't the latest, and threw it down again.

"That cover looks a little out of focus," Cy grunted. I think your art director needs to enroll at the Paturzo School for the Blind. Get him a cane and a dog."

Cy's five day growth of beard made him look like a scowling owl, all camouflage and eyes.

"When was the last time you saw Larry alive, Cy?"

"The dead man? I don't remember. In the summer all the days just melt together into one dumb fuckin' numb one. You think I killed him?"

"No, I don't think that."

"You got that squirrelly reporter look on your face. If you were such a great reporter you wouldn't be here.

So drop it. I don't dislike you, Rob, so why don't we keep it that way?"

"Thanks. That's a fine way to talk to an editor. What if I got offended?"

"Oh, fuck you. Offended."

Rob laughed.

"Where are you going, Rob. You've been looking at your watch a dozen times already. You're waiting for 6:30 so Mickey Mouse can get a hardon? Do you have any checks for me? Slezak was starving me to death, the asshole."

"I'll check into it. We're not the only place that owes you money, are we? Didn't you say that publisher —"

"Publishers are all scum. This weasel, he says write some stuff for me, write some stuff. Then after he publishes three stories, and he's stalled me all along, he says he can't pay. Then he begs me for three more! Says he'll get a check to me when I bring them down. I bring 'em down, he gives me a check for half of what he owes me, and the check bounces. I could kill the scumbag."

"I know how you feel."

"I need money, you know," Cy said. "Even a crappy apartment costs a bundle. Do you believe it, a damn walk-up near Avenue A, a studio, and it's $650."

"Nobody has a cheap apartment anymore. Toby's had to borrow money from his parents. His rent is a couple hundred bucks more than yours."

"Yeah, but he's living over on West 72nd. They've got some cheap fruit and vegetable stores around there. And they've got guys selling clothes and books on the sidewalk. That's pretty good. It's like open-air thrift shops."

"Only you would appreciate something like that.

Look, Cy, I'm on deadline here. I've got so much I have to do, and I hate having to be here late."

"Take the stuff home."

"Can't. My girlfriend really doesn't want to see tons of nude photos all over the place, and copies of Rabbit lying around —"

"Oh yeah? She thinks it's bad or something?"

Cy's blue eyes were like ice. "She thinks women are being exploited? Listen, are women paying five bucks for a lousy sex magazine? No. Men are. Are women exploited when they walk down the streets in their fuck-me summer outfits with their tits wobbling and their nipples poking through and their shorts halfway up their assholes? Or is it the guys that are walking into traffic watching them? She doesn't like Rabbit? What about the crap she's into? Vanity Fair or some trendy shit, with pregnant women and smirking dykes on the cover? If Rabbit did that stuff, we'd be under fucking arrest.

"Entire industries are built on cunt. Magazines, ripoff topless bars, strip clubs. They've got these dating services run by slimeball guys to trap other slimeball guys into wasting hundreds of bucks. Some guy knows one of these pricks — a millionaire in Boston pulling scams all over the country. And swing clubs! If women are so into sex, how come the guy pays $50 to get in but a woman can get in free? Why is it streetcorners are all full of hookers exploiting men? Why is the supply and demand is so fucked. Exploitation? Women withold sex. They use it like a weapon."

"You know, a psychologist would charge you $55 an hour for this."

"I'd rather pay it to a whore. At least you definitely leave with less stress than when you came in. I don't mind exploitation if I can at least get something out of it."

"Like gonorrhea?"

Rob realized he was only making Cy angrier.

Like a feverish country preacher, the man in black with the fierce eyes and scruffy growth of beard rose to his full height. "I wrote a porn novel once and the weasel publisher promised me $500, and then he never even paid and I had to sue in Small Claims. Some bitch gets a million bucks for a summer novel that's nothing but sex, but it's phony, and it's by a woman, so she gets rich. You judge men by their porn, and call them crude and savage and exploiting. What if we judge women by their porn? They have porn, you know. That's what those trash romance novels are. Judge them by their porn, and they're stupid, shallow, brainless bitches!"

"Cy — you're getting yourself all upset here —"

"Look," Cy Kottick said, turning his angry glare at Rob, "Rabbit does a service. It keeps about a hundred thousand guys jerking off, and that keeps them from putting their hands around a woman's throat. If you don't want to defend porn, and if you don't really think that this magazine is important, then why the hell don't you get out? I'll take over right now!"

"I'll take that under advisement," Rob said mildly. "You might wait until Larry Slezak's murdered body is at least cold."

Cy sat down.

"I have to let off a little steam," Cy said without apology. "Otherwise I just let out farts."

"I have to go out soon. God, I'm not used to sitting around an office all day."

Rob took a piece of paper and rolled it into the typewriter. There was already some typing on it. Cy craned his neck to read it upside down.

"What's that stuff?"

"Cover lines for the new issue: "Trench whorefare with two fighting lezzies...Massage Parlor Madness: an appointment for an anointment with ointment...Pictorial: Biggest Tits in Pittsburgh..."

Rob stuck the paper in the typewriter and stood up.

"This is a little trick," Rob said. "If you're leaving the office always look like you left in a hurry. Make sure your desk is cluttered and piled high with work. Put something in the typewriter to make it look like you just stepped away and you'll be right back."

Cy nodded, unimpressed. "When will I be able to use this information? Only if you'll hurry up and resign. Why'd you take this job, anyway?"

They walked out of the office together. Cy was a foot taller than Rob, but with his bad posture and vulture-like look to his eyes, he seemed the same height.

"Look at that. Holy shit," Cy said. Walking by was a girl in a pair of snug yellow shorts. She was wearing a tank top, her small breasts soft rubber cones shuddering sideways like two look-outs as she walked. Cy looked as if he was going to take a bite out of her ass as she minced past.

"You don't think she knows that she's driving me nuts?" Cy complained. "Bet she has orgasms just walking in those little pants. Wouldn't you want to be her maxipad?"

Two yuppies on their lunch hour hurried past Rob and Cy, one of them knocking into Cy's leg with his briefcase.

"Scussmee," the yuppie said.

"See?" Cy grumbled. "Nobody knows how to speak. This fuckin' city, everybody's on top of each other. And not where it matters."

"It must be 90 degrees out."

"I don't want to know," Cy said, scratching at his beard. "The humidity is on me like mold on a peach."

It was like walking into an exhaust fan from a laundry, a hot blast that hit them and stayed on them, making their clothes wilt on their bodies. The air in midtown was especially foul today, the city a yawning mouth of smells and heat. Cy and Rob walked along a while, then without a word Cy drifted off into the crowd, a black form swirling in the vibrating pattern of colors crossing the street.

Business men shook their heads, walking together, talking business. Newsstand dealers stared out from their dark grottos, faces framed by lurid hanging magazines and scare newspaper headlines. A fat, pink-faced snub-nosed bum with dirty blond hair dragged along the street on a broken leg, holding a paper cup, whispering to passersby. The fast food places had sweaty lines stretching thickly toward the revolving doors. A bus stalled nearby, spewing out black carbon monoxide with every snort of the motor.

The number of porn stores on 42nd Street had decreased sharply over the last few years, but their ranks were not replaced with anything better. Cheap clothing and sneaker stores caught the attention of pimps and drug dealers, the fast food joints got the spare change money begged for by bums, and the movie theaters showing R-rated violence attracted hooky-playing school kids and bored teenagers.

Rob took the bus that moved slowly across 42nd

street, edging from the Port Authority on 8th Avenue to the United Nations on 1st Avenue. It was almost a sight-seeing bus, but no native New Yorker thought so, suffering as it crawled past the huge library building on 5th Avenue, then slowly jerked past the landmark Grand Central Station. It didn't seem like much of a landmark with bums haranguing the pedestrians, street vendors spreading shabby used paperbacks and magazines out on the sidewalk, and con men trying to hustle unwary tourists into cabs — gypsy cabs that would charge triple rates for a ride.

The bus cranked slowly past the Daily News building, stopping short to exhale an exhaust fart that seeped carbon monoxide in through the open windows. Nobody on the bus seemed to notice. It stalled again and as the bus lurched toward Second Avenue, stopped in the gridlock. A 'Fink Means Good Bread' truck had stopped in the huge puddle made by a broken fire hydrant and cars honked their horns furiously as they went around.

Finally The United Nations building came into view.

It was really just another bland big box of a building, standing like a huge domino at the end of 42nd Street. Across the way, in the small vest-pocket park, a camera crew was set up, with huge vans blocking one of the traffic lanes on 1st Avenue. Rob crossed the street and eased past the small crowd that had formed to watch the movie being made. In spite of the blazing sun, there were lights set up and trained on the park benches where a scene was going to be shot.

Some kid was hurrying by with a heavy crate full of canned sodas. A picnic table was set up with sandwiches and fruit for the camera crew and the cast. Rob looked at the trailers parked nearby. The nicest looking ones had to be for the major stars. Carrie was billed third or fourth. Rob moved down the line of trailers, careful to look casual. Each one was informally guarded by hangers-on and people with clipboards, most everyone munching sandwiches and talking.

"I'll tell Carrie," Rob heard someone say. The man jogged slowly up to one of the trailers. "Tell Carrie that we start up again in a half-hour. Here's the good news: we're quitting early. We'll be through by four, and that'll be it."

"They keep saying that," a dour, matronly woman said, standing on the steps leading up to the trailer. She saw Rob. "What do *you* want?"

"Carrie's expecting me."

"Carrie's having lunch now. She doesn't have any appointments scheduled."

"She does, with me."

Rob bounded up the stairs and past the woman.

"Security!" she shouted out.

Carrie was sitting in the trailer with a salad on the table in front of her.

"Your bodyguards off for the day?" Rob said.

Carrie looked up at him, startled momentarily. When she recognized him, a look of loathing clouded her features. She stood up and walked over to him, her right arm flying up.

"Don't slap me, this time I'll slap back," Rob said. "Your pals came to my house yesterday. What kind of army have you got, anyway?" Rob heard cries and noise outside, but he kept talking. "Do I tell the police you sent them? Is that the kind of free publicity you want?"

Carrie looked out the window.

"You've got ten seconds," she hissed. "Leave or they'll throw you out!"

"Get some cops! Maybe you want me to tell them that you authorized a murder!"

"Oh my God," Carrie gasped.

Rob wasn't prepared for such a reaction. The young actress seemed to sink, fainting, and she leaned against Rob heavily. She let out a moan and then stumbled toward the couch where she sat down, her face in her hands.

"Miss Sinclair," the tubby matron said through the half-opened trailer door, "Security's here."

A private security guard climbed the steps two at a time. He pushed open the door and clamped his hand on Rob's shoulder.

"All right, let's go..." the guard said.

"I'm staying, right Carrie?"

"It's OK, Rafael," Carrie said. "I know this man. But I don't know him that *well.* So if you would, just stay right outside the door."

"Very smart," Rob said, nodding his head. "You know how to keep your cool in a crisis."

The guard gave a hard, warning look to Rob and walked out.

Rob sat down next to Carrie. She was wearing a light scent of perfume. Her skin was smooth with theatrical make-up, a light, doll-like shade of beige. It was strange and alluring and brought out the deep green of her eyes. The varied shades of green that danced in her eyes seemed to kaleidoscope together, drawing Rob in toward her black pupils. Carrie blinked.

"Don't just sit there staring at me," she said. She said it coldly, and it snapped Rob out of it.

"Let's start with the murder. Deny it all you want — you might have an alibi, but I bet your pals don't. Think they'll take the rap for you? They're too stupid to stand up to questioning."

"You're crazy," Carrie said, her voice straining, her eyes searching Rob's. It unnerved him. Even in her anger she was beautiful. Her eyes shimmered and danced so brightly. Her hair was fine, soft, delicately blonde. Her teeth were clearly clenched, but clenched behind soft lips, deep red, the reality of every cliche about ripe twin cherries.

"I'm talking about a murder," Rob said. She knew that. He said it to remind himself why he was there. She had set him up, she had watched him take a beating, but there was something about her that was so hard to resist.

Carrie's eyes were moist, her voice was tearful.

"You saw the film. You saw the *film,* damn you! I didn't kill anybody."

Carrie turned away from him, tears trickling down her cheeks.

Rob touched her face and brought away wetness.

"You're not acting."

"I don't know what you're trying to do to me," Carrie blurted, her words coming between sobs, "you blackmail me, you— you come and threaten me with a film I made years and years ago. All you cared about was *sex.* Yes, I was going to make a stupid little sex film! Yes! You didn't care what happened, you didn't care, you and your horrible magazine! And now? Now you're raising the stakes. Now you're trying to blackmail me for murder!"

She turned to face Rob, her lips quivering with hurt,

but her wet eyes blazing and hateful.

"I couldn't sleep last night," she said. "I've had to take oh, oh, GOD knows how many pills, just to be able to function today."

"You seem to have an appetite," Rob challenged.

Carrie shot her slim arm out from her side, toppling the salad bowl on the floor. It made an ear-splitting crash.

"I haven't eaten a damn thing! They sent it to my trailer and I couldn't eat a bite!"

The door pounded open, the guard had his gun drawn.

The guard stared down at the floor.

"Relax," Rob told him, "it's salad."

Carrie waved him off impatiently and the guard reluctantly backed away. Rob closed the door.

The actress stood near the window of the trailer and looked out. The shadows from the window screen made a solemn veil across her pale white face. Rob moved a few steps closer to her.

"You thought I was going to blackmail you, Carrie. I wasn't. I never was. I really am a reporter. Or I was."

She looked at him carefully.

"I didn't know what to do with the film. I didn't want to give it to Larry, at Rabbit magazine, even if he promised me a job."

Carrie put her hands to her face, wiping at the tears.

"I came to you. I just wanted to find out what it was all about," Rob said. "I was excited. I didn't know for sure what the hell to do. I still thought I had a story, I really did. I just wanted to talk to you. I probably would've just given you the film. Like when I was a reporter, and I let a woman go without interrogating her. Because I just didn't have the heart."

"Well, why didn't you then?"

"You didn't give me a chance," Rob said, his anger replacing his sympathy for the crying star, "you can still see the marks on my face from your goons. And that wasn't good enough for you, either. You sent them out to murder!"

The actress was silent, one hand rubbing her eye like a sleepy, confused child. But Rob wasn't falling for any of it now.

"But all bets are off," Rob said. "Did you use those two goons that worked me over in the hotel? Or did you use the other two, the ones that got to me at my house? Which pair did the dirty work for you? Which pair killed Larry Slezak?"

"You're crazy, you're just a crazy man!" Carrie said. "I don't know what you're talking about! I don't know, I don't know! Stop it, please stop! You're getting me crazy with all this crazy, crazy talk!"

"Where are they now? Those two guys in the hotel?"

"They're at the hotel," Carrie said numbly.

"OK, and what about the other two?"

"I don't know who you're talking about!" Carrie wailed, her voice quivering.

"There was an old guy, about 60, with a white moustache. He's got a round face. Tired eyes. And there was a greaser, a guy about half his age, with black hair and a big nose and a mean mouth that turns down at the corners like fish hooks are pulling at them. He called the older guy "Brains" or something, like he was the boss. Two men. You know them."

Carrie rushed to Rob, her trembling lips were inches

from his. She started to shake Rob violently. "You know about the murder! Didn't you watch the film? You know I didn't kill James Sledge! What did you do to that film? Did they doctor it? Oh, oh Jesus, didn't it *show you* who did it? Don't you know?"

Rob impulsively held Carrie in his arms for a moment. She shrugged out of his grasp and they both backed off, afraid to touch someone they couldn't trust.

Carrie Sinclair began to sob. She sat down, holding her head in her hands.

"What are you trying to do to me," she wept. "You know what was on that film."

"Who is James Sledge?"

"The man with me. Maybe he had another name. I don't know. I didn't know him. I'd never even seen him before. We were making...a movie. What did I know? I wanted to be an actress, I wanted to make films...I was no runaway. I was no virgin. I knew what I was doing, or I thought I did...anyway, we were making this film, and God, I was a little high, I had a couple of joints before they started shooting. I was just, *doing* it, and then — and then —"

Hot tears were coming down Carrie's face, her mouth was open, but only a hoarse, moaning cry came out.

"He was rough with me. He was just using me. I wanted him to stop. My face was next to his — they wanted him to keep going. He was going to get on top of me. And I looked into his face, I was looking into his eyes — and that's when I heard the shot. It was so loud, it almost made me deaf it was so loud. It was right in front of my face like a cannon shot. And suddenly, his face wasn't there. It was just blood, and gore, and red all over, and I felt wet rain on me and it was bits of his skin and his blood...a dying man's blood on my face."

She gasped in revulsion, reliving it.

"I was so frightened, I just froze. And then I had to run, I had to get up. His body — it was falling on top of me, falling over me, with the face burned away from the gunfire, and the blood on me. I heard more shots — I just made for the door. Somehow I made it to the door! I thought maybe it was a raid; they said that when they made movies like that, sometimes cops were tipped off. I thought it was the cops." She began sobbing again, her voice coming out strangled. "The cops or it was one of *them!"*

Carrie looked up at him.

"I have to know...What happened?" she asked.

"I don't know," Rob said, swallowing hard. "I didn't know about any of this. Because there was nothing on the film. It just ended suddenly."

"*Nothing*?"

"One minute you're with this guy and the next, nothing. It was just black."

Carrie stared at him.

"They stopped filming," she said, her eyes widening. "When you first came to me in the hotel I couldn't believe you didn't care about the murder. I couldn't believe you were going to blackmail me for making a stag film. That's why..." her voice softened. "That's why I lost it and called my bodyguards in. Don't you see?"

"You're telling me there was a murder at the end of this stag film," Rob said slowly. He looked into Carrie's eyes. He noticed the black mascara, the false lashes that drew him into her luminous green gaze. "Well, there was no murder. It wasn't on the film. The filming already stopped. The film just stayed in the camera until somebody developed it. But," he added, an edge creeping into his voice, "there was a murder ten years after that film was made. Larry Slezak, the editor of Rabbit Magazine."

"You think I ordered it?"

"Because you thought that's where the film was — with Larry Slezak, the editor of Rabbit Magazine. So you sent your bodyguards out to find it. They knew that Larry, being the editor, would know all about it. So they went to his house that night. And when they didn't find the film, they shot him!"

"My bodyguards were with *me* all night."

"I haven't told you the date."

"They're always with me."

"They're not with you now."

"Not when I'm on the set, no. They work all afternoon and evening. And every evening I've been at these, these stupid stupid publicity things. Dinners and banquets and parties."

"It would be pretty easy for your bodyguards to slip away."

"They were with me. What are you trying to say?"

"Okay, the guards were with you. So you hired two more. They killed Larry. And then they came after me, next. If Larry didn't have the film, they had to figure that I did, because I was the one that met with you. They tried to get the film away from me. Who else could have known about the film? Only you, and me, and Larry Slezak. So this old guy with the moustache, and this mug, this thug with him, they came after me!"

"Oh Jesus," Carrie said, getting up. "Keefer. And Joe Pantera. Don't you understand? I never hired them.

They were never my bodyguards! They were the two men in the hotel room with me! The man with the moustache, he was the brains. He got the room and the actor and me — and the young one, Joe Pantera, he was the camera man! Those two men you think I sent — they were the ones who *made* the film."

Somebody was knocking on the trailer door.

"Five minutes, Miss Sinclair."

Carrie Sinclair whispered, "Those two men are killers."

Rob touched her hand, held it for a moment. It was cold. She was terrified, or she was just a cool, calculating actress.

CHAPTER TEN

The brakes squealed as the bus came to a stop at the corner of 42nd and 8th. Passengers lumbered out to get across the street to the Port Authority. Rob watched as a few of them moved out through the back exit door.

Just then two figures slipped onto the bus, having held the back door open for the passengers getting out. Rob got to his feet.

The two men who had nearly killed him in Riverdale!

No, it looked nothing like them. It was two Puerto Rican guys. They hustled toward the back of the bus and sat down. The bus driver hadn't noticed.

Rob felt his heart pounding. He walked up to the front of the bus and got out. He didn't want to go back to the Rabbit magazine office, not now. But Carrie was going back to work, as shaken up as she was. And in the midst of all this craziness, he was an editor now and there was a magazine to get out.

Rob glanced back briefly to make sure that no two men of any description were following him.

He thought about what Carrie had said. He thought about the two men who tried to kill him in Riverdale. Whether they were sent by Carrie or not, no matter if he believed her story or he didn't, one fact was the same. They were at large and they'd try again.

She said their names were Keefer and Pantera. She said the man who was killed was named James Sledge.

There was one way to check on it. To really be a reporter again.

"Hi, Elise. I'd like to see Michael Krebs. You do recognize me, right?"

The receptionist gave him a sour look.

"Ex-employees are not allowed —"

"Look, get him on the phone, will you? Tell him to come down into the lobby!"

Elise adjusted her headset and put the call through.

"Michael?" she said. "It's Rob Streusel. He wants to see you." She told Rob with great satisfaction, "He's on deadline now. He can't talk to you."

"Tell him I have to talk to him. Right now."

"I'm not a messenger service!" she snapped. "Michael? Are you still there? Rob insists he wants to *speak* to you."

She said it as if it had been an obscene proposition.

The girl pointed to the service phone perched on the corner of the reception desk. Rob picked it up.

"Hi, Michael, it's Rob. I need to get in here."

"Can't do it, Rob. You don't work here. I could get into a lot of trouble and it just isn't worth it."

"Is murder worth it?"

"Murder? Are you threatening me?"

"No, no, dammit I'm not threatening you, Michael. I'm investigating a murder."

"Not for us. Otherwise you'd have clearance."

"Oh, you're real smart. God *dammit*, Michael. I need to look up some back issues."

"Then go to the library. They have everything on microfilm."

"It'll be a lot fuckin' easier to find it out from here, Michael. Everything's keyed by name, by subject, cross-referenced every damn which way. I don't know for sure what I'm looking for and I have to go run some names through the computer files before I know which issues I need."

"Rob, I'm on deadline here, you remember what that's like —"

"Michael, I've never really asked a favor before."

"I can't, Rob, I can't. Let go of it, Rob. You're not a reporter anymore. You're not with The City Daily anymore."

Rob began to laugh. He winked at the switchboard girl.

"OK, Michael, that's great."

"No hard feelings?"

"No."

"Good. I gotta go. Take care, Rob."

Michael hung up. Rob said, "It'll only take two minutes, I promise. Great. Thanks a lot."

He signed his name on the register sheet in front of him, marking down the floor and the time. Before Elise could say anything, Rob said to her, "Michael Krebs said he'd take responsibility for me coming up. But don't worry. I might be getting my old job back. Then you'll see lots more of me."

He walked confidently toward the elevator bank, convincing himself he wouldn't hear Elise squawking after him.

She didn't. She studied him carefully as he walked into the elevator. Then she turned back to the switchboard.

Rob knew which room had the back date issues

stored on microfilm. There were microfilm reading machines just like a library, and next to them a few computer terminals. He tried to remember the code, known only to employees, that would gain access to the computers. Only a few people were using the computers in the big, steel-gray room that hummed with the sound of the machinery. He sat down, poked a few buttons, and watched the screen in front of him glow green. Finally the sentence came up that he was waiting for:

"TYPE: Name of SUBJECT."

He typed in the name that Carrie Sinclair had spoken: Joe Pantera.

Joe Pantera, the young, mean-mouthed strong arm. The one who grabbed the keys from him and tried to break into the apartment. The guy who liked to punch and kick.

Carrie hadn't told Rob much, but she did say he had been the camera man on the film, a creep even then, a leering stud wanna-be who wanted her, and bad. That lust continued until he had to sit there and watch her making it with the black guy.

"NO FILE."

Rob quickly typed in another spelling of the name.

"NO FILE."

He tried another spelling, then quit.

There was nothing on Joe Pantera in The City Daily files.

Carl Keefer was the other one, now about 60 or 65, a broken down film "producer" way back when, having drifted from loansharking and petty schemes to the porn world. His hair was now gray and his moustache white.

There was nothing on him in The City Daily files.

There was one more name. Rob punched it into the computer.

It came up JAMES SLEDGE: 8/28/81 7.3

Rob checked the date again. There was no mistake. August of 1981.

"Can't be," he said to himself.

Rob checked the metal file cabinet and brought out the microfilm spool for August, 1981. He threaded it into the machine quickly. He pushed a few buttons and the film automatically began to spool to August 28th, and then to page seven.

The door to the computer room opened, and two men stood in the doorway, one of them a uniformed guard.

Rob pressed PRINT and the machine began to whir, and from the bottom, a long, newspaper-sized sheet of paper began to quiver out, starting from the top. It was a replica of The City Daily for August 28, 1981, page Seven.

"Okay Rob, I'm afraid you're going to have to leave," Michael Krebs said.

"You wouldn't have said that if your friend wasn't standing there," Rob said. The security guard stepped forward, shaking his head with a "let's not make a scene" look of weariness.

Rob folded up the copy of page seven.

"You've got a lot of nerve, Rob," Michael said, stepping back as the security guard gripped Rob's arm.

"What was that you put in your pocket?" he said.

"I'm going, I'm on my way out," Rob said, "no problem." He began to walk briskly and the security guard lurched forward to keep up with him.

"Thanks for the favor, Mike!" Rob called out.

"Don't get me into trouble," Michael Krebs shouted,

"I didn't tell you it was ok."

"You're a real company boy, Michael."

"At least I have a job, pal! I'm not a fuck-up like you were."

"I don't need a lousy press card to be a reporter," Rob said. "I'm going to solve a murder — and when I do, I'll give you a copy of the story. And I'll shove it down your throat!"

The guard pushed Rob forward.

"That'll be the only way you'll ever have the right words on the tip of your tongue!" Rob called out.

Krebs followed Rob and the security guard to the elevators.

The security guard pushed Rob into the elevator. Michael watched the doors close, saying, "Don't come back Rob. Now I'm going back to work. *I work here!*"

"Where? At a computer or at a urinal? There's a difference between being a reporter and being a prick!"

"That's enough," the guard said.

The elevator doors began to close.

"I could've said a lot more," Rob said.

"I held the door so you could get that last shot in," the guard said. Rob looked at him.

"He really is a prick," the guard said. He smiled amiably at Rob. But when they reached the first floor, he said "Don't come back ever again. I mean it."

Elise was standing at the elevator, waiting for them. There was an offended look on her face. She had been betrayed. Lied to. Abused. Used. She glared at Rob.

Rob brought his hands together into balled up fists, one next to the other, as if he was handcuffed. He showed them to her that way.

Then he extended the middle fingers on both hands.

CHAPTER ELEVEN

"Would you turn that down, please?"

Rob looked up and saw Julie rustling across the bedroom in her white lace nightgown. She slid the dial on the stereo and the room became tensely quiet.

"I can't concentrate without the radio on," Rob said.

"That's no reason to blast my ears off."

"I can hear people outside talking. I can hear the people upstairs walking. We're living in a dump and I'm sick of this shit. Can't you see I'm trying to read something?"

Julie put the sound on softly.

"It's after midnight," she said. "I need my sleep. I've been under a lot of stress lately. And it's all your fault."

"What do you think I'm working on?"

He moved his thumb across each line of the short newspaper story on page seven of The City Daily.

Julie leaned over and said "Please, Rob, they beat you up twice. Next time they might just do what they did to Larry. No talk. Just a bullet in the head."

Somehow, her caring was not the same as being comforting. Rather than making it worse by arguing with her, Rob just nodded his head. She padded back into the bedroom.

The story that he had quickly xeroxed in that decade-old issue of The City Daily was a familiar one.

Headline: KIDS PLAY HIDE & SEEK, FIND CORPSE.

"The body of a man identified as James Sledge, 27, an ex-con with several arrests for drug dealing, was found in the alley of an apartment building on 42nd Street and 10th Avenue by three children as they played hide and seek. The grisly discovery was made by eight year-old Eusebio Colon and his two friends. The boy called his mother who in turn informed the police. She later said, 'Eusebio wasn't scared or nothing. He's a big movie fan and I guess that prepared him to see something like this. I'm glad I didn't see (the corpse) because I don't like those gory movies.' Reportedly half of Sledge's face was hollowed by the pistol shot fired at point-blank range."

It wasn't a big story, just one of a half-dozen or more a reporter had to write each week. Some guy who got killed. Nobody knew what he did for a living, but some kind of drug or sleaze connection seemed obvious. And nobody was hunting too hard for the killer. The story was not exactly something for the scrapbook of the man who had written it.

The byline for the story belonged to a young reporter by the name of Robert Streusel.

Rob remembered it now. He followed the cops who had gotten a lead that James Sledge was seen in a hotel lobby a block away, one of his frequent hang-outs.

The cops had interviewed a cleaning woman.

Rob had spoken to her right after.

"I don't know what happened to the man," she'd said. Rob could tell that she knew plenty. He wasn't the police; she wasn't as careful with what she said and the way she said it.

When Rob had finally gotten her talking, she just broke down.

"I need this job," she said, "it won't do no good if I tell. I don't know the name of the person that did it and I can't even tell you anything that would help. And it won't bring back James Sledge. Rest his soul. He had no family. He had no friends. He had no nothing."

He told that story to his senior editor. He was ordered back to harrass the maid and get her to make more of a statement. Rob felt so bad for her, he said no.

"Then write up what she told you already," the editor said.

Rob refused.

"Are you a newspaper man? Or are you gutless? You can't let your personal feelings get in the way, kid. Maybe a two week suspension, without pay, will change your mind."

"It won't."

"Then I'll make it a permanent suspension."

The maid kept her job. Rob lost his.

Rob was wondering now. Were they both living in crummy apartments going nowhere?

Julie came to sit down next to Rob.

"Now I can't sleep," she said. "What are you doing? Reading?"

"I'm through."

"Good. You know how I get when I'm under stress," Julie said softly. "I can't sleep, I just toss and turn, and I need some kind of mmm, distraction." She spoke softly, with a teasing touch of humor to her voice. "I need something, something that'll take my mind off my problems. Do you know what that could be?"

She leaned over to kiss his neck, her long hair getting into his eyes, preventing him from reading. The hair tickled his eyes and he tried to push the hair away. Julie sensuously kissed his neck and ear. Rob held the paper off to the side, trying to read it again.

"Tickle-tickle," Julie whispered, nibbling her tongue into Rob's ear. "Tickle you tickle you."

Rob swiped at the mosquito-like itch he felt. Julie giggled.

"You like that...tickle you!" She swabbed her hot tongue at his ear again. "Tickle!" She swabbed at it again.

"Will you GET THE FUCK AWAY?" Rob shouted, standing up.

Julie looked down at the floor.

"I thought you liked it when I did that," she muttered.

"I *never* liked it, if you want to know, and I especially don't like it *now*. I'm trying to work, all right?"

Rob turned off the stereo and went into the bathroom. He tried to re-read the newspaper article, but he'd looked it over so many times he couldn't stand reading it again. He stuck a finger in his ear trying to wipe out some of Julie's saliva.

Carrie was at least telling the truth about one thing. James Sledge was killed. And from what he knew of the case, it seemed to have happened as she said it did. He definitely was killed in the hotel and the body dumped a block away. But there was nothing on the film to give him a clue, nothing but that opening seen of her with Sledge.

And there was no comfort in knowing that whoever

had the film had a good chance of ending up beaten up or dead.

One bullet in Larry Slezak's head. That was the mark of a professional, wasn't it? The only mark on him. The killers had looked over some of those films in his bookcase, looking for the Carrie Sinclair movie. They'd turned the lamp on his desk up to look through the magnifying lupe and check the frames, and when they didn't find what they wanted, they shot him. No pleading, no struggle. Just a bullet in the head.

They shot Larry. And then they came after him. And they would be back.

A chill shot through Rob and he dropped the newspaper. He turned on the hot water in the shower, stripped quickly and got in. The hot water didn't feel hot. It wouldn't warm up. He was actually shivering. He stared at his hands. They were shaking.

Michael Krebs, the weasel ex-friend of his on The City Daily was right. Trembling like this — he was no reporter.

The idea of someone out to get him sent another chill through him, one even worse than the first. He pushed his face under the steaming shower and tried to steam the fear away. He suddenly felt a wave of burning electrcity shooting all over him. He rushed from the tub, half scalded.

He stood dripping wet naked.

He tried to reach for the tap but the hissing water stung his hand.

Rob draped a towel across the toilet seat and sat down.

What about James Sledge, the porn actor who was killed?

What about Larry?

What about the men who were out to get him? What did they all have in common?

And what about the roll of film that seemed to start it all?

The questions tumbled one after another and then kept rolling and rolling around in his head.

"You're no reporter," Michael Krebs had said. Rob was hearing it over and over now.

Maybe he was right.

Then he thought about creep, Krebs. What if all this happened to him? Krebs would probably take a bus to Staten Island somewhere and go into hiding.

He wouldn't stay and take it.

Rob felt the sting of the hot water on the bruises that were still sore on his face. There were several black and blue marks on his ribs. He'd taken a beating and he hadn't stopped. He was nearly killed at his own front door, and he hadn't stopped.

He thought about that. It took some guts to keep going, and he hadn't even thought about it.

He got up and looked at himself in the mirror. He looked into his eyes.

"You took a licking and you kept on ticking," he said to himself, with bitter humor. It was only now, in a quiet moment, that the fear came back.

Rob wrenched the shower tap and turned it back to the middle setting. He got in the shower and energetically began to lather up. Then he quickly rinsed off and got out.

"I've got to think my way out," he said as he shrugged into his bathrobe.

He went into the living room. Down below a few

kids were still laughing, talking, pushing each other around on a street corner. It was midnight but it was warm outside and everyone was restless. Air conditioners rattled in apartment windows and every now and then a car would crawl by with hot salsa music pounding from its speakers. His was one of the "luxury" buildings, and it had central air conditioning. Which was always broken.

The warm, still air clung to him like a mitten and he pulled his bathrobe back off. He still felt suffocated.

"What if I believe Carrie?" he said out loud. "That doesn't make it any better. If Carrie didn't send Joe Pantera and Carl Keefer after me, then they did it on their own. And they'll try again. They killed Larry and they want to kill me, too."

He thought about Larry's death. It couldn't have been done by Carrie's bodyguards. The way they roughed him up, almost for the fun of it. They surely would have given Larry a beating, just to make damn sure that he wasn't holding anything back. They wouldn't have just shot him, cold-blooded like that.

He thought of Carrie. How vulnerable she looked, how near to tears, how underneath it all, she seemed just as worried, just as confused as he was. She put on the tough act the first time only because she thought he was tougher.

There was a way of making sure about Carrie.

There was a sound at the front door. He stopped.

In the dim light he could see movement, darkness blocking the light from under the door, something in the way. Somebody was at the front door.

Rob dashed quickly toward the bathroom. He snapped the lid off the hamper and rooted around for his underpants. He slipped them on. He grabbed the toilet plunger next to the john and brandished it. It felt pretty heavy in his hand. A crack on the neck with the wooden stick — it might be enough to knock a man unconscious.

He stared at it. Better take the plunger end of it off. He jammed his foot down on the rubber plunger and pulled hard, trying to pull the stick loose.

It wouldn't come loose. The plunger was somehow screwed onto the stick.

Rob held the plunger end so he could hit with the stick part of it. But the rubber just bent in his hand.

The key was in the lock.

The door was opening.

Rob wrestled with the toilet plunger one last time.

The door opened wide.

"Toilet stopped up?" Julie asked.

Rob exhaled heavily.

"How did you get out there?" he asked.

"How do you think," she said, carrying a small bundle into the kitchen. "While you decided to go take a shower I went down to that new bodega that opened up down the street and I bought myself some cold beers. There's some for you, if you want. One good thing about the way the neighborhood's going. The bodega is open all night. The Associated closes at 9 p.m."

"Cervezas," Rob said. "Muy bien. Gracias."

"Do you mind telling me what's the matter with you?"

Julie twisted off the cap of a cold beer and handed it to Rob. Rob sipped it.

"You know I don't bring my troubles home from work."

"Oh, no, not you. When that little kid was run over by that guy wheeling a cart full of fur coats on 38th Street where all those garment center warehouses are — you didn't spend days and days with the family and their lawyers and stuff? And when you started doing reports on Times Square, you didn't start bringing home those porn videos and magazines?"

"That was fun, wasn't it?"

"For a while. Yeah. But I got tired of watching them a lot sooner than you did."

Rob drained the beer.

Julie sat down next to Rob on the sofa.

"Rob, I don't like men trying to break my door down. What are you trying to do to us?"

"I'm a reporter, dammit."

"What's that supposed to mean? You're not a reporter. A reporter gets paid to report. And nobody's paying you. Nobody's paying you to get yourself killed and take me with you!"

"I'm still a reporter, Julie. I can't shut my eyes like turning off a TV set."

"Then tell me what's going on. Who were those guys?"

"I can't. It's better if you don't know."

"But I *do* know. There's this film, and if somebody wants to get it, I'll damn well give it to 'em!"

"Look, I have a lot on my mind."

"Yeah."

"I have to make a phone call."

"You mind telling me who you're going to call at this hour?"

"A hotel."

"I'm not staying in a hotel!"

"I didn't say that, did I? Will you just leave me alone for a minute?"

Julie didn't argue. Rob looked up the number of the joint where Carrie said the porn film was made. The hotel on 42nd Street. The name of it wasn't familiar to him. It had been so long.

Julie waited in the bedroom and listened to him talking on the phone: "Do you know who Carrie Sinclair is? You don't. I see. No, I was just curious. No, I'm not a reporter. And I'm not with the police department. I'm a private detective — yes — and I'm trying to find the girl. I know it's been over ten years. Her parents hired a number of detectives before me, but as you can see, I'm the first to talk to you. So I've made more progress than they have...Can I just speak with you in person? I can come down now, if you want. I just have two or three questions I hope you can help me on. Well, all right. I'll ask you now, then.

"You were working in the hotel when James Sledge was shot? Hello? James Sledge. They were making a film. I'll tell you exactly what I'm talking about. Joe Pantera was behind the camera, and Carl Keefer was there, too...Please — just hang on for a second, ok? Hello?"

Rob checked his watch.

He put the phone down and rushed over to his desk. He came back with his Rolodex.

"Dayan Limo? I'd like a car. Meadow Road in Riverdale down to 42nd Street as soon as you can. Right. Thanks. No, not a limo, just a regular car. Thanks a lot..."

"Good luck," Julie said.

"Thanks. I wish I could tell you more."

"So do I," Julie said. "When armed men come to my door — because of something *you* did — I think I deserve an answer."

Rob began to get dressed.

"You're right," he said. "I think I have enough time before the cab comes."

CHAPTER TWELVE

The name had changed twice over the years, but the maid had stayed. Now called The West Side Inn, what hadn't changed was the building, the carpeting, or the clientele. It was after 1am by the time Rob arrived downtown but traffic in the lobby was brisk.

"That is thirty dollar" the driver said in a heavy accent.

"Isn't that for a limousine? I said just a regular car."

"This isn't a regular car. Is a four door. That is limo."

"Yeah, ok, ok," Rob said, counting out the money.

The driver smiled.

"I hope she's worth it."

Rob shot him a tired glance of contempt.

"What's the big deal," the driver said affably. "Who cares. Do I care? You want I should wait?"

The lobby of the hotel had a strange, strong smell of musky perfume masking cleaning fluid. A couple had just left the front desk, and as for the other couple now talking to the clerk, it didn't take Rob a second glance to realize the lanky white woman hanging on the arm of the Middle Eastern man with the white pillbox hat wasn't a woman.

The creature was as tall as the man, the shoulders clearly modeled, the make-up on her face successfully hiding any trace of razor stubble but applied as thick as plastic. The lipstick and eye make-up were exaggerated beyond garish. The only thing Rob wasn't completely sure of was whether the transvestite was a hooker or not.

He noticed the way they talked to each other, the way they moved. The transvestite's eyes glowed, the conversation whispered with the excitement and dirty glamor of a pick-up. For the transvestite, it was slutty surrender into the arms of an exotic man. For the dark-eyed stranger from the Middle East, any white flesh was a conquest, and he wasn't considering himself gay at all. If anything, he was showing his mastery of a weak white man, so weak he was dressed like a woman, ready to get butted. When it was the transvestite who paid for the room, Rob's suspicions were further confirmed.

The couple got into the elevator as the maid was getting off.

Rob crossed the lobby.

"I spoke to you on the phone a little while ago," he said.

The maid walked quickly to the counter, standing behind the counterman, a tough man with tattoos on his arms and a rack of earrings jammed into one lobe. He immediately walked around the counter and confronted Rob.

"Can I help you?" he said irritably.

"I wanted to speak to your maid over there."

"You a cop?"

"No."

"You want to talk to this guy?" he asked the maid. The maid shook her head. "She don't want to talk to you. Get out."

"Why don't you want to talk to me?" Rob shouted to her. "Are you afraid? Look, I know everything that happened. Do you remember me? Do I look familiar to you?"

The maid shook her head.

"I was there! I was a reporter on The City Daily. You asked me not to write anything that would get you fired. Remember that?"

The maid looked at him closely.

"Remember what you said? That you couldn't identify the murderer, and you didn't want to get into trouble?"

"It's been so long. What good's it gonna do to bring all that up again?"

"Someone who kills once will kill again. And it's happened again! Only this time, there might be some clues. This time something can be done if you'll trust me."

"I told you, I hardly saw a thing. Don't remember a thing."

"I'm trying to help the girl. The girl who was in that room. Do you know the hell she's been living with all these years?"

The maid nodded coolly. "Being a murderer!" she said.

"What? You can't believe she killed James Sledge!"

The maid stormed toward him, tears in her eyes.

"There was blood on her dress. Blood all over the damn thing. But it's not gonna bring him back from the grave. I don't want no revenge, I just want to be left in peace. That's all I got to say."

Rob had to choose his questions well — make her mad enough to keep talking — not mad enough to stop.

"If she tried to kill everyone why didn't she try to kill you, too?"

"I don't know," the maid said. "She dropped the gun is why. Thank the Lord she dropped the gun in the room and ran. She could've killed me! The second shot ripped into the door..."

"The *second* shot?" Rob looked into the angry faces of the maid and the counter man. "That's in keeping with exactly how it happened!" he said.

"What would you know about it? What *she* told you?"

"What do you really know about it?" Rob answered evenly. "What Joe Pantera told you? What Carl Keefer told you?"

The woman looked at the man, who moved menacingly forward.

"Wait a second," Rob said quickly, "listen to this. A girl is making love in bed with this guy. She doesn't care that it's a black guy. She doesn't care that anybody's filming it."

The counter man put his arms across his chest. He was listening to this. The maid was looking away, trying not to.

"She's making love to him. That's all she's doing. I have the film. I've seen it."

The maid's eyes widened.

"Now think carefully. How long was she in that room? Come on, *remember*. She was in there a long time, wasn't she? Before the shots? All right then! She was making this film. She was making love and something went wrong."

"Yeah, she got afraid or something. She got hurt or something. And she damn went crazy!"

"Did you see it? Then how do you know? How?

What if it wasn't her? There's a shot, point blank range. The man she's making love with is killed. The girl is shocked, the blood is all over her.

"She doesn't know what's going on, but the two men are fighting. A second shot is fired. It rips into the door. That bullet could've killed you, an innocent bystander.

"The girl's in shock. There's a dead man. There's gunfire. She's not sure if maybe she's been shot, too. She sees blood. There's blood all over. She rushes out. She thinks she's dying. She hurries away..."

Rob couldn't tell if the maid believed this version of the story or not.

"Does it make sense to you?" he asked. "Could it have happened that way?"

The maid didn't nod yes or no.

"Maybe Joe Pantera told you something else. Or Carl Keefer."

"You better go."

"Don't you see? You didn't want to talk, you didn't want to get involved. And I never confronted you. And that was my job. You were busy saving yours, and I was busy thinking I knew mine. No communication at all. And what has it gotten us? More misery, more hell, and more murder!"

"Leave me alone!"

"Ten years later, and you're barely hanging on to a night shift job. The hotel's changed managers and names, and nobody gives a damn about you. Nobody gives a damn about me, either. They fired me for not getting the story. I've wasted ten years of my life since."

"You gotta go," the maid said. "Please! I can't talk no more now."

Rob backed away, looking carefully at the maid. If

he left now, would she still be here tomorrow night?

He opened the lobby door. When he looked back at the maid, he saw that she and the desk clerk were talking. The way he was pointing his finger at her, and the way she was answering, he knew that it meant trouble. Trouble was all that hotel ever saw, and there would be more of it.

CHAPTER THIRTEEN

"What, we've got guys dying for pussy?" Rob said sourly.

The art director sighed and answered, "We've got to get this book shipped on time. Or else."

"Or else what? They'll buy Nugget instead?"

Raymond Fitzgerald theatrically pinched at his nose right between his eyes. He looked like he just got out of bed, with his fashionable bird's nest mess of thinning hair on top, cut short on the sides. He had foresaken his bowtie in favor of a slim leather tie dyed light blue, which either was in fashion, or was in fashion in his own determined mind.

"Check these pages for typos," the art director said. "Please, Robert, don't give me the kind of static Lawrence did. Working in this place is bad enough. But," he emphasized "But" with a click of his tongue against the roof of his mouth, "we must do what we *must* do."

"Yeah. Yeah. I got about four hours of sleep last night. I could be out trying to solve Larry's murder."

"That will be the day."

Rob looked at Raymond.

"I didn't mean that you couldn't solve a crime," the art director enunciated, "I mean that there are so many killings every day. And some of them probably deserve it. You know, Lawrence didn't have the nicest personality in the world. There are ex-girlfriends who hated him, men who hated him for spoiling their women, and then there were people like me, who hated him out of principle. The lack of it. The important thing, Robert, is to avoid me having similar feelings about you. So please, if you'd concentrate on your work and help me get this book out on time?"

Rob grabbed a handful of boards and tried to focus on them.

The magazine copy had been mounted, two pages a time, on white manila boards. The columns of type were on resin-coated paper stuck down with a rubbery gum adhesive. Black and white "stats," photostat versions of the photos, were stuck in place so that the printer would know where each color slide was to be, and what size. The only blank spots were for the ads, which were stripped in later.

The ads were almost all rip-offs, as Larry used to cheerfully admit. He liked handing Rob the latest irate letter from a putzy reader: "I sent away for a movie, "Teen Lesbians" for $14.95 and nothing happened." The biggest joke was the company that sold "spurious Spanish Fly, guaranteed" for $9.95 a tube. The readers had no idea what the word "spurious" meant. If the company ever got a complaint from the postal department, they could point to their ad and say that they were doing nothing wrong at all. "Spurious" was right there, in the text. The product, they would insist, was being sold as a novelty.

Rob glanced over the copy: "I stabbed my cock into her tight little ditch. She began to babble like a backed up sink, so I planted my lips on hers to shut her up, drilling my tongue down her throat till I was using her uvula for a punching bag."

That had to be one of Cy Kottick's stories. "The bed creaked. Gloria groaned and gasped. I shot my load, a jolt of jizz coiling out of my shaft, spitting into her womb. She let out a long low gap of air."

Rob circled the word "gap" but then changed his mind. There wasn't enough time to get it changed to "gasp" and it didn't make that much difference anyway. Cy once told Larry how he loved the typo that turned "cunt" into "cut." It went great with slit and gash.

"...Just as I slid my cock out I erupted again with two or three convulsive spurts of come. They flew through the air, plopping soggily onto her pubic thatch and belly, one long spurt lying like wet white string from her navel down to her crotch."

Rob put the board on top of the pile on the side of his desk.

Rob had moved the desk and chair to a different wall in Larry's cubicle. He hated the idea of sitting in the exact same spot as the murdered editor. He checked his watch. He wanted to get the hell out of the office and get back on the case. He opened a drawer to get a fresh grease pencil. He noticed a yellow Post-it note with a phone number. The area code was 516, which meant Long Island. He punched it in.

A woman answered. She seemed an older woman.

"Hello?" Rob said.

"Yes," the woman said, "can I help you? This is Mrs. Molanski."

The name clicked. Tee's mother.

"Hi, Mrs. Molanski, this is Rob Streusel, I'm the new editor at Rabbit Magazine."

"Oh."

"I was just calling to check on your daughter. Is she all right? Can I speak with her?"

"She's all right, thank you," the woman said, an edge to her voice. "She's not home. She's living in the city again."

"Do you have a number for her?"

"No," the woman said abruptly. Then she continued, unable to leave it at that. "My daughter is over 18, and she tells me that she doesn't need my advice. I didn't even know she was living with Larry until she came home crying." Mrs. Molanski barely controlled her anger as she added, "Tee only comes back here when there's a crisis."

"I'm sorry to bother you Mrs. Molanski."

The art director came by with more boards that his assistant had finished pasting down. "This over here is really fouled up," he said, pointing to a few lines. "It's a whole sentence. We don't have enough press type to change it, we'll have to send it out."

"Let's see," Rob said. He read the line out loud: "She sucked jars ron it, the pomk spft wet wit cmm — hey, this *is* fucked up. Just cut it out entirely."

"Then it'll be too short at the bottom of the page."

"Well then leave it in," Rob replied amiably. "Leave it in, leave it in, like a good American."

"You have to make a decision here," he said.

"Then take it out. Why don't you slip one of those public service ads in? Join the Army, or join the March of Dimes or something? That's good for a few inches at the bottom of a column."

"Now I'll have to go and clip one from a back issue," Raymond Fitzgerald huffed. "It doesn't matter to you, does it, when you burden me with extra work?"

"Tell you what. Don't change it then."

The art director rolled his eyes and left.

From the front of the office there was a long, low growl. A guttural whine rose that sounded like a vacuum cleaner being turned off. Rob looked up. There was another eerie growl, this time shorter, fiercer, punctuated at the end with a sudden ear-shattering bark.

A police dog! The cops were coming in with dogs!

Rob sat motionless in the cubicle.

But now, there was nothing. No sound at all.

Rob waited, his pen poised in his hand. Pressure. That's what it was. He hadn't heard anything at all.

Rob looked at the boards in front of him. "He rubbed his stiff cock, while she lowered her delicately laced panties down around her angles..."

Rob didn't bother changing it to ankles. This was one of Toby's stories. Maybe angles would only make it seem more poetic. It was odd that Toby had a desire to write romantic short stories and yet was also so reserved and scientific, with his collection of science books and his preoccupations with mechanical gizmos.

Rob settled back in his chair. Then it started again — a jolting bark that made his heart race. Sudden frantic yelping echoed loudly all over the office, shattering the quiet drone of the fluorescent lights and the dull mumble of the radio from the art department.

Rob slipped out into the hallway and tried to peer around the corner. He remembered Larry talking about moral majority groups and feminists and pickets. "They'll come and kill us all," he joked.

The door to Krantz's office suddenly began to creak open. Rob stopped. The door opened wider, but there was nobody there. Rob craned his neck to look inside. And suddenly, right at his feet, the barking erupted. It was a wire-haired terrier, its black button eyes trained on him, its hungry little mouth open, fringed with urine-colored fur. It barked relentlessly.

Somebody came up behind Rob.

"Rob, please close the door," the art director said.

"I didn't know Krantz had a dog," Rob managed to say.

"It's Mrs. Krantz's dog, but he has the rights for the *baby*. He gets the dog every other month."

"He's divorced?"

"Yes. Bernice Publications is Bernice Krantz, the ex-wife."

"Oh fine, if he dies the dog'll inherit the business and we'll be putting out Fire Hydrant Illustrated."

"Just close the door," the art director said. "Mr. Krantz keeps the dog in there when he goes out."

"Where the hell does he go?"

"The less you know the better. Some of the people in the distribution end of this business are less than savory. If he doesn't join them now and then for drinks and lunch and things like that, and if he doesn't bring them a little 'off the books' check, they get cranky. Which means Mr. Krantz turns into 265 pounds of Hudson River fish food."

"Look, I've got to go out. This magazine can run itself."

"But the corrections. They'll take all day."

"I'm saving Irwin money. If I make corrections, it'll cost a fortune at this point. Just go through the boards yourself. If there are no glaring mistakes, fine."

"I am the creative director, Robert. My job is not to

find mistakes and/or correct them!"

"Make it easy on yourself. Leave 'em. If Krantz notices, just blame me. I don't care."

Rob walked back to his cubicle, Raymond Fitzgerald muttering and fussing behind him.

"If you walk out that door, then I'll go too," the art director said. "I could find better things to do with myself on such a nice day. I don't like being cooped up in the office."

"Look, Raymond," Rob said, "I think it's more important to solve a murder — and stop another one from happening. I've got to find a lead on a couple of guys."

Rob checked the address on the xeroxed letter that had arrived a few days earlier. It was from Magnum Sound Studios, 612 West 57th. The invitation said "2pm: Luncheon Buffet, Film at 3pm." There weren't many porn screenings anymore, especially with videos being cranked out at the rate of dozens each week. There was a good reason to go to this one. It wasn't the star. It was one of the producers, an old timer who'd been in the business for years.

The screening room was small, holding only about 50 people. There weren't that many sex magazine film reviewers or film distributors.

"I think I'll try the chopped liver," one of the reviewers said. "It looks like you know what, though."

It was Timmy Hecker, pudgy-faced with wiry, woolly white blonde hair. His skin was almost as white as his hair, and there were unhealthy gray circles under his eyes. His nostrils were wide and his nose thick, and his upper lip was unnaturally thick. He was about 44, now an "old timer" in the business.

"Did you bring your Kleenex? Waterproof hat?"

Timmy asked with a leering, open-mouthed grin. He didn't speak; he loomed. He was 5'6" and had the habit of craning his face up into the face of the person he was talking to. He wore a red blazer and his yellow shirt pinched in at his chubby neck, making his head seem to balloon off his neck.

"I didn't see you at that Midnight Blue party at Paddles. They had a dominatrix with a cat's head tattooed on her mound. It was wild. She let her pussy hair grow in a little for the fur. It was great. I mean, there were some creeps hanging around."

Timmy grinned, showing soggy bread adhering between each tooth. He took another enthusiastic bite of his sandwich. He was one of the few who really loved the business and had no aspirations for anything else. He liked meeting porn starlets, even if they only talked about sex with him instead of performing it.

That was good enough for Timmy. He'd insinuate in his articles that he and the porn star "had a real good time" during the interview. It wasn't good for the readers' fantasy to realize that this really was a business, and that porn stars didn't fuck everybody in sight, especially skeevy writers for men's mags.

Timmy collected vintage men's magazines from the 50's and 60's on up, and could even tell the difference between the editors — the issues of Swank when Bruce Jay Friedman was the editor, versus a Stan Bernstein or a Manny Neuhaus.

He heaped a dollop of the liver onto a slice of ryebread and folded it over. He tasted it and smiled at Rob. "I've now decided to give the film a good review." A few specks of the brown adhered to his prominent upper lip, as if he had been rooting in the soil.

Rob watched the crowd, the magazine film critics and the exhibitors and distributors who booked the films for theaters. The disparity between the two was great.

The magazine writers were mostly under 30. Rob recognized a few of them; 'Squeamy' Ellis, Joe Marselli and Paul Lowe. They came to the screenings alone, barely talking to each other. 'Squeamy' sometimes played violin on the street, stationing himself in front of a fruit store on Broadway in the West 70's and making forty or fifty bucks for the day. He was proud of his nickname and used it on all his reviews, not realizing that it marked him as the same kind of loser as the various nerds and jerks who insisted on being 'Ace' or "Ratso.'

Some tried to look bored or macho, as though they really didn't need to go to a film to see naked women. It was just a job. Some tried for the Guccione look, with gold chains, open shirts and highly polished black shoes. Some others were just out of college, getting the first writing jobs they could find, looking at it all with eager eyes and slightly abashed smiles.

The theater owners and distributors were almost all in their 50's or older, pink in the cheek after downing the hard stuff at the buffet table, talking with nudges and forced loud laughter. They were far away from their wives. The girls on the screen were all young.

"When you've been in the business as long as I have," one older voice boomed, "you can tell if it's a good flick after the first fuck." A hoarse chuckled agreed with him, adding, "I can tell by the music on the opening credits!"

The two groups didn't mix. The old men eyed the young with wistful jealousy, jealous of them for being hip and being able to do everything with the *new women* — the hotsy totsies who gave blow jobs routinely and actually said they enjoyed doing it. The young writers looked at the old businessmen with feral anger. The guys with the pinky rings and the $500 suits had it made. These illiterates had the money, they were the ones with the fancy East Side apartments and mistresses on the side, buying all the pussy they wanted. The fat cats could piss away $100 for a night of fucking. But writing porn stories — especially now that most men's magazines printed pictures without the "redeeming social value" of even a porn story — that $100 was getting harder and harder to get.

"I've seen you around," a film critic said to Rob, "Who're you with?"

"Rabbit," he said. "I'm the editor."

"I'm with Flame. You do all the reviews for Rabbit?"

Rob shook his head. "We don't use many film reviews anyway."

"How about stories? Yesterday I interviewed one of the stars of this film, Tina Volva. She seemed really out of it, but I got a few hot quotes. Worst breath in the world."

"Maybe you caught her just after working hours. Did you ever work with a guy named Larry Slezak?"

The kid was too wired to answer. "If I get to the other one, Mindy Hooters, do you think you might be able to use it in Rabbit as a feature?"

"No. Thanks for thinking of us, though."

Mindy Hooters and several members of the cast came through the double doors and into the waiting lobby. The film's publicist greeted them effusively and there was a lot of kissing. It was as though they were part of a real Hollywood premiere.

Mindy was flanked by an Oriental girl, Jako, supposedly her real-life lover, and another woman, a blonde. They all wore shimmering satin evening gowns with lace at the cleavage. They wore heavy pink blush makeup and seemed like high priced, exquisite call girls or models, if not Hollywood starlets.

"Hello *Mr. Schleifer!*" Mindy gushed, rushing over to peck the cheek of the film's producer. "Amber? Jako?" The girls on either side of her took turns giving him kisses on the cheek, too. Rob checked the mimeographed cast list. The names the actresses used were always either exotic or jokes, but ridiculous either way. The one on the left was Amber Hare, the Asian girl on the right just went by the single name of Jako, which someone insisted was short for Jackoff. They looked more like little girls, made up for a party, giggling over their dresses and made-up names.

The guy from Flame stopped Amber Hare and introduced himself. He said, "I just want to say that you are, without a doubt, one of the brightest young stars working in films today. I really enjoy your work."

Amber pursed her lips, politely waiting for him to finish whatever it was that he was trying to say.

"Can we do an interview after the film?" he said, finally.

The glamorous porn actress shrugged and said, "Ask the publicist. It's up to her."

Rob slipped past them to the producer.

"Mr. Schleifer?"

Lou Schleifer was close to 70, still ruddily handsome, quite able to charm any slut waitress or cokehead hippie chick into doing some pornies. He had a very good salt and pepper toupee combed carefully into the real hair that formed a ring around his head. His face glowed with a dark tan. He wore a slim moustache and his aviator-styled glasses gave him a fresher look than the old black rims he used to wear. He wore an expensive red sweater, a shirt and tie underneath it.

"What can I do for you?" the producer said with a pleasant, practiced smile. "You're one of the reviewers."

"Uh, yeah. I'm Rob Streusel, from Rabbit. I know this is going to be a great film. I'm planning to do at least four pages using all the chromes I got in the mail the other day. Lots of great shots."

"Good, thanks," the producer said, a trace of impatience in his voice. "If you want to do interviews, you have to ask—"

"I have a question. It has nothing to do with the film. We do a sort of "whatever became of" column sometimes. Fans write in about actresses they haven't seen in a while. That kind of thing. Whatever became of Betty Page and Irving Klaw."

"Uh huh."

"Someone mentioned seeing some loops produced by some guys a long time ago, and I don't think they've made any films in a long time. I was wondering if you might know if they're still in the business."

"Yeah? Who."

"Carl Keefer? Or Joe Pantera?"

The producer looked at Rob very carefully for a moment. Then he chuckled.

"Boy, that's going back a hell of a long time." He sipped his drink. "They never even made features."

"Are they still in the business?"

"Nooooo," the producer said emphatically. He brightened and added with a laugh, "they may still be in jail."

"Gee, I didn't know that."

"Oh yeah. I'm not sure what went down, but it had nothing to do with the business. Armed robbery or something. I'm sure it was all Pantera's idea. He was one tough bastard. Christ, Carl Keefer and Joe Pantera. Haven't heard those names in *years*."

"Did you know them at all?"

"Carl, a little. He made loops mostly. He was big when 8mm was the main thing on Times Square. He didn't even do stuff for Prettygirl or Diamond Collection or any of the major outfits. He'd just shoot some stuff and if it was halfway hot, somebody'd buy it and dupe it. Just plain white box stuff. I didn't make loops very long. You see, I always had a vision. I always wanted quality. You don't get quality with 8mm or 16mm. You know, I still shoot all my features on film stock, not video. Carl was just one of a lot of small timers who made quickies."

"And the cameraman? Joe Pantera?"

"Well, since Carl wasn't really well versed in film, he needed a good cameraman so he found Joe. Maybe they met in jail to begin with, I don't remember. Pantera was just a thug who happened to know how to run a camera the right way. Carl could as easily have owned a book shop, been an accountant. That is, if he had any real brains. He was always a loser. He drifted into whatever was making money, and way back then you could make a decent living making quickies like he did. They didn't really have any feel for cinema, you know. Did you see the reviews I got in Penthouse? They loved my last film. There aren't many of us who are real auteurs."

"I guess not. Not too many directors mean anything to the average porn buyer. John Leslie. Paul Thomas. I guess some people only know Russ Meyer or Bruce Seven."

Schleifer forced a chuckle. "I'm the one who wins the adult film awards every year!"

"Where do you think Keefer and Pantera are today?"

"Dead. Probably dead."

"Or else maybe in the business of making somebody else dead?"

Schleifer called out, "Mindy! You look wonderful, darling." He said "Pardon me," to Rob and made his way toward his leading lady.

Everyone was filing into the darkened screening room. Rob sat in an aisle seat toward the back. Within a minute of the opening credits, Mindy was seen languidly lying around in her bedroom, dolled up in garterbelt, stockings and see-through bra. The front door rang and she walked over, threw the door open wide, and stood there. "Everyman's fantasy" films were never subtle. A plumber was standing there, a happy smile on his boyish face.

"Excuse me, miss. You called the Lyonhart Plumbing Company?"

"I think I need some pipe," Mindy said. Several snickers came out of the audience. The plumber reached into his bag and picked up a pipe.

"Something like this?"

"That's nice and hard. But do you have something bigger?"

Thundering, Latin-tinged jazz began to play as the

camera followed Mindy's undulating ass as she walked toward the bedroom. The plumber took his pants down, his cock already hard. She got down on her knees and purred, her eyes closed, her mouth open. She inched her lips down the shaft, further and further. The music rose rhythmically, and a vocalist was singing "I ain't waiting anymore, baby, I ain't waiting, go down!"

She eased her mouth off the cock and jerked it with businesslike efficiency until sperm began to spurt in slow motion just across her cheek.

Rob glanced at his watch and left the screening room unnoticed, all eyes glued to the pattern of goo that was dripping into the siliconed valley between Mindy's hooters.

At the Rabbit office he started to make a few notes to himself about Pantera and Keefer. He stopped when he heard a noise at the front door.

Somebody was punching at the combination lock.

"I was just checking if the new issue was out," Toby Shell said. He actually had a half grin on his face. He even had a polo shirt on and jeans, instead of his usual schoolboy outfit.

"You look relaxed," Rob said. Toby's face clouded, as if that wasn't such a good thing. "You look like you're going to Central Park or something. The jeans, I mean."

"Oh," Toby said, looking down self-consciously. "That's not a bad idea. It could be fun, going to Central Park."

He pondered the thought for a moment, just standing there. He said, "I used to fly a kite there when I was a kid. I studied all about air currents, and airplanes and flying. I still have all my science textbooks and my books on airplanes."

"Really? You're one of those guys who never throws anything away? Where do you keep all that stuff?"

"Bookcases," Toby said. "They're built in. I don't know what would happen if I moved."

Rob remembered Larry saying something about how Toby was getting a few articles accepted in Popular Mechanics, and they paid quadruple what Rabbit paid.

Toby still was just standing outside Rob's cubicle, as if he was afraid to come in and sit down.

"I guess the new issue didn't come in."

"No. Anything else I can do for you?"

"Uh. How's it going?"

"I don't want to burden you with my problems, Toby," Rob said. "Let's just say that being the editor of Rabbit, on top of everything else that's going on, is not making me too happy. Taking Larry's place is kind of weird."

The thin writer gave a little spasm of a chuckle, as if he was trying to acknowledge and agree with Rob. Rob couldn't tell for sure what it was.

Toby backed away, and mumbled something about having some more stories soon.

A moment later, there was some commotion down the hall. Voices. Rob got up from the desk and raced to the front door.

Cy was standing there.

"A welcoming committee," Cy muttered. "I don't want applause, I want money."

"Irwin's not here, Cy."

"I thought I was going to get a check today. I'm behind in my payments at the V.D. clinic. They're going to take away my dick. I told them to just wait till it falls off. This is terrible. That fuck down on 22nd Street is still stalling me, and now another publisher's in hiding. They're always on the phone, out of town or on the toilet."

"It's deadline day, Cy. Things are a little crazy. You have any stories to drop off?"

"No. I'm not writing anything till I get paid."

"Well, that's good news. Look, I was heading out for a while, so if you want back issues or anything, just get them. Or ask Raymond. What was going on out here? I heard voices."

"That's a bad sign," Cy said. "It was just me. I come in, and that creep Toby was going out, and we did a goddam samba here till he finally went around me. I can never make eye contact with that jerk. He's saying 'Scussmee, scussmee,' like a little bug."

"Don't take this the wrong way," Rob said, "but excuse me. I've got to get out of here for a while."

Rob slipped past Cy and opened the door. Cy followed him down to the elevator bank.

"What's the matter with you, Rob? You're acting like some kind of asshole."

Rob pressed the elevator button. He remembered an Army-Navy store down around 9th Avenue. He walked down there, not paying much attention to Cy.

"Come on, Rob, what's going on? It's not like you to just take off. You're supposed to sit at the editor's desk, like the captain going down on the ship."

"Going down *with* the ship. You've been writing porn too long."

Rob stopped in the middle of the sidewalk.

"Cy, what did you really think of Larry Slezak?"

"Slezak? I don't know. He was ok. Too bad about him. But at least he never knew what hit him."

"How do you know?"

"Because he was shot in the head, right? Now that's quick and easy. Better that way than getting scrotal cancer or something. Or having your girl knife you while you're sleeping, and you lose all your oxygen and turn into a vegetable."

"Oh come on."

"It's true. It's happened. Larry had a friend who knew this guy. Jeff somebody. His girlfriend was crazy. And one night for no fucking reason, she starts choking him while he was asleep, and she broke his windpipe or something and he lost his oxygen and his brain just rotted faster than a cabbage in a microwave."

"And Larry was worried about that?"

"Sure. All the chicks he picked up? These teenagers, they get turned on, they move in, and a few weeks later, out they go. He had the attention span of a road runner."

"I thought he had a good thing going with Tee."

"Yeah. I guess. But I don't think he was the only one. A chick like that, she has lots of guys interested."

Cy looked around. "Christ, it's getting hot out. It's going to be about 90 again today. What are we standing around for sweating like this? Are you such a big fan of B.O.? Look at that."

A homeless man was sitting a few feet away, a fresh wet stain in his lap. People walked briskly by. Cy chuckled. "That guy knows how to keep cool. He's taking a swim in his underpants."

"Cy, I'm investigating Larry's murder."

"You want to help? I stick my neck out for nobody. Is that what you're up to?"

"I'm not kidding. If you could walk me over to The

West Side Inn right now. Just hang around by the door while I go in."

Cy looked at Rob carefully.

"That fuck and suck motel? What's going on there?"

"I don't know. First we go in here."

Rob and Cy walked into the Army-Navy shop. Like every other shop on the Square, porn or straight, it had a certain smell to it, and a palpable hostility to the patrons who did their browsing with quiet rage and disgust. Racks of green khaki jackets and camouflage coats were against one wall, but the main fascination for the young punks in the store were the knives, machetes and axes in the glass cases up front.

There was a non-stop whispered mutter from the young kids as they pointed to the hatchets and axes and hunting knives. "Ay," somebody laughed, "you could really do some damage with that one." "Yeah? How about this?" "Man, that's too big to even carry." "Naw man, it hangs down off your thigh. You wear a long coat. Nobody knows."

Rob motioned to the clerk. One display case had a bunch of Swiss Army knives and other paraphernalia. A gun was hanging from a peg, the price tag marked $9.95. Rob pointed to it.

The man mechanically pulled it off the peg and held it.

Rob tossed a ten dollar bill onto the counter.

"They been around checkin' tax," the counter man grunted. "Gotta charge tax."

Rob put down an extra buck.

"I don't need a bag," Rob said, pocketing the gun and scooping up the meager change.

Cy followed Rob out of the store, squinting as the

bright sunlight bathed his face, showing every line and every peppery spot of stubble on his chin.

"Didn't know you smoked," Cy said, spitting on the sidewalk.

"You recognized it was a lighter?"

"Only because the fuckin' sign said "Lighter" underneath it. It looks plenty real. Listen, if I do this for you, I expect to average at least *two* stories per issue from now on. Payment on acceptance."

"Yeah. Listen, just stand outside. That's all. I just want it to look like I've got a partner."

"How long is this gonna take? I mean, do I have to wait a long time before somebody shoots you in the head?"

At The West Side Inn, Rob asked the desk clerk for Joe Pantera's room.

"Pantera? Nobody by that name here."

"Maybe I got it wrong. It sounded like Pantera. Could you check and see if any name on the register sounds like that?"

The desk clerk shook his head politely.

Rob reached into his wallet and pulled out a ten dollar bill.

The desk clerk took the bill and shook his head politely, adding, "But thanks for the tip."

Rob put another ten dollar bill on the counter.

"That should do it," Rob said. Then he elaborately smoothed down the front of his shirt, molding the outline of the lighter-gun that he had tucked into his belt.

"Here, *you* look," the clerk said, snatching up the bill. He turned the register around.

Rob glanced down the list of names. Sheldon, Coates, Sturdivant, Peterson, Shantz, Downing... Nothing remotely like Pantera. Nothing remotely like Keefer.

"You got two men staying in the same room somewhere?"

"All the time," the clerk replied. "Live and let live."

Rob checked for two names arriving at the same time and the same suite.

He found two names but pretended he didn't.

"I've been checking every motel and hotel in the area," Rob said, "and all it's done is cost me a lot of bucks."

"Too bad," the desk clerk said, shutting the register.

Rob walked outside and met Cy.

"There's a chance two guys staying here murdered Larry," Rob said.

"So you're going in there with a cigarette lighter and try and get 'em to smoke enough to get cancer and die?"

"Yeah."

"Rob, you wave a fake gun at a pair of hired killers, they'll take out theirs and before you know it you're pizza. These guys have real guns, right?"

"I don't know," Rob said, "they didn't show any when they tried to break into my place."

"When they tried to what?"

"Forget it, Cy. Go home. I'm going to hang around here for a while."

"Watch your step," Cy said.

"Thanks."

"I mean it." Cy pointed to a lump of dogshit just inches away from Rob's foot.

CHAPTER FOURTEEN

"Can't you remember anything about the shooting?"

Carrie Sinclair immediately answered, "No." She put the phone down for a moment. Her two bodyguards were talking with her publicist.

"After the shooting in New York, Carrie's going directly back to California," the publicist said.

Carrie said into the phone, "Look, Rob, I really can't talk now. I don't have the time."

"I don't either, Carrie. Not if I believe what you told me. Keefer and his friend tried to get me once, and I don't think they'll waste any time trying again. Try it from the beginning, ok, when you first got into the room. Let's see where it goes."

"Rob, I can't talk about it now. I'm needed on the set."

Rob sat at his desk at Rabbit staring down at the pile of incoming mail and manuscripts. On top of it was the xerox of the news story on James Sledge.

"I know, Carrie, I know. I've got to be here working, I have a job too. My boss doesn't want me out of the office. Over the weekend I can try and keep an eye on Pantera and Keefer, but I can't do it today. At least give me some more stuff to work with. You're in on this, too. What if they get a hold of the film?"

"They haven't gotten it yet."

"No. Look, why don't I just give it back to you?"

"You keep it, Rob. I trust you. You've hidden it in a safe place."

"Right. And everybody knows that I have it, not you."

"What are you saying?"

"I don't want them to try and beat it out of me. Please, Carrie, just one time from the top."

The publicist walked out. The bodyguards were standing outside of her trailer, each flanking one side of the door.

"Rob, I was just a kid. It was ten years ago. I was getting high every day. There are *years* I practically don't remember. I was in New York, I wanted to go to one of those dramatic schools. Only when I got here, I heard they were a con. You get a diploma after appearing in a few shabby plays, and that's it. Joe Pantera was a hustler, I guess. I was hanging out, I met the guy. Maybe we slept together once or twice. I had no money, I was getting panicky, and he told me about how he filmed movies sometimes. He said he could get me a lot for it. So he introduced me to Mr. Keefer, and he talked to me about it over dinner somewhere."

"So you agreed to make a porn film."

"Yeah," Carrie said, her voice rising, "I did."

"I'm not being judg—"

"What do you call what you're doing, Rob? You're making money off sex and you don't feel bad doing it."

"Carrie. Before somebody comes in here and tries to beat me up again — Jesus, you know I'm not blaming you."

"Don't push me! Please, they're calling for me."

"Think for a minute, just think about it. You're

making a film for the first time. Are you nervous? Excited? What's being said?"

Rob heard Carrie sigh heavily. He waited for her to come up with something.

"All right. Joe brought me to Carl Keefer that day, and we met in the early afternoon. I remember that. He seemed ok. Just your average middle-aged guy. He could've been my father, for God's sake. He had that little moustache like my father, and his hair was thining a little. He wore those baggy kind of clothes, you know, with his belt up tight like it was going around his chest. He was interested in me, I could tell. But I wasn't interested in him. He was chain smoking. "We were at, I don't know, a coffee shop or something. And Keefer told Joe to get over to the hotel room right away, and get the cameras and stuff set it up. He kept telling me that he'd give me the money before the filming started. He kept talking money. I guess he didn't want me backing out. Who knows, if I was off my high, maybe I would've changed my mind. I don't know. It was flattering. It was a *movie*. I know it doesn't sound like much, but being told you're beautiful, that you'd be the star of a movie. That's all I heard at first. And it sounded more exciting than scary. And I was going to get paid, like, like more for an hour than I could've gotten for a week. You've got to remember, Rob, this was the late 70's. It was still like, hip to be free with your body.

"So Joe went out to get his camera stuff, and get a camera man and set up lights —"

"Get a camera man? But Joe was a camera man, right?"

"Yeah. Yeah."

"Was he going to make the film with you?"

"Rob, it was so long ago. I don't even remember. I guess not. I don't know. Nobody talked about the actor. I didn't even know who they'd hired. I thought maybe Joe was going to do the film and Keefer was going to film it.

"I think Joe said something about how he wanted us to do it together, as a sign of love. A testament. A celebration. We hardly knew each other, but he was so intense, he said crazy things.

"When he left and I was alone with Carl, Carl began telling me how pretty I was, and what nice blonde hair I had, and he asked if I was a natural blonde. Then he asked me if I'd mind making it with this black guy he knew. And he even said he'd throw in another fifty bucks. He had a paper bag with lingerie in it. I'd never seen stuff like that before. He told me he bought it especially for me, and it was mine to keep."

"OK, so you went to the motel."

"No, not right away."

"No?"

"No, Keefer told me to sit in the lobby for a minute. I guess he wanted to make sure the hotel room was set up, or safe, or something. I remember that. It was really hot and humid out, and I didn't want to stay alone in the lobby 'cause there were some really scuzzy types there. I wanted to stay outside, but it was so hot."

"How long were you down there?"

"I don't know."

"The time it would take to smoke a cigarette?"

"I didn't smoke cigarettes."

"Two minutes? Three?"

"About that. I don't know. Carl Keefer came down and got me."

"Was he alone?"

"I don't *remember*, Rob. Please, let me go —"

"Just a little more, Carrie. What happened next?"

"They set up the lights, and Joe was talking to me and he seemed really excited, and I was a little nervous I guess, I tried not to show it. Keefer was the director, I guess, but he didn't really say anything about what to do. It was like, we all know what to do so let's do it. Then James Sledge showed up."

"What can you tell me about him?"

"Nothing, nothing at all. Just a guy. He smiled a lot. He shook my hand. I thought that was a nice show of respect, you know? And then it started. And there was so much going on, it was overwhelming. I just can't be sure what happened next. Maybe it was — the trauma. I remember the shot. I remember his face. But I don't remember everything that happened, I just don't."

"Try to imagine yourself back then, imagine yourself back in that room."

"I don't want to! I don't ever want to!"

"You're an actress, Carrie, you're a good actress. You were a good actress then. You knew the lights were on you. You knew there were other people in the room. Where were they? What were they doing? You couldn't have been paying attention only to James Sledge, not with the other people around, and the lights. Somebody was giving you directions, right?"

"Yes. Yes, somebody was giving instructions but I can't *remember*. Honestly, I just can't."

"Maybe if somebody else asks you the questions. My girlfriend could do it. Maybe that'll relax you more."

"It's not that, Rob. I can tell you're trying to be sensitive about this. I feel comfortable talking to you on the phone this way. I'd tell you anything, no matter how intimate. But I just don't remember!"

Rob could hear the sound of someone knocking on Carrie's trailer door. "All right, Carrie, all right. I'm almost through. Just tell me about the room. OK?"

"Please..."

"Just answer this for me. Where was Pantera and where was Keefer the last you remember?"

"Joe Pantera was behind the camera. It was at the foot of the bed. He wasn't even looking into the camera, he was just staring at us. He had the camera on the tripod, and he was just staring. And Carl Keefer...he was off to the side. Near the door. He was giving the instructions."

"Then there was the shot, and you just lost it."

"Rob, goodbye, ok? Thanks —just, goodbye."

Rob put the phone back and sat at Larry's desk. Discarded stories and copy was lying all over it, including a fragment Larry had been working on, an "editorial" for an upcoming issue: "It's summer, and it's time for Sluts! Those double-dare do it for the hell of it sleazeteasers who heat up and fry every guy who sees 'em. Flip through the new issue in your hot hands and enjoy non-stop nookie! Here are sluts on parade!"

"Fuckin' asshole," Rob said, crumpling up the paper. "It's not funny, Larry. None of it is a joke."

The art director had left a blow-up of the new issue's cover.

It featured a fairly ugly brunette with tremendous siliconed breasts. Blue veins ran thickly through them and a keloid scar, white and lump, was visible at the side of her left breast. She was glaring up from the page, half-taunting, her lipsticked mouth forming a perfect "o."

"Now *those* are blow job lips," Cy Kottick said. He was wearing the same old black frock coat he always wore, no matter what the weather. His jeans were the same too, dark gray with white at the knees, the fabric at one knee just about to fray.

Cy eased into the chair next to the desk and said, "We're falling dangerously behind, here, payment-wise. A ditch digger does better than I do. A fuckin' men's room attendant does better. A unionized ass wipe does better."

"What the fuck do you want from me?"

"What are you so pissed about?"

"Look, I'm not the accountant I'm the god damned editor."

"If you don't like it, why don't you quit?"

"Cy, I am the editor, at the moment, and that means I can pick and choose how I spend my time and with who."

"Oh, oh, well listen, I'm really scared."

"Cy, I'm really not in the mood."

Cy blinked in surprise, and his voice became conspiratorial.

"Are you under pressure? What happened with the Times Square motel and everything?"

"Nothing yet. I've been too busy in this fucking toilet to get a chance to check it out."

"Uh huh."

"Look at all this junk."

Rob yanked open the top drawer of Larry's desk, which was still littered with match books, old pens, a smattering of pennies, a few copper Show World peep show tokens, a bottle of nasal spray, condoms, Tic-Tacs and cigarette ashes. Rob slammed the door shut and opened the second drawer, which was filled with rejected manuscripts Larry had been too lazy to send back, dirty pictures ripped out of other men's magazines, and a lot of bent and creased Rabbit stationery.

"You just go like this," Cy said, reaching into the second drawer. He hauled out a pile of papers and slammed them into the garbage can.

A few post-it notes, the glue on the back long since wiped dry, rocked gently side to side to the floor like leaves. A color slide danced on its edge for a moment and tipped over like a dead butterfly.

"I don't know what half that stuff was," Rob said angrily, going to retrieve it all.

"What do you care? That was Larry's business, and Larry's dead."

Rob picked up the slide.

"A slut!" Cy said, "I can tell from here."

Rob looked at him. Then he held up the slide to the light.

"How did you know it was a nude?"

"What else would Larry have in his desk?"

Rob recognized the girl in the photo.

"This was one of the shots of Tee," he said. "It must've gotten
lost in the desk."

Cy snatched the slide from Rob's hand and held it up to the light.

"What a cunt," he said.

"Did you know her?"

"Just a bimbo with no fuckin' sense."

"How did you know she had no sense?"

"She wasn't fucking me, was she?"

"Was she?"

Rob snatched the slide back with as much precision as Cy. Rob took out his magnifying lupe and gave the slide another look.

"You know, Tee really didn't seem all that broken up about Larry's death."

"So?"

"It was so sudden. You hear about somebody dying and even if you don't know them well, it's a shock, isn't it? She was living with him, and she was thinking about where she was going to live next. I remember her asking me about the West Side. When I called her mother, she said she'd already left home again. That's short grief."

"Women," Cy said. "What do you expect. They're always thinking practical. They have that gut instinct for survival. Me, my reaction would be from the heart. If my girl got blown away, I'd be down on my hands and knees."

Cy looked deadly serious.

"Yes, Rob, I'd be down on my hands and knees; fucking her corpse till the coroner pulled me off."

"Oh come on."

"Well it's the last time I'll ever see her, isn't it?"

Cy looked dead serious about it, too.

"This slide wasn't taken in Larry's apartment, I know that for a fact. Look at all these books. The pictures Larry showed me of Tee, they were all like this. All taken up against a bookcase with all kinds of fancy books in them. I thought Larry had taken them in his apartment, but he didn't."

"So? Larry was no photographer. He couldn't take a

picture in an automatic photo booth. While you puzzle that over, I've got a better one for you. When's Krantz going to sign some checks for me? Do I have to beat his stupid head in for him? I was down at 22nd Street today."

"Did you get your money from the weasel?"

"I told him I wouldn't leave without a check, and I didn't want a rubber one."

"What did he say?"

"He said he was filing for bankruptcy. Meanwhile he's living in a fucking townhouse on the East Side. These creeps who hide behind their grinning lawyers — they give it all to the lawyers. If they just paid their debts they'd have more money and they'd probably live longer. I won't let your idiot boss Krantz get away with it."

"We're not going under, Cy. Calm down."

"I've written for that prick for so long I should be on retainer, that's what. Give me five hundred bucks the first of every month."

"If Krantz ever gave you five hundred dollars all in one check, you'd probably go on a binge."

Rob sat back in his chair. "What would you do with that kind of money, Cy? Go to some whorehouse five nights in a row? Or would you buy the fanciest hooker you could find and spend the full five hundred on her? A beautiful woman who'd do everything you've ever wanted."

"I can write my own fantasies, thanks. And getting money out of this fuckin' magazine is a big fantasy."

"For that kind of money, maybe you could get to fuck somebody famous. Who'd you like to make it with, Cy? Somebody like Carrie Sinclair?"

Cy look at Rob carefully, cocking his head to one side.

"You're up to something," he said. "Like buying a cigarette lighter and pretending it's a gun. You better watch it. You *don't* know who you're dealing with."

"Pretty big talk when I'm the only one accepting your stories these days."

"Oh, I give a shit."

"Ever go to the movies, Cy? Ever see Carrie Sinclair?"

"I don't know what's on your mind," Cy answered. "So you don't get to know what's on mine. Let me see that cover. What a dog. The covers for Rabbit have really gone downhill lately. Raymond is getting senile. I'm surprised Krantz hasn't fired him. I know Larry was ready to let him go."

"Really? Why?"

"You didn't know about the great knife cover?"

Cy left the cubicle and emerged a few minutes later with a handful of back issues.

"Special butt man's bonanza issue, Mistress Jessica's Porcine Training, this was a good issue: two of my stories in it. Nude beaches. Here. Here, take a look at this. This issue nearly lost Rabbit its place on the newsstand."

The issue of Rabbit had a nude girl lying in bed. And superimposed onto the cover, a huge knife. Cy grinned. "Nice, huh? A real big no-no. You don't mix sex and violence on the cover of a men's magazine. Not ever."

"I never thought of that. But you're right. I can't remember seeing a cover like that on a skin mag."

"These stupid stroke books have enough trouble getting into newsstands and convenience stores as it is, even when the girl's nipples are covered. You don't realize it in when you're in New York, but most parts of the country are still so conservative that you couldn't get away with putting two scoops of vanilla ice cream on the cover of Popular Cooking. And look who's operating some of our fine newsstands. Fundamentalist psychopaths from the Middle East who refuse to carry any magazines they don't like. Especially infidel sex magazines."

"And Larry was ready to kill Raymond Fitzgerald for this? Why didn't he stop him before it went to the plant?"

"Because that's when Raymond had changed the masthead and called himself "creative director." He was so full of himself that when Larry told him to change it, he didn't! Can you believe it? He said it was such a great looking cover, and he'd worked on it for like, what, an extra hour or something, and he got into a big snit."

"But why did he put a knife on the cover, anyway?"

"I don't know. That idiot Toby Shell wrote some wacko story about a guy who's in love with a blonde and he does all this fantasizing, and in the end he shoots himself. The big twist was that all these horny thoughts were running through his mind the instant the bullet went into his brain."

"A rip-off of "Occurrence at Owl Creek Bridge." The old Ambrose Bierce short story."

"It was the featured story, and our creative director got carried away. So he put the knife on the cover."

"But in the story it was a gun."

"He couldn't find a good enough photo of a gun. Well, they pulled as many copies as they could and put a new cover on, but most of them went out. Krantz had to do some fancy talking with the distributor. There's a lesson for you. What you see and what you get are two damn different things."

"There are a lot of lessons in that, if you look for them."

"What I'm looking for right now is money. How about it? Next time I'm in, have a check ready for me. I don't need much, Rob. Take a look at this shirt."

Cy opened his coat. He was wearing a surprisingly new looking white shirt with blue pinstripes.

"A Pierre Cardin label. And just five bucks. Listen to me and check out the thrift shops. These yuppie scum buy a shirt, wear it once or twice and get bored. Then chuck it for a tax deduction."

"Wait a minute, look at that thing over there."

Rob pointed to a carefully stitched slit that was about an inch long near Cy's heart.

"That shirt had a rip in it."

"It's ok now," Cy said calmly. "You can hardly notice it. So maybe the guy didn't donate it. Maybe his next of kin did. Maybe he was stabbed to death. Point is, I'm wearing it now, and I'm ok."

As Cy walked out, Rob flipped the color slide of Tee onto the desk. He picked up the phone.

"Julie? Listen, I'll be late for dinner, but I'll definitely by home by — what time is it now? By nine. I'll definitely be home by nine." He tried to phrase it without alarming her, but he couldn't. He said, "If I'm not home by nine, tell the police to go to the West Side Inn."

"Rob! Rob, you're not a detective —"

"No, but I'm a good reporter. Don't worry, Julie. I

love you. And I won't put you through another night of this. It's got to end."

Rob walked out to the elevator bank. Cy Kottick was already gone. The elevator filled up by the time it reached the lobby. Rob moved with the moist, warm flow of people spilling out into the streets. The Port Authority was teeming, the cross-town busses unloading a painfully slow vomit of flesh, in black suits, brown suits, faded summer dresses, the bodies oozing off the narrow bus doorways like lumpy syrup. The mottled traffic flowed awkwardly across the street, winding in swirling eddies of people, finally flushing into the Port Authority building.

Rob felt the sweat glisten on his forehead and drip down the side of his face, and he wasn't sure if it was the heat or nerves. He turned west. Fewer people were walking home in this direction. Down ninth there were still mostly office buildings and stores and some off-Broadway theaters. There weren't many homes that office workers would want to live in. There were a few tenements. And there was a hotel called The West Side Inn.

CHAPTER FIFTEEN

Rob tapped the cigarette lighter-gun in his waist band. He pulled his belt an inch tighter. Now the gun wasn't slipping down the leg of his pants. Now his stomach was in knots.

He walked by the motel and gave a quick look inside. The same angry-looking desk clerk was on duty, staring down at a piece of paper and trying to make sense of it. A bell boy in a shabby maroon coat, the gold piping uneven at the cuffs, stood at the counter talking to him.

A family of Puerto Ricans came out of the elevator. The father was a heavy set man wearing a white embroidered shirt that was thin enough to let his dark nylon undershirt show through. The mother, heavily made up with orange tinting streaked through her hair, shouted to the kids, who were all struggling with large suitcases.

The bell boy followed them out, almost pleading with them to let him carry something. He was a black kid with a little lightning bolt shaved into the side of his skull. His expression flickered between sullen depression and annoyance. He held the door for the family and followed them out into the street. He dashed out toward the gutter.

The bell boy saw a cab coming and waved.

"We go home on the bus," the father shouted, pointing to the Port Authority building.

The bell boy shook his head and started back inside.

Rob blocked his way and with a meaningful look in his eyes eased him just to the side of the door, away from the sight of the desk clerk.

"Why don't you make twenty bucks the easy way," he said to the kid. "I need a little information."

The bell boy flashed his own dangerous look, but was listening.

"Yeah?"

"Yeah. I'm a reporter. There are two guys staying in the hotel under assumed names. One's about 35, sort of greasy tan complexion like he just got back from the beach. A mean mouth. Thick black hair combed straight back. The other guy's older, around 60, graying hair, little white moustache, brown eyes. Looks like he hasn't slept too well in about thirty years."

The bell boy looked like he knew what Rob was talking about.

"You know them?" Rob asked.

The bell boy shrugged.

Rob had the twenty dollar bill ready and he dug it out of his pocket, folded, and slipped it to the bell boy.

"What room are they in?"

The bell boy pocketed the bill and snorted a rueful half-laugh through his nose.

"You're no reporter."

His eyes lowered to Rob's waist where the bulge of the gun was.

"So what does that mean," Rob said evenly.

"Another twenty," the kid answered confidently.

Rob leaned against the building and wearily fished his wallet out and scraped together a ten, a five and five ones.

"Hope you get some money out o' them," the bell boy said, shoving the money inside his jacket pocket. "Room 405."

"Is there a back way into this place?"

The bell boy began walking away.

Rob clamped his arm on the kid's wrist.

"If you know I'm not a reporter, then you know I'm not fucking around," he said tensely.

The kid looked him over carefully. He started walking, moving down the block and around the corner. Rob followed. The alley way had a service entrance. The kid looked around, then used his key on the locked gate.

Piles of plastic garbage bags were lining the narrow hallway, the place smelling of wet cement and trash. There was a strange sound, a gushing sound like the wind. It was cool in the dank service area which was lit by two low-watt glaring light bulbs that seemed to turn the air a buttery yellow. Rob could see in the distance a causeway leading directly to the lobby, and another that went off on a twisted, dark course to the right.

"Take the stairs," the kid told Rob. He pointed a finger at him and added, "We never met." Then with a little hurried skip, he rushed past Rob and quickly arched away from a huge pile of garbage and slipped down the causeway toward the front lobby.

The desk clerk, glaring impatiently, said in a loud voice, "Sneakin' a smoke again?"

Rob inched his way closer.

"Well? Is that what you were doin' on my time?" the desk clerk said again.

Rob strained to hear the small, muttery voice of the bell boy.

"Yeah well...sorry boss. Won't happen again."

The motel stairway was dim, and the second floor entrance was completely dark, the bulb not burned out but shattered. Rob could make out a crown of broken glass still in the socket. There was no glass on the floor. Somebody had swept up the mess but had decided that trying to unscrew the broken bulb was too much work.

The drone of Jamaican rap music came loud from the second floor and Rob didn't have to walk softly to hide the sound of his footsteps as he raced up to the fourth. He opened the door cautiously. He recognized the maid as she made the rounds. He hung back in the stairway as she slowly made her way down the hall. When she dragged her supply cart to the next door and walked in with some towels over her arm, Rob quickly dashed out to check the number.

The numbers were moving downward. 405 was toward the far end, a good thirty feet away from the stairway. Rob glanced at his watch and then slipped back to the stairway. As the maid came out, he closed the door. He pressed his ear against it and waited for the sound of the next door opening. He ventured a quick look then ducked back into the darkness.

He breathed in, the lighter-gun slipping from his belt again. He pulled out the mock weapon and put it in his pants pocket. He tapped at his pocket, then tried to see how fast he could reach in for it.

He brought his hand back out to his waist. Then he reached into the pocket quickly, like a western gunslinger. Soundlessly he tried it again, and again, seeing how fast he could get to it.

"Hello, Mr. Keefer," the maid said, pulling her cart up to 405. "Should I make the bed now?"

Rob opened the door wider but couldn't make out everything she was saying. He heard the sound of a click, and the windy air currents seemed to get louder. Somebody was in the stairway. The click seemed like it came from below, but it might have been from above.

The echo of footsteps was loud. Rob instinctively closed the door so the maid wouldn't hear it. The footsteps echoed all over the place, but standing perfectly still and trying to fight against his own panic, Rob concentrated.

The sound of the music on the second floor was still muffled. That meant nobody had opened the stairwell door. The rhythm and speed of the footsteps meant that the person was coming downstairs. Nobody walked upstairs with that cadence.

That person was hurrying down stairs. And Rob was standing right in the way, loitering behind the stairway door to the fourth floor.

Rob pushed the door open a crack, wincing when it made a slight squeak. The maid was inside the room. The cart was still parked next to it, with a bag containing soiled linen hanging off it.

The maid was making the bed, having obviously taken the sheets off and dumped them in the bag.

The footsteps got louder.

Rob swung the door open and slipped out into the hallway, crouching slightly. There was mumbled conversation from within the room. Rob made out the voice of the maid, then one man.

A long, dark brown arm jutted out from the room, and dipped into a silvery tray on the cart. The maid was getting fresh soap.

Rob pressed his ear to the stairway door and heard the footsteps pass by. He opened the door cautiously and saw a figure moving down to the next landing, a heavy set man with big shoulders and big arms, wearing a black suit. He was a light-skinned black man, the top of his bald head glistening slightly in the dim light. He entered on the second floor; the rap music getting loud and then muffled again.

A moment later the maid emerged from the room, busily wiping her hands having tossed a used little piece of soap into a plastic garbage pail under the cart. When she let herself into the next room, Rob made a rush for Room 405 and gave a brisk knock.

"Yeah, Sandra," Mr. Keefer said as he opened it.

Rob pushed his way in and shut the door. He reached into his pocket and flashed the gun, waving it wildly. He shoved it back in his pants hoping that Keefer hadn't gotten a real good look at it.

"Don't try anything!" he shouted.

"Calm down, kid," Mr. Keefer said, moving back, his hands limply in front of his chest in a placating gesture.

Rob pushed past him to check the bathroom, then he whipped open the one closet door.

"You're spinning like a top, kid. Take care of yourself. There's nobody hiding in there."

The twin beds were freshly made and tucked in. It was plain to see that nothing was underneath the beds except one suitcase and a pair of shoes.

"Your friend isn't around," Rob said.

"My friend? I have no friends."

"You know who I mean. Joe Pantera."

Keefer looked mildly surprised that Rob knew the name.

Rob kept his hand jammed in his pants pocket, gripping the gun. He pulled the chair roughly away from the desk and steadied himself in back of it, leaning on it with his free hand. Keefer's eyes shifted from Rob's pocket to the door and back.

Keefer took a stutter-step toward Rob, and Rob moved back, pulling the gun out of his pocket. In an instant Keefer turned to his right and grabbed for the door knob. In the second it took for Rob to react, the older man had the door pulled open and was nearly out.

Rob pocketed the gun-lighter and flew forward, lunging desperately toward the fleeing man. Rob caught Keefer around the knees, knocking the older man into the door frame. They both toppled to the ground.

Keefer was strong, and once he saw his escape blocked, he began to fight. A bony fist slammed at Rob, hitting him full in the chest. Rob let out a grunt of pain and felt his head kick backward and bounce off the thin carpet. Keefer pushed his forearm against Rob's throat and dug his free hand hard into the pit of Rob's stomach. The air went out of him, not even a wheeze finding its way through the vacuum made in his throat.

Now that he had the advantage, Keefer was going for the kill. He kept his forearm crushing against Rob's throat, watching dispassionately as the young writer gagged for air, his eyes popping pleadingly.

He reached into Rob's pocket for the gun. He eyed it for a moment and grimaced.

"A wise guy," Keefer grunted contemptuously. "This is a pretty old trick, kid."

Keefer held the gun out and pulled the trigger.

"YAH! JEEZ!"

A sudden burst of blue flame shot up, flickering with a wild burst of orange.

The cheap lighter, broken in the struggle, vomited out a flame as fuel leaked all over Keefer's hand and down the side of his jacket. Blue flame danced on his hand like water.

Keefer rushed back into the room and yanked the blanket off the bed, smothering it against his flesh.

"Jeez fuckin' CHRIST!"

Rob limped to his feet, forcing air through his crushed neck and windpipe.

He braced himself for a moment, and then threw a punch.

The sick sound of bone hitting teeth made for one juicy click noise. Keefer sank, moaning.

Rob, his legs and stomach weak, sank to his knees after landing the shot. His stomach felt as empty as a ditch. His mouth worked like a dying fish. He tried to breath but the air was like humid gauze, hanging in the air, too thick to be sucked into his lungs. He couldn't get anything past his straining lips and into his mouth.

He strained his eyes to catch the grimacing Keefer who began to retch and cough loudly, blood spattering out of his mouth. Keefer crawled towards Rob, bright red blood coursing down his chin.

Keefer's face was only inches away from Rob's.

"Fuckin' PRICK!" Keefer spat clots of blood. One tooth hung precariously tilted, cemented into the reddened bloody pudding of his lip like a misplaced Chiclet.

Keefer spat and the tooth dropped away from his mouth. He looked toward the escape route; the door closed on its hinges and clicked shut.

Rob struggled, crab-like to his feet. He cocked his

fist and advanced on Keefer, who sat forlornly where he was, one hand up in a supplicating position.

Keefer grimaced, his mouth juicy with his blood, the words gurgling in his lips, "tha's fi- hunad doll—sh."

"Five hundred dollars?"

"Ma parsh-sh-shal," Keefer grumbled, picking his partial bridge up a few teeth that had been held in place with some gold wiring.

Keefer took out a handkerchief and balled the bloody teeth up in it.

He gave Rob a rueful look and went to lie down on one of the twin beds, shutting his eyes and letting out with a moaning sigh, blood still pumping from his mouth, down the side of his face, making an ever wet, ever widening ring of dark red on the pillow.

Rob crossed the bed. He quickly ducked into the bathroom and pulled a towel from the rack, shoving it into the sink. He turned on the water and soaked it for a moment. Then he carried the dripping towel to the bed. He handed it to Keefer, who took it with resignation and softly pressed it to his jaw.

"Can you speak?"

"Yeah, uh huh."

Rob took a deep breath. His heart was beating hard. This was his last chance and he knew it. He waited, gasping, until the flood of questions he wanted to ask stopped spiraling through his mind. He just stood there for a minute, watching Keefer press the pink-tinged towel to his jaw and mouth.

The man on the bed could be Larry's killer. He could be hired by Carrie, somehow. One question, asked wrong, could blow everything.

"You expecting Pantera soon?"

Keefer shook his head.

"You don't think he might walk through that door any minute?"

Keefer shook his head but yes or no meant nothing anymore.

"Let's hear your fuckin' version," Rob said. His legs still felt weak. He eyed the overturned chair near the desk. He knew that if he sat down he might not be able to get up. He pulled the chair out and leaned against it.

"When you made that film with Carrie Sinclair and James Sledge, this place wasn't called the The West Side Inn."

Keefer stared at the ceiling. Rob reached down and pushed the wet towel hard against his jaw, making him cry out.

"I said talk!"

"OK already," Keefer said. He stared at Rob's wrist, trying to make out the time on Rob's watch.

"Waiting for somebody?" Rob said.

He couldn't tell if it was a twisted grimace or a painful smile on Keefer's face.

"Start from the beginning. The filming. You and Pantera were making a porn film with Carrie Sinclair."

Keefer nodded cautiously.

"Then what happened."

Keefer stared at Rob.

"I said, then what happened."

"You got the film," Keefer said disgustedly. "You know."

"Yeah, I got the film, and you'll never get it. No matter what you do. How much did you think you'd get out of Carrie Sinclair for it? A hundred thousand? A million?"

Keefer didn't answer.

"How much did Carrie want for it?"

"I don't know how much we could've gotten out of her."

Rob nodded his head. That was the clincher for Carrie, he thought. Keefer and Pantera hadn't approached her. That proved they weren't working for her. A surge of strength shot through him as he stood in front of Keefer. There was at least somebody in the mess that he could believe in.

Rob chose his words carefully.

"You guys broke into the Rabbit office — the night before you came looking for me."

"Yeah. I tried to get Joe to listen to me and stay away, but he didn't. We looked for the film, and then we figured that we should just go after the editor. If you didn't have it with you, you'd tell us where it was."

"Or else. So after you broke into my apartment and didn't find it, you decided to come back again when I'd be home."

Keefer nodded.

"You hadn't seen Carrie since you made that film."

"No," Keefer said simply.

"But you figured if you got a hold of the film she'd want to see you."

"Stop playing games with me, kid," Keefer said. "What's on that film is no good for any of us. Do the cops have it?"

Rob kept his mouth shut.

Keefer said, "Pantera saw that story in the paper about the guy at Rabbit magazine finding Carrie's film. That got him crazy, even after all these years. Maybe because of it. We spent the last seven in the can. Seven years with that crazy fuck Pantera. Seven years on a 15-20 sentence. Armed robbery. I didn't do a damn fuckin' thing, I was just there with him. The fucker. We robbed a camera store. Yeah. Big bucks. Lots of cameras to hock. But the prick, he used to shop in that camera store. He pulled the job to get even 'cause he hated the prick who ran it. And the prick recognized us. We got away, but the cops knew who to look for. We didn't get far.

"You know what it's like to rot for seven years? That fuckin' film. Pantera held it over me for years and he's still doing it now. I don't have another seven years to spend. I can't do any more time."

Keefer was getting hysterical. "If they put me away at my age I might as well be dead. I have nothing to lose!"

Keefer suddenly bolted from the bed. Rob lashed out with his left hand, chopping into Keefer's bloodied jaw. With a single strangled cry, like a puppy run over, Keefer crumpled back to the bed, face down.

"Tell me about the filming," Rob said coldly.

There was only a weird, wet gurgling sound coming from Keefer, and it made Rob shiver. Keefer moved on the bed. At least he wasn't dead. Blood was pouring out of his mouth.

"Where were you in that room? Were you near the door?"

"What do you care," Keefer mumbled.

"Tell me."

"OK. Yeah."

"Pantera was behind the camera."

"Yeah, yeah."

Rob clutched the back of the chair and took a breath.

"Then there was the first shot. Right into James Sledge, blowing half his head away."

There was no answer from Keefer.

"The second one went through the door, nearly hitting the maid. And after the third one, Carrie Sinclair ran out of there. She didn't know who was dead and who was alive."

"The chick was scared to death," Keefer said, clutching a pillow up to the side of his face, sitting up on the bed.

Rob could understand that all right. Just looking at the blood oozing in Keefer's mouth was getting him rattled. Carrie had been only a few feet away when the sudden explosion blew into Sledge's face.

The gray in Keefer's moustache was red-tinged, clots the size of buttons adhered to his cheek and chin.

"All right, Keefer. The first shot that was fired killed James Sledge. That leaves you and Joe Pantera."

"Fuckin' Pantera. I should've known better. I didn't know just how much of a crazy psycho he was till then. I didn't know he was so stuck on her."

"On Carrie Sinclair?"

"You've seen her. Christ, she was just as beautiful then. Maybe more. So young she was. I didn't know Pantera was a killer. I swear I didn't. Poppin' guys — it didn't mean a fuckin' thing to him. He'd done it before, only I didn't know. I got James Sledge for the film 'cause I thought it would be a nice touch. She was so young and blonde. Black on blonde."

Keefer moaned as he prodded the towel against his mouth.

"You *know*," he said, his pained eyes pleading with Rob. "I didn't have a chance. He was crazy. Watching that black guy fuck her. He wanted her for himself! He just went crazy when Sledge started to use her, and rough her up. Then he comes after *me*! Jesus Christ."

Keefer cocked his head. "Did you hear something? There's somebody outside."

Rob backed up to the door.

With one eye on Keefer, he pulled it open quickly.

Just out of sight, the maid stood next to her cart. Her eyes were wide.

"Nobody out here," Rob said.

He closed the door again.

Rob looked around the room. It was similar to the one in the film. He stood up and moved to the foot of the bed. "The first shot was Pantera, coming from behind his camera. The camera was at the foot of the bed. He came around and fired point blank into Sledge's skull. Sledge probably didn't even see it coming. Pantera was behind Carrie. She definitely didn't see what was going on. She just saw his head explode.

"Then he fired the second shot. He was at the bed, pointing the gun at you, Keefer. You were watching the action from the side of the bed, behind the lights. That gunshot went right through you into the door and nearly caught the maid. And the third shot?"

"He thought I was finished. I grabbed the gun."

Keefer stopped himself. The old man looked puzzled.

"You didn't know *any* of this," he said to Rob. "What was on that fuckin' film?"

Rob blinked.

Keefer, his eyes wild with misery and horror, said"The film — the film you got hold of — it DIDN'T show the killing!"

"It stopped dead, it went black," Rob shouted,

"Pantera stopped it when he went in front of the camera to kill."

"Son of a BITCH!"

Keefer cradled his head in his hands. "Pantera said he had me in the picture. He said he'd moved the camera and caught a shot of me, and that if I didn't help him get the film, I'd go to jail again. Until I saw that thing in the paper, I thought he had the film. And he never did! But — you don't walk away from Pantera. Never. He was my assistant, but I never could control him."

"Help me catch Pantera," Rob said.

"No."

"Dammit, you've got to help me!"

"No, no," Keefer moaned. He flailed one arm at Rob, begging, "Leave me alone. Go away! I didn't do anything! It was him. It was all him. He saw that item in the paper, the one that said that Carrie Sinclair made a porn film. That's when he started to get that crazy idea about revenge. He wanted to get that film so he could blackmail Carrie with it. He knew all along that the only thing on it was her having sex."

Keefer wiped at his bloody jaw. "When we were in jail," he said, "We heard about Carrie's career taking off. It drove Joe nuts to read about it in the magazines and see her picture. Nobody in the can believed that he could ever have made it with a movie star. When we got out, he kept talking about how much he wanted her, but there was no way we could make it to California. Then she came here. And there was the story about the film. He was gonna make her pay. Not money. More than a pound of flesh. That's what Pantera wanted from her! But he had to get the film."

"Pantera forced you to help him," Rob said, "I'll tell the cops."

"The cops! No, my God...I can't double cross Joe!"

"Damn right," came a loud voice behind Rob.

Joe Pantera stood in the doorway.

"Lemme get out, Joe," Keefer cried. "Before you kill this kid, lemme out. That's all I ask — just lemme go!"

"Don't go yellow, Keefer," Pantera said sternly.

"They can't prove anything against me," Keefer gasped, "I'm not on that film. And — and I'm not gonna ever say anything against you, Joe. You know I wouldn't. I could go to the west coast."

Keefer pulled a suitcase from under the bed. It was big and awkward, and he could barely lug it out,one hand up to his shattered jaw, the other pulling weakly.

Pantera pulled out a gun.

It was much bigger than the gun shaped like a cigarette lighter. He was made out of black-blue steel. It was thick, bristling with the gun chambers containing six high caliber bullets.

Pantera grabbed Keefer's face, pinching his mouth and jaw, the blood spurting with a horrible squeaking sound.

Keefer screamed hoarsely. Pantera raised the gun and brought it down against the old man's skull. As the old man slumped to the ground, Pantera kicked him hard in the chest, the inert body tumbling backward.

"Leave him alone," Rob shouted.

Pantera turned his fierce eyes on him, the gun swinging around to point at his chest.

"I beat you up once and I'll do it again. You bleed *real* easy."

Pantera waited on Rob's silence. He smiled, deliberately. Rob kept his mouth shut.

"I could kick you around for the fun of it," Pantera hissed.

Rob didn't move a muscle. Pantera pushed him into the wall with his free hand, then pointed the gun.

"I want the film," he said.

"I couldn't give it to you if I wanted to," Rob said.

"Oh yes you could," Pantera said, advancing toward him. "And believe me, scumbag, you want to!"

"It's burned. Destroyed."

"I don't think so."

"Listen to me, listen! Why would I keep it? So you and this guy could come after me and beat me up?"

"I won't beat you up again. This time I'll flat out kill you!"

"But — listen — there's *nothing* on that film! Nothing! You don't see any murder!"

"I know that," Pantera said calmly, now directly in front of Rob. "I stopped filming the minute I decided to blow that nigger's head off. Keefer thought I was crazy."

Keefer rolled over with a muffled moan.

The gunman looked at his partner with contempt. "Shut up, old man!"

Rob suddenly swung his right fist down, punching into the bone of Pantera's wrist.

The gun went off with a deafening blast.

CHAPTER SIXTEEN

The bullet connected with the TV set in the corner of the room and slammed into the tube, leaving a neat bullet hole surrounded by spidery cracks.

The gun lay smoking on the floor.

Pantera shoved Rob out of the way and made a grab for it, but Keefer, still on the floor, lunged in desperation. He fumbled for it, nearly getting a hold of it in his bloodstained hands.

The front door suddenly smashed open, and a voice barked out "HOLD IT!"

Keefer's fingers darted away from the gun as if it were a hot coal.

Rob tried to focus his eyes as he sat, his legs twisted under him, against the desk.

Pantera was breathing heavily, cursing under his breath, his hulking frame turned toward the intruder.

Rob had never seen the man before, but behind him, Rob made out the skinny young bellboy, and to the other side, peeking over the man's shoulder anxiously, the hotel maid, a worried look on her face.

Pantera put up his hands. Keefer closed his eyes, unable to re-open them until several deep breaths had pumped the oxygen back into his wracked body.

The stranger had a gun. But it didn't matter. This was a baleful black man about 40, round-shouldered with powerful, thick arms. He had a stubbly thin moustache under his broken, wide-splayed nose. His scowling face meant business. He was wearing a black suit. He had a shaven skull with just the slightest trace of stubble on it.

Rob knew him now. It was the man he had seen hurrying down the stairway. Rob figured it out. The house detective.

The maid rushed into the room, kneeling down beside Keefer. She whispered something to him, and he groggily murmured something back.

She looked over at Pantera. Her eyes told the detective something. The detective walked right up to the burly young thug. The detective was shorter, but stockier, looking as if he could punch Joe in half with one shot. His deep voice was resonant and clipped.

"You got your bags packed?" the detective said, kicking the suitcase over.

Pantera shook his head.

"That's not mine," he said.

"Well find yours," the detective said. "And get packing."

Pantera looked around. Rob was on one side. Keefer was on the floor to his right. And straight ahead, the detective and the bellboy. Behind him was a window, four flights up.

He slowly creaked open one of the faded bureau drawers and dumped some lumpy piles of clothing onto the counter top. He pointed to the closet door, the detective nodded carefully, and Pantera opened it, pulling out a dirty brown duffel bag from the top shelf. He began to stuff the clothes into it.

"Pack it up," the detective said.

"Yeah, yeah," Pantera sulked.

A siren began to howl in the distance, and it seemed to be getting louder and louder.

Pantera glanced at the door and then at the window, his fists clenched.

The detective went to the window and gave a look. The siren noise got louder still, wailing and screaming out its two alternate notes. The siren noise began to get softer.

"Police car heading east," the detective said. "It can come back damn quick."

Pantera shoved some more clothes into the duffel bag.

"Now get out," the detective said.

Pantera looked at Keefer.

"Maybe I'll see you again, Carl," he said.

Keefer steadied himself on one elbow.

"Joe, you had me working for you like a dog. All you had on me was my own fear."

"Guess you weren't so smart. Not even when you were *my* boss."

"Ten years out of my life. I should kill you."

Keefer eyed the gun lying on the floor.

"You won't try it," Pantera said, stalking toward the door.

"Don't ever come to this place again," the detective said. "He didn't kill you, but don't tempt *me*."

Pantera stared coldly at Rob.

"I'll get you and that bitch!"

"That's enough," the detective said.

Pantera looked away, his eyes smouldering with hate. He didn't look back. The detective pointed a finger at the bellboy who obediently began walking behind

Pantera, far behind Pantera, but enough to make him know to keep on going, out of the lobby and out into the street.

"Thanks, Sandra," Keefer said to the maid.

"You okay?"

Keefer nodded.

"The guy's a killer," Rob said to the detective, suddenly finding his voice, hoarse and strangely high.

"Got enough trouble in this place without bringing the cops around," he said. He gave the room a once-over, picked the gun up, and walked.

Sandra tried to help Mr. Keefer up, and Rob took his left arm. They helped get Keefer over to a chair.

"Now you got your answers, kid," Keefer sighed. He winced as the maid applied fresh, cold wet wash clothes to his face.

"I can't stay here," he said to the maid.

"Yes you can. Joe ain't coming back. He's gonna go after that movie star. No way he's coming back. You stay."

"Joe was holding all the money," he said to her. "That's the way it was when he became the boss."

The maid touched his cheek.

"I got nothing but my clothes," he said. "I got a prison record. I don't know much about anything except surviving. Maybe out in California I can learn how to make videos. Maybe they can use somebody with my kind of experience."

"You can stay here long as you like," the maid said.

"If 3,000 miles is as far from Joe Pantera as I can travel, I better start going soon as I can. But I won't forget you, Sandra. For a while there, it was like the old days. You looking out for me."

"Well now we're even, Mr. Keefer." She looked at

Rob. "What you said to me the other day, I listened. And I listened when you were talking behind the door. You were right about that girl. She didn't do it. I should've tried to help you a lot sooner. Ten years sooner."

Twilight was in the air in Times Square. Rob looked out the window. The sunset going down over New Jersey had traces of yellow and pink, but was soiled by a dirty ring of brown that muddied the horizon.

When Rob got down to the lobby of The West Side Inn he saw that it was getting busy, swelling with transient night couples, hookers and their johns. Somewhere in the hotel, the detective was making his rounds, along the hallways or down the stairways.

Rob looked around the lobby. Nobody was paying any attention to him. The desk counter clerk was busy writing in the big book he kept on the counter. Some hooker was at the soda machine getting herself a Dr. Pepper and swishing the soda in her mouth with every sip, smacking her lips with her tongue, then swishing the soda in her mouth again.

Rob pushed through the front door and looked sharply from side to side.

Joe Pantera was long gone. But he was somewhere.

The bellboy pushed through the glass doors and went to the curb. A cab pulled up immediately but it was a gypsy, painted blue with a meter machine hooked up to the dashboard. The bellboy looked back at a pleasant looking elderly man waiting just outside the hotel. He shook his head to the driver and sent him off. A legit cab pulled up and the bellboy motioned for the elderly man who peeled a dollar bill from his wallet and handed it to the kid.

Rob waited till the kid had slammed the cab door.

"The guy who was thrown out of here," Rob whispered, "Did—"

"Never saw him," the bellboy said, walking briskly past.

It was warm out, and in twilight, the gray had a quieting effect. The few working people, late in coming home, walked slower. The bums were listless as they stood or sat, looking with idle resignation down the street. The city eased up. But only for a few moments. Night was coming down quick and dark.

When it got really dark, it all came angrily alive again with renewed desperation. Out of the blackness the painted faces were more striking in the harsh glare of headlights, the shabbiness more threatening when it came out of the night and the gutter.

Neon lights, dormant in the day, switched on in front of Rob as he stood in the street. In bright green neon one sex shop began to flash "GIRLS, GIRLS, GIRLS." In bright red next door, another sign lit up: "PIZZA, PIZZA, PIZZA."

He felt his body ache. He stared at the knuckles of his right hand, which were bright pink. Little scraped shards of skin stuck up from them like little bits of pink grapefruit pulp. He tapped at the edges with his left hand and they gave off mild stings.

His back felt sore, and his ribs.

Up a few blocks was The City Daily. Some reporters were working there right now, sitting in front of luminescent green and white computer screens, typing out their stories.

A chill swept up from his bones and crawled up the back of his neck. Cold sweat burst on him. Under cover of night, Joe Pantera was out to fulfill his promise:

"I'll get you and that bitch."

Maddened beyond all reason and desperate to get revenge before it was too late, Joe Pantera would do anything. With Keefer out of the picture, nobody could reason with him now. If he couldn't destroy the beautiful girl with blackmail, he would just destroy her!

Rob tried to think. Pantera had to know where Carrie was staying. It was probably in the paper somewhere. There were some publicity pictures in the paper of her in front of the Waldorf.

After he pulled the sticky phone away from the gummy receiver Rob listened for the dial tone. He heard it and with a sense of relief put a quarter in the slot. It stuck there, jammed. He pounded it a few times, then raced down the block, looking for a restaurant, a fast food joint, someplace with a phone. Across the street he saw another pay phone.

"Hello?"

"It's me."

"Oh, God," Julie said. "Where are you?"

"Downtown. Took a while to find a phone around here that works. I'm on the Square."

"Are you OK?"

Julie's voice on the other end of the phone was the only thing that made any sense for him, for all the sense that he had finally made of Carrie Sinclair's porn film and the murder of the leading man, James Sledge. He sketched it in for Julie as quickly as he could.

"Those guys who tried to break into the apartment. They were Joe Pantera and Carl Keefer. Pantera is out on the streets, a goddam maniac. He's going after Carrie Sinclair, I know it!"

"She has body guards, doesn't she?" Julie suddenly interrupted.

"Yeah, she does. I don't know if they're around all night —"

"Let her body guards handle it, Rob! You came within inches of getting killed tonight, don't you realize that? You're in danger!"

Rob looked around; every face was a nightmare to him. There was a pack of shouting teenagers on the corner, an old wino holding a broken bottle, a pair of six-foot hookers in stomping high heels, a feverish nerdish guy with glasses and a hand stuffed deep into his jacket pocket. A cab squealed its tires as it made a killer fast turn at the corner and hurtled away.

"I'll be home as soon as I can," he said.

"Rob? Oh, Rob, say you're coming right home!"

"There are a couple of things I have to do," Rob said.

"Does she mean that much to you? Why do you care so much about Carrie Sinclair?"

"Julie, come on!"

"Well?"

"You've got to be kidding! What do you think, we've had sex together?"

"You *have*," Julie said, her voice rising up tearfully. "You've watched her have sex — "

"That was on the *screen*, damn it! It was only a movie."

"That wasn't acting. She was having sex and you watched!"

"I don't believe I'm having this conversation! I nearly got killed tonight."

"Yes! Yes! Remember that, Rob!"

"PLEASE DEPOSIT—"

"I gotta go. I don't have any change. Julie. Julie?"

She hung up. Rob shook his head.

Some porn actor just wanted to have some fun, and fuck and make a few bucks. He was murdered.

Some guy who edited a men's magazine also just wanted to have some fun, and fuck and make a few bucks. He was dead, too.

"Carrie's got to know!" Rob said into the dead phone. "Nobody can help her but me."

CHAPTER SEVENTEEN

Carrie Sinclair was coming out of the hotel, elegant in a green silk gown covered in white spangles that reached modestly to her ankles. Wearing a tux, the tall, suntanned co-star of her new movie escorted her down the steps leading to the limousine. In their way was a throng of paparazzi waving cameras that had brick-sized electronic flashes clamped to the sides. Behind the photographers, crowds six or seven deep stood in a wide, buzzing circle, anxious to see what all the fuss was about.

Rob burrowed into the crowd and came up just behind a member of the hotel security team.

"Back up, come on, back it up," the guard said, giving Rob a shove.

There was a line of limousines. Everyone in the cast of the new picture was going to some kind of party. A few limousines had already taken off with members of the cast.

"Carrie!" Rob shouted, but voices all around him were shouting her name too, and a lot of frantic gibberish.

Carrie Sinclair, smiling at the crowd, seemed to look right through Rob. The camera flashes splashed white light onto her face again and again. Her teeth were white, her skin was bright white, her hair was platinum-white. The flashes were coming a lot faster the closer as she got to the limo. The spattering fireworks of white light intensified, batting brightly at her face and hair and the spangles of her gown, throwing weird shadows behind her.

"Carrie!"

Rob reached his hand around the guard's head and tugged him on the right ear. When the guard turned, Rob ducked underneath his left arm and slipped in front of Carrie.

"Carrie I've got to speak to you!" he called out.

Carrie's face went grim. As she slipped into the limo she motioned for the doorman to keep it open. She told her escort to move over as Rob made his way towards her. Photographers swarmed in front of Rob, snapping their flashes in his face. Rob slammed the door shut.

"Pantera and Keefer were at that Times Square hotel. There was a big fight. Pantera's on the loose. He's crazy."

"And you think he might come after me?"

"I don't know. It's pretty easy to find out where a movie star is staying."

"Don't worry, Rob. I've got bodyguards. He can't get into the hotel. Even if he did, he couldn't get into my suite."

Rob nodded, but he wasn't convinced.

Carrie looked at him. "Rob," she said softly, "why do you care what happens to me?"

Rob was stunned for a moment. Carrie's perfume was sweet as he sat beside her.

"Are you infatuated with me?" she asked.

"First you thought I only cared about the money. Now you think I'm doing this to get closer to you."

Rob looked out the window at the throng mobbing

the movie star's limo. "I guess it's real easy to lose track of what's important in your life." He looked into Carrie's beautiful eyes. "I love my girlfriend,"he said.

A cameraman smacked against the window of the limo, jarring everyone in side.

"We better take off," the escort shouted to the driver.

"Listen, Carrie — Joe Pantera is out on the street somewhere, right now! It's been over ten years. You might not recognize him until it's too late."

"Don't try to frighten me."

"There! Right over there!" Rob said, lunging at the glass on his side of the car.

"Pantera!"

Rob leaned forward to protect Carrie, putting his hands against the glass.

The figure just outside the door on the driver's side began to smile and wave. A flash blinded Rob for a moment, and when he blinked, he saw that the photographer, now happy to have gotten one last shot, was not Joe Pantera.

"It looked like him," Rob said.

"Can we drop you off someplace?" Carrie's escort said.

"Really, Rob," Carrie added, "don't worry about me. I'll be fine. I'm going to be surrounded by people all night, and I'll be safe in the hotel. And then I'll be going back to California."

"And that's it? Pantera is still out there. He doesn't care about the film anymore. He's gone crazy. Crazy!"

"Driver?" Carrie's escort said. "Let's take off. When we get away from the crowd, we'll stop again and let this man out. Anyplace in particular you'd like us to drop you?"

Rob sat back in the limousine. Carrie's co-star inspected the fully equipped bar and poured himself a drink.

"Where are you going?" Rob asked Carrie.

"Where else. A party."

"Where?"

"It's at The Twilight Calzone."

Rob knew about it. It was a trendy Italian place with $50 pasta that was really spaghetti.

The limo pulled up at the corner. Carrie squeezed Rob's hand. She said, "Thanks."

Rob watched the limo take off. He waited a moment or two and hailed a cab.

The party, which had started earlier, was in full swing. Limousines were lined along the block. A sign in the restaurant said "Closed: Private Party," and a feverish-looking publicist balding and pebble-eyed behind thick glasses. from the film company stood at the door with a sheet of paper in his hand, scanning the list before letting people inside.

There were fans gathered along either side of the entrance way. Some had Instamatics and were waiting to take snapshots. A few had pens and paper, and one older man had a gift package of some kind tied up with a ribbon. It was a square package and evidently very heavy for him. He held it front of himself carefully.

Rob stood across the street, back in the blurred darkness of the humid night. A few people skulked along the street, not even glancing across the way at the brightness and the lights and the faint sound of the dance beat echoing from behind the closed doors of the fancy restaurant.

Standing in the shadows, Rob waited and as each

figure came into view, it seemed to be Joe Pantera. At least, until the person stepped into the glow of the of lamp light. After a while, the chill of expecting to come face to face with a murderer wore off. That heavy set punk chick stuffed into black Spandex was definitely not Pantera. There was no way Pantera could get into that private party. No way he could get into the hotel after.

The slow limousine with Carrie and her co-star arrived and Rob quickly re-crossed the street. With the fresh limo in sight, the crowd began to come to life like a swarm of bees. The old man with the square package moved forward just as Carrie made her way between the velvet ropes at the entranceway.

"It's Miss Carrie Sinclair and Mr. Jack Kenneally!" the publicist with the clipboard cried out, evidently for the benefit of the crowd. They let out a little burst of applause and people cried out to one star or the other. There was a momentary burst of flashing light from the scattered cameras.

"I"ll give that to Carrie," the publicist said, trying to take the square, brightly wrapped package from the older man next to the velvet ropes.

"No," he insisted, "let me through."

"Nobody's allowed through!" the publicist said loudly.

Rob moved through the crowd, trying to get a closer look at the old man. The man had thinning hair and a white moustache.

"I said I'll give it to Carrie," the publicist hissed.

"No! No!" said the old man, becoming agitated, "I said let me through!"

Rob rushed up alongside the publicist. "Leave Carrie Sinclair alone!" he shouted, making a grab for the mysterious package.

The stubborn old man tugged the package back and held it tight. "I'd love to leave her alone," he said. "What's the matter with you people? Can't a citizen get across a sidewalk without having to go into the gutter? What's the idea of blocking the way?"

"This isn't for Miss Sinclair?" the publicist said meekly.

"No! I live in the apartment on the other side of the restaurant. I thought I could get through this mob, and then you stopped me! This gift is for my wife, not for any movie star! Will you move this rope so I can pass?"

"Oh, excuse me," the publicist said, grinning idiotically.

"What's in there?" Rob asked.

"Fruitcake," the old man answered. "Damn heavy one, too."

Rob helped the old man through the swelter of fans and held the door as he slowly made his way into the lobby of his building. Rob continued on down the block, away from the crowd.

He wasn't too far away from the subway station.

He found a seat on the #1 local and looked across the way at the blackened mirror-reflection of himself. His hair was messed beyond its usual tangle of curls, the lights above made his deep-set eyes appear shadowed and tired in their sockets.

He closed his eyes for a moment.

When he opened them as the train pulled into the next stop, a sullen-looking kid in a leather jacket sat down opposite him. Immediately the kid began combing his hair, then fidgeting with the cuffs of the jacket.

The kid looked a little like Pantera. It was enough

to make Rob tense. He remembered the fierce look on Pantera's face. It was like a trapped animal. When he got out of the hotel room, there was no question that he was still an animal, not freed to run away, but let loose. Let loose to kill.

The kid stared at Rob.

Rob looked away.

There weren't many people on the train by the time it got to the Riverdale stop. The hilly streets were nearly deserted, too. But with all the trees clumped together between private houses and along the slate pathways on the smaller streets, the quiet was eerie. There were many places for muggers to hide.

Rob made his way from the subway, nobody in sight. The night was sultry, the humidity heavy. Clots of dog shit pocked the narrow pavements; the law about cleaning up after pets was a joke in the Bronx, along with most every other law. A net of gnats circled Rob's face as he walked past a vacant lot.

The pitch blackness of some of the unlit streets and the faint police-whistle chirp of the crickets gave him a feeling of vulnerability. One minute, anyone could be blown away.

Pantera had killed James Sledge in a sudden blind rage. The cruelty and unpredictability of the thug was obvious. When he and Keefer had tried to break into the apartment, he took sadistic pleasure in kicking and punching, and trying to sever Rob's fingers with the slam of a door.

Larry was lucky that in that rage, Pantera didn't try to torture him. Didn't pistol whip him. As Larry sat at his desk, Pantera just put a bullet to his head. Larry probably wasn't even looking.

Rob's footsteps sounded hollow against the pavement. He stopped.

There had been no sign of a break-in at Larry's place. No sign of a struggle. And the bullet wound had been to the side of the head, at close range.

Rob took a deep breath. It had been a long day. He just wasn't thinking straight anymore. He felt dizzy and hungry.

A Chinese kid in a white linen jacket was in the vestibule, holding a big brown bag full of food in white squared containers. Rob could smell the delicious scent of the steam. The intercom had just buzzed. The kid looked back and saw Rob. He bowed slightly and held the door.

"Thanks. Thanks," Rob said. "That stuff smells great."

The kid instantly produced a take-out menu from his inside pocket and handed it to him.

The kid pressed the second floor button. As he left, Rob said, "That really smells good. I might call in an order. If you come back to this address for an order on the fourth floor, it'll be me."

The kid gave a little nod. The elevator doors closed and the car lurched upward.

When Rob opened the front door, there stood Julie, her eyes wide, her blouse stained with clots of red, her legs red, and red on the floor.

She was trussed tightly, belts winding around her ankles, rope around her wrists which were pulled behind her back. She stood propped up just a few feet from the door, a gag in her mouth.

The gag was red, smears of it were dry on her throat, looking like finger marks.

"Surprise!"

Joe Pantera stepped out from the kitchen. He grinned as he bashed down an aluminum pot that clattered loudly on the polished wood floor.

"You were a little late for dinner," he said.

Julie, forced to stand at the door for hours, gave out and fainted. Rob held her in his arms, bringing her slowly toward the carpeted floor.

The strange smell of tomatoes was in the air. He could see now — that red stuff all over her. It was...

"Spaghetti sauce," Pantera said. He let out a snorting laugh."It could'a been real blood, and it will be, if you don't give me the film."

Rob rushed at the thug and tried to grab him around the throat. Pantera easily side-stepped Rob and grabbed him by the hair, jerking his head back, making him gag.

"No more heroics," Pantera said. He kept Rob's head bent back. "Where's the film."

"Haven't got—"

Pantera slammed Rob down and kicked him as he fell over. The sickening sound of the foot against Rob's head was lost on Rob, who could only hear an insane, high-pitched ringing in his ears as he tumbled over and over, everything white and yellow and now red in his eyes.

Then came the pain, which throbbed up into his eyes and exploded over and over as if his brains were boiling. Hot blood pumped down the side of his face. He wiped at the warm runniness at the side of his face. The red on his hand was much darker, much redder than the tomato sauce that Pantera had smeared all over his girlfriend.

The room whirled around and around and Rob silently spilled back, face first, to the floor.

Pantera hauled him up into a kneeling position.

"I said you bleed easy. What about her? Get the film," he said, "or I start kicking your girlfriend's pretty face in."

Rob nodded, and steadying himself, blinking at the blood dripping in his eye, sleepwalked into the bathroom. He winced turning on the bathroom light. In front of him in the mirror was a face masked and dripping, unrecognizable.

Pantera snatched the film out of the box.

"Sure this is it? We're gonna have a show," Pantera sneered. Rob wiped his face with his sleeved forearm, the whole sleeve turning red instantly.

"You! Bitch!" Pantera shouted at Julie, "got any pot in the house? Coke?"

She shook her head.

"Booze? Let's make this a fuckin' party. Get a bottle over here. Make it quick. And don't try anything."

She went to the kitchen cabinet where a few liquor bottles stood on a back shelf. She grabbed the first one, a half full bottle of J&B. She put it down on the table. Pantera's face was hard to see in the dark gray of the room, but his black eyes shone, and his frowning lips formed a dark smear. He grabbed the bottle, twisted off the cap and took a swig. He turned to Rob.

"Where's the projector?"

Rob pointed to the hall closet. Pantera stalked over and flung the door open. He saw the old projector on the floor.

"What's this, from like, 1950? You lug the fuckin' thing out. Set it up." He grinned nastily.

Rob hauled the projector up and began to set it on the table facing the living room wall. Pantera came over, the reel in his hand, his downturned mouth working in a chewing motion.

"I always wondered what happened to this little reel," he said, nodding his head with satisfaction as he held it in his palm. "After the shooting, the maid stashed our equipment with one of the guys who bought our stuff for his porn store. By the time we were able to get out of the hospital, it was gone. Before they hocked the camera, they developed the film, I guess. Where'd you find it?"

"In a box of films at Girl-a-Rama, on 42nd, Rob mumbled hoarsely.

"Yeah, that was the building all right. The fuckin' film was just lying around all this time, waiting for me."

Pantera flipped the film onto the spindle and snapped the machine on. It whirred noisily. A cockeyed rectangle of white light fluttered against the wall. Pantera reached for the Scotch bottle and took another swig. He watched intently as the film began to play.

"The two of you!" Pantera suddenly barked. "Stand right here on my right side, where I can keep an eye on you!"

Rob and Julie stared at each other and shuffled close by.

"She hasn't changed," Pantera said, the images dancing in his black eyes. "I should've taken her back to Sheepshead Bay. Married her. Right after the first time we fucked. Well, maybe it's not too late."

Carrie smiled at the camera.

"She was smiling at *me*."

Pantera watched the way he had photographed the pretty young girl.

The camera moved back, then zoomed in on her breasts.

The camera panned slowly up to her face for a moment and then retreated for a long shot as she undulated on the bed, still putting on her best smile.

A harsh growl issued from Pantera as the black man began to make love to her.

"I should've killed that asshole Keefer for bringing the bastard in. Right then and there before he touched her, I should've killed him. I couldn't stand lookin' at it. I had to stop it. I had to!"

He took another drink.

"I'll kill Carrie Sinclair," he said calmly. "Here, or out in California. She can't hide. I've got the film now. She'll have a choice. Me, or nothing. Nothing!"

Pantera reached out suddenly, grabbing Julie by the arm.

"Get something else," he shouted, "I'm tired of drinking this shit!"

He turned the bottle over and whiskey puddled all over the table, dripping to the floor. He looked at the flickering image of the naked actress and cursed silently. He stared at Julie, looking down her body, his eyes hard on the outline of her breasts.

"Come on, Bitch," he said. "Get me something!"

"I don't know what you want," Julie said coldly.

"Maybe I want THIS!" Pantera said, lunging for her, kissing her harshly, then pulling back, spit hanging off his bottom lip.

Pantera pulled Julie closer and gave her another vicious kiss. "You don't like it? I'll kill you if you don't!"

Pantera grabbed the whiskey bottle and broke it against the table, sending shards of green glass splintering through the air. He held the broken bottle up against Julie's face.

"I'll kill you right here and now," Pantera said. He held the bottle against her cheek. The jagged edge had fine slivers, like shark teeth, and it didn't take any pressure to start a trickle of blood squirting down the side of her face.

On the living room wall the distorted picture of the naked actress Carrie Sinclair and James Sledge suddenly flickered, and the fleshy images shot upward to the ceiling. The projector spun around as Rob pulled the projector cord tightly around Pantera's throat.

The bottle fell.

Pantera's hands lurched up to his neck, his eyes wide in the dark gray of the room.

"You're a dead man," Pantera grunted through clenched teeth. Rob could instantly feel the stronger man's fingers beginning to pry at his own. Pantera pulled at the cord and Rob clung to it, watching as the makeshift electrical tape began to fall away.

A glint of copper appeared on a segment of the frayed cord and Rob pulled the wire taut, inching the exposed patch closer and closer to Pantera's sweaty neck.

The shock stopped the thug for a split second.

The naked images projected on the wall slid away as the projector came crashing down from its perch on the table. The 500 watt bulb sounded like a pistol shot as it broke, sparks flying up from the groaning machinery. The lights in the apartment went out, the room aglow with sparks and the emerging orange of a crackling flame from deep within the machinery.

Pantera fell to his knees. Rob pulled the wire from the wall, and with the few feet of cord he held, instantly garroted the dazed hoodlum, pulling the cord tighter and tighter. He gripped the projector cord tight in his wet, blood soaked hands, held it so tight he could feel his knuckles breaking through the skin.

The air smelled of burned rubber and smoke. The broken motor and machinery crackled as searing blue flames waved upward and over the plastic and the metal.

Rob kept the pressure up, the wire biting into Pantera's neck. The hulking thug was no longer moving.

Finally, reluctantly, he loosened his grip.

Pantera's head flipped forward down onto his chest. Slowly, his body tipped over and fell heavily to the floor.

Rob held Julie in his trembling hands. They held each other long after the projector's melted plastic had cooled and the film of Carrie Sinclair lay shriveled in the last curls of foul black smoke.

CHAPTER EIGHTEEN

A stack of letters and envelopes were waiting for Rob at the Rabbit office. In the back room the tinny radio in the art department was turned up and music played. Somebody had left a copy of The City Daily lying on a table.

There was a little squib about Carrie Sinclair leaving for the Coast, and a photo of her.

"Don't hang around the house," Rob had told Julie. "Go in and teach. It's better if you keep busy. I'm going to the office today. It's the only thing you can do."

Julie had nodded uncertainly. She felt the little scratch on her cheek, still stinging.

"Look, Julie, there's nothing more to worry about. Pantera was crazy. A killer. He would've killed us. He would've killed Carrie Sinclair. Who knows how many people he really did kill over the years? The cops had a rap sheet on him. They saw the apartment and everything. They knew what we went through. And it's over. He's dead. His partner's on the run. Nobody's going to come after us now." He looked in to her eyes. "He deserved what he got."

"He did," Julie said softly, holding him close to her.

But when Rob sat down at Larry's desk, shivers of ice and heat began to run around in his body like alternating current. His heart began to pound.

"Rob," the art director called, "I'm going to send back those chromes from that photographer, Andy Novick, the ones we're not using. He's with the Southampton Agency. You have the address on the Rolodex?"

"Come in here a second, would you? What did you say?"

Rob wanted any diversion, a conversation, something to take his mind off everything else.

"I'm sending the extra chromes back to that photographer, Novick," Raymond Fitzgerald said with some degree of petulance. His white shirt was crisp and starched and he wore a black tie that made him look like a waiter.

"There anything I need to look at?"

"Not at the moment," the art director answered, turning his back, walking off.

Rob's rising irritation with the art director was at least some kind of emotional break.

He looked at the clutter on his desk, the porn waiting to be digested. The envelopes were different sizes, the paper different quality, the query letters all different too, and all the same. "Dear Sir, Enclosed please find a story I think would suit the needs of your readers..." "Dear Mr. Slezak, my story, 'Her Pet' as the name implies, tells the tale of a woman and her schnauzer..." "Dear Editor, if you use the following story, do not use my real name, but the pseudonym Axel Varney that appears under the title..."

Rob remembered Larry going through the mail once. "I don't tell 'em why it's crap. They'll write back. I send their shit back like Roto Rooter, no rejection slip." Larry didn't even lick the return envelope, convinced some skeeve might have put poison or excretion of some kind on it. He sealed it with tape.

Rob heard the front door shut, and then another door slam.

He fingered the slide in the right hand desk drawer, then held it up to the light. He put it in a box with some other slides. He took a deep breath and lurched up from his chair, his fist clenched around the box.

Irwin Krantz was seated behind his desk, his heavy fingers re-arranging the morning mail in order of importance. His breathing was raspy this early in the morning and he cleared his throat several times, sighing deeply after the last cough began to pinken his face and bring water to his eyes.

"Eh, Streusel," he said.

The room was stuffy. Rob saw that the window sill had a layer of dust and had not been opened in a long time. The view was the rooftops of a series of low-rising stores. Vague white-gray light came through the window, most of it spilling just around Krantz's desk, leaving the rest of the office in clammy shade.

"These girls are all candidates for the next cover," Rob said.

Irwin nodded and held out his hand for the box of slides.

"Want to go back to the art department to look at these, Mr. Krantz?"

The publisher wearily shook his head, his lips curling sourly. He spilled the slides out on his desk, picking each one up at random. There was a yellowy lamp on his desk. He held each color slide up and exhaled deeply before steadying his hand to look. He didn't need the magnifying glass of a lupe.

The slides were small, but his tired, practiced eye could instantly size up each girl. Rob had not seen Krantz go through the motions before. He knew the slides well enough to know exactly which ones Krantz tossed down quickly, and which ones he paused over.

Krantz pushed his heavy paw against the slides on his desk, separating them into two piles. He scooped up one pile and, tilting the box, let them fall in. The others he held in his hand.

"These," he said, "are ok."

Rob held out his cupped palm and Krantz dropped four slides into it. He walked back to his desk and put the four slides down on the desk blotter.

All four were from various photo agencies.

There was nothing but flaccid disinterest in Krantz's face the whole time.

"Here!"

Rob jumped in his chair when he heard something slap heavily inches in front of him. The art director had tossed down a bunch of copies of the new issue of Rabbit and they spilled in a fan across the desk.

The art director, acting as if he had just unloaded his week's worth of dirty laundry, stared down at the pile in muted disgust. Rob flipped through the pages quickly, muttering "thanks." The masthead of Rabbit bore the name of the deceased editor.

"Larry Slezak's last issue," Rob said, looking up.

"He got so much out of life," the art director announced. He began to walk away.

"I'll need a few more copies," Rob called. "I'm expecting a few of our writers."

The art director shrugged his shoulders and continued down the hallway. "There's a box full in my office," he said. "You can come and get them if you need them."

"Wait a second," Rob said, scooping up the four slides, "take these. These are the slides Krantz ok'd as possible cover girls. Why don't we make it easy on ourselves and use all four of them, one after the other?"

The art director flattened his mouth, one nostril flaring up as if he smelled something bad.

"Because we're working on winter issues now. So after this issue, we have to ask the photo agencies for a lady wearing a ski cap or something. Irwin likes his magazines to look *timely*."

The art director tossed the four slides down on his light box and after pressing the white button on the side, the glass box fluttered to life, glowing white. He took out his lupe and studied all four pictures.

"On this one, there's not enough room on the top for the Rabbit logo, and we can't afford the extra charge in matching the background color and extending it. This is all right and this is all right, too. But I think the redhead is the sexiest. You always get a lot of attention with a redhead."

"Great," Rob said. "Listen, it's getting late."

"It is?"

"Krantz left already for lunch, and he's not coming back. I'm going to leave soon too. I have some errands to run this afternoon. So I'm hereby giving the art department the afternoon off."

The art director looked surprised.

"On whose authority? If you'll notice, the creative director is ahead of the editor on the masthead. And besides, we've got a lot of work to do."

"Would you rather work, or do you have stuff you'd

rather be doing?"

The art director cautiously answered, "I'd rather be doing *anything* than working in this toilet."

"So, go." Rob said.

Rob waited at Larry's desk.

He looked down the hallway, wondering what was keeping everyone. Finally, the art director emerged, his hand on the back of his assistant, pushing her along.

"This is a special *treat*," he told her, "but remember, we will be back here 9am *sharp* tomorrow morning, won't we!"

The girl shifted her eyes to the ceiling and nodded her head emphatically.

"Don't forget to lock up when you leave," Raymond Fitzgerald told Rob.

When he heard the front door close, Rob got up from Larry's chair and turned out the bank of lights leading down the hallway to the art department. The office was quiet and empty.

He looked at his watch.

Krantz never put in more than an hour or two at the office. The art director was gone. The freelancers were a little more erratic. Rob checked his watch again.

He sat back in the chair and waited.

He heard it, clear as a bone breaking, when the combination to the outside door lock began to click.

Footsteps moved quickly down toward his cubicle.

"What's going on, a fuckin' blackout?"

Cy sat down in the chair opposite Rob.

"Nobody's in but me," Rob said. He clicked on a tape recorder concealed in the desk drawer. "I'm all alone."

"That's too bad about you, Rob. Oh good, another

issue for my collection." Cy grabbed a copy of the September Rabbit from Rob's desk. "There should be Pulitzers given out for porn. You ever read James Joyce's letters? Real good gross shit. But they didn't give him awards for *that*."

"D.H. Lawrence said that pornography is the laughter of genius."

"I didn't know he had a sense of humor. Jeez it's hot out today. Humid. You feel your eyebrows crawl. I may have to shave this off."

Cy scratched at his short growth of hay-colored beard, the errant untrimmed hairs running upward on his cheeks, a few of them glinting just an inch or two under his eyes. He had on faded blue jeans that were light brown on the thighs from were he would wipe his hands. "I took the subway up. This guy in a wheelchair came on. I was going to offer him my seat."

"OK, Cy." Rob looked at the slides on his desk. He selected two of them and handed them to the glowering figure across the way. "Some cover mag possibilities."

"I get to see?"

"Sure."

Cy held the first one up to the light. "I wouldn't mind fucking her face." Then he held up the second. "Hey. That's, what's her name, isn't it? That's Slezak's chick."

"Is it?"

Cy reached for the lupe on Rob's desk. He put the slide behind it and held it up to his eye.

"Yeah, sure it is. Look at those little tits. The nipples are nice and big. Why is it that chicks with little tits have the big nipples? Looks so weird. Fuckin' hot, too. I'd recognize those tits anywhere."

"Larry showed you the nude shots of Tee?"

"Sure he did. He always showed me the nude shots of his girlfriends."

"Always slides?"

"No," Cy said. "He had a cheap Polaroid camera. He took Polaroids. I guess that's why he had the slides done this time, so he could actually put the bitch in the magazine. What a putz. So what's this, the Slezak memorial issue or something?"

"You know who took the slides?"

"Who? How the hell should I know?"

Rob nodded. Cy put down the slide. He frowned, his eyes glistening from behind the hooded sockets. "What the hell are you asking me for? What the fuck are you staring at *me* for?"

"I'm not."

"You've been acting like a nut ever since I came in, Rob. In fact you've been acting strange toward me for days, and I don't like it."

Cy rolled up the copy of Rabbit and waved it menacingly.

"I don't like what you're doing."

Rob leaned back in his chair.

"Cy, you don't even know what I'm doing, do you."

"No," Cy answered belligerantly. "That doesn't mean I can't not like it. And another thing, I'm owed for the last issue, and now for this issue."

He glared at Rob.

Rob put his palm out, signalling Cy to keep still.

The sound of the front door was faint this time. The person pushing the combination buttons did it gently. The door opened quietly.

"You want the money?" Rob whispered, "and a bonus?"

"Sure as shit," Cy said.

"Then duck into the closet. "

"Come on —"

"Go! I'm not kidding!"

Cy took the copy of Rabbit with him and hurried across the way to the closet where the coats and umbrellas were kept. He closed the door.

Rob turned up the lamp on his desk.

"I thought the office was closed. I didn't see any lights. It's spooky in here," Toby said, sitting down. "Thanks for calling me. I have two new stories. Is this the new issue?"

"Yes. Just in."

Toby placed a pair of neatly typed stories on Rob's desk. He blinked at the bright light of Rob's upturned lamp, the surrounding office in almost total darkness.

"I invited all the writers down to get copies of the magazine," Rob said. "I also spoke to the art director. And to Krantz."

Rob shoved a copy of the new issue across the desk.

"The last issue that Larry Slezak worked on."

Toby looked at Rob, then down at the magazine.

"I've got the cover girl for the next issue," Rob added. He gave Toby the slide.

Toby held it up briefly, then put it down.

"That's not the way to look at a slide, Toby. See, I do it like Larry did it. I turn the lamp around. Then I put the magnifying lupe up to my eye, and I look at the slide right up close to the lamp."

Rob looked back at Toby, but it was hard to see him because of the glare from the bright lamp.

"She's going to make a great cover girl," Rob said. "Take a look. Take a good look."

Toby gingerly held the slide up and peered into the lamp light.

"You —.you can't use that slide," Toby said.

"Why not? Larry's not going to mind."

"That's Tee."

"I know."

"She's not going to give permission."

"How do you know?"

"She wouldn't."

"She already did. You know Larry. I came across a paper in his desk. A model release for her, with her signature on it."

"But that's just one picture. What good's it going to do to print one picture?"

"When *you* have the rest?"

Rob turned the lamp around. The light was yellow on Toby's skin. The young writer blinked and bit his lower lip. His eyes turned away from the brightness and stared off at nothing.

"You took those photos of Tee," Rob said. "You're the only one who has any interest in science. When I first saw those pictures of Tee, and the ones up against the bookcase, I read some of the book jackets. Airplane books. Science books."

"Lots of people have books like that —"

"That's just the start of it, Toby. Larry knew you were a photographer. He wanted some professional pictures, but he wanted them cheap. He figured he didn't have any competition from a guy like you. What happened at the photo session? You couldn't control yourself? You tried to make love to her?"

Rob saw the look in Toby's face.

"You didn't have to *try*. Tee and Larry's relationship was never so strong. She just went along. What did she care? But she wasn't going to leave Larry just for a fling. She wasn't that serious about you, was she? She just figured she'd have a little fun with you. You were in love with Tee. It didn't mean a thing to her."

Toby remained silent.

"You knew the kind of personality Larry was. Overpowering. You couldn't compete with it. Larry knew it. But he was a little too confident, wasn't he? Guys like Larry are like that. If they don't hear barking, they figure they won't get bit. Especially by somebody as quiet and toothless as you."

Toby Shell didn't move, his face deliberately blank, as if he wasn't even listening. Rob couldn't tell anything from the eyes, or the now slack mouth.

"Larry told me all about you, Toby. You just wrote these porn fantasies. And they kept you going, too. Until you got a chance at the real thing."

Toby just stood there.

"And then you heard about the porn film with Carrie Sinclair in it. Larry told you. He told everybody. He was calling everyone he knew trying to find somebody with connections, somebody who would buy the film for big bucks. You knew he had dynamite. Maybe you told him so. Maybe you offered to come over — on the pretext of talking to him about ways he could make money with it. That was just a way of getting to Larry alone, and away from the office where there wouldn't be any witnesses. Wasn't that it?"

Toby stared down at the slide of Tee on the desk.

He said softly to Rob, "Larry was talking about making a killing off the film, if he could get it away from you. He pretended to be your friend. He just wanted to get you to bring the film to the office so he could steal it. He was going to pretend it was stolen by a cleaning man, or a writer. Then he'd sell it and you'd never be able to trace where the money went."

"You and Larry plotted exactly what to do."

"Something like that. I told him I knew friends of friends who might buy the film for a big price. And all I wanted was a little percentage. And then we talked about getting it away from you."

"See, Toby, that was another little mistake. When Tee told me about Larry making all those calls, she said he spent all night at it. He couldn't have called any New York businesses. They were all closed. And people out on the West Coast couldn't fly into New York within a few hours and kill him. It wasn't Carrie's bodyguards, or Joe Pantera. He didn't even know who Larry was when he read about the film. It had to be one of his freelancers living in New York."

"The film you found, Rob, it made killing him so much easier," Toby said. "I fantasized about killing Larry, but I knew I'd be a suspect. I didn't want Tee to ever suspect a thing. As he got on the phone with me I knew what I had to do. If Larry died, everybody would think it had to do with the porn film. And I was right. The cops were looking at you. And you were looking at Carrie Sinclair. I knew that whoever had the film would be the prime suspect, and that wasn't me."

"I understand Toby," Rob said, trying to keep calm, "I really do. You couldn't stand Larry having such a sweet young blonde thing like Tee. With him gone, she'd have no other choice but to run to a guy she could trust. The guy who had taken those pictures of her, and showed her how much he loved her. It didn't take long, did it?

Right after Larry died she was asking me how it was to live on the West Side. Where *you* live. And when I called up her parents, that's what they said. She was living on the West Side someplace, but they didn't know exactly where."

"You really aren't such a bad reporter, Rob."

"One last thing. The murder scene. Larry knew his killer. Nothing was disturbed in the apartment. Nothing was out of place. Except the lamp. Like this one. Turned up. Turned up for only one reason — for Larry to examine slides, not film. You couldn't just walk in and shoot him. You didn't have that kind of nerve. So you waited till he was occupied with something. The murder scene proved it. Larry was killed sitting at his desk, with his lamp upturned. He was looking at slides when you put a bullet through the side of his head."

Toby touched the slide lying on the desk.

"I missed this one."

"But Larry had the rest of them at home, didn't he?"

"I wanted him to give me back the slides before I killed him. They were taken in my apartment. I knew they were clues. I asked him if the slides were at the office or at home. He told me he'd brought them all home. They were in his desk drawer. I asked him if he wanted any more poses; if there was anything I missed. He took them out and started drooling over them."

"I'll bet that got you steamed, Toby."

"He kept pointing at Tee and saying what a good fuck she was."

Toby's face in the lamp light was expressionless. He gazed directly at Rob.

"I didn't want to kill him, Rob," Toby said simply. "I did, but at that moment, I wanted to give him...a reprieve. Do you know what I did? I told him that Tee was interested in me. I told him that we'd made love after the session. That...I loved her. And Larry didn't even look up at me. He just laughed. He wasn't even jealous. He said it didn't mean a thing."

Toby's left hand moved inside his bulky white shirt. In his waistband was his gun. Rob could see the glint of it in the darkness.

"I'm glad I confessed to someone," Toby said. "You're a writer. You know how good it feels to get the words out of you. I feel better now."

"Good, good Toby. You can tell the police. You can get it all off your chest —"

"No, Rob."

"Does Tee know that you killed Larry?"

"No, Rob. Only you. And everyone will think that you were killed because of that porn film. The only evidence against me is that slide of Tee you kept."

"You better look around, Toby. You better be more careful this time. Anybody see you enter the building? Will anybody see you leave? Will you try to make it look like a robbery this time?"

"All I care about is Tee! Don't you understand? She is...everything! Without her, I am not alive."

"Don't do it, Toby."

"I can't let you live, Rob," he said almost apologetically.

A voice shot out of the darkness.

"For Chrissake, live and let live!" Cy Kottick shouted. He slammed the light switch near the closet and the flourescents popped to life.

Rob grabbed Toby's wrist.

In an instant Cy was on the other side of Toby. The

Vietnam veteran's hold was strong and he forced the gun out of Toby's hand.

Cy pushed Toby down into the vacant chair at Larry's desk. He kicked the gun away.

Toby didn't look up. He stared at the color slide of the beautiful young blonde. His trembling fingers reached for it. The image was so tiny in his hand.

CHAPTER NINETEEN

The police and Toby were long gone.

The only lights in the office building down on Times Square were in the offices of Rabbit magazine on the 6th floor.

Cy leaned back in his chair and watched Rob on the phone.

"Got everything?" Rob asked. "Great. So the story will run tomorrow? OK. Thanks." Rob hung up the phone.

"That was good writing, for over the phone," Cy said. "You know, I could never dictate a story to someone. I have to type it out."

"I'm a reporter," Rob said. "I've had to phone in a story before. They say it'll be in the morning edition. My first person account of Larry's murder and Toby's arrest."

"I'll bet they were impressed."

"This isn't just one story. I'm going to send them samples of my old stuff. They said they might have an opening for me. It's too bad The City Daily wouldn't talk to me. They could've gotten the scoop instead. But you know, they have a policy. They just don't like to talk with ex-employees."

"Now here's an opening for *me*," Cy said, pointing at the centerfold in Rabbit. "I like this part you wrote here: 'Our centerfold girl, Senta Folla from Italy..." real cute, Rob."

"Her name was Thelma and she's a waitress in a waffle house in Los Angeles."

Cy laughed. "Are you sure you want to give up editing Rabbit? You're good at this stuff. Admit it, it's fun."

"Maybe I'll write you a story once in a while. You don't have a bad staff to work with. Just keep an eye on your creative director and make sure he doesn't do anything stupid on the cover."

"I'll get him to promise. Just stick the naked woman on the cover and forget the knife. But you have to admit, it would be a good challenge to come up with some kind of excuse if he did."

"You'll get along with Irwin Krantz, Cy. I guess he's ok. He's just a businessman, that's all. Just don't go too crazy, ok? Take it easy. You're the editor of Rabbit — assign the stories and relax."

"I'll get along with Irwin Krantz? The fucker owed me money!"

"You're on salary now."

Cy nodded dismally. "With some publishers, that still means you don't get paid." Then he brightened up.

"I can still write stories can't I? I could make an extra few hundred a month. This could turn into real money!"

"I don't know if that's ethical, Cy," Rob said, removing a few of his pens from the desk. "Don't get carried away, all right?" He closed the desk drawer. "It's all yours, Cy."

"I'll use a front," Cy was saying. "Yeah. Krantz would never know. I'll find somebody who'll pretend to write the stories and give 'em a percentage..."

The slide of Tee was still on the desk. Rob noticed the picture of Carrie Sinclair in the newspaper and the caption about her new movie. He left them in the office.

Rob walked down 42nd Street. He wasn't planning on being around the area any time soon. The offices of the newspaper that took Rob's story weren't anywhere near Times Square. They were down in a big, shambling old building near the Seaport, which, come to think of it, was almost as lousy an area as this one.

He used a pay phone to call Julie.

"I'll be home in a half hour," he said.

"Where are you?" she answered, her voice sweetly concerned and confused, "You can't get all the way up here from mid-town in a half hour."

"I'm taking a cab," Rob answered.

"A cab!" Julie laughed. "What are you celebrating?"

"Coming home to you," he said.